P9-CSE-739

ECLIPSE

RICHARD S. WHEELER

A TOM DOHERTY ASSOCIATES BOOK

NEW YORK

ECLIPSE

Copyright © 2002 by Richard S. Wheeler

Design by Heidi Eriksen

A Forge Book
Published by Tom Doherty Associates, LLC
175 Fifth Avenue
New York, NY 10010

www.tor.com

Forge® is a registered trademark of Tom Doherty Associates, LLC.

Library of Congress Cataloging-in-Publication Data

Wheeler, Richard S.
    Eclipse / Richard S. Wheeler.—1st ed.
        p. cm.
    "A Tom Doherty Associates book."
    ISBN 0-312-87846-X (acid-free paper)
    1. Lewis, Meriwether, 1774–1809—Fiction. 2. Lewis and Clark Expedition (1804–1806)—Fiction. 3. West (U.S.)—History—To 1848—Fiction. 4. Clark, William, 1770–1838—Fiction. 5. Explorers—Fiction.
I. Title.

PS3573.H4345 E28   2002
813'.54—dc21

                                                                2001058978

First Edition: June 2002

Printed in the United States of America

0 9 8 7 6 5 4 3 2 1

For my friend and editor Dale L. Walker,
eminent historian, Jack London scholar, biographer,
critic, journalist, teacher, and bookman

PART I

1 LEWIS

I knew myself to be the most luminous man on earth. The sun was at its zenith, and so was I, but like the setting sun, my light would lessen soon. At this moment, surely, I shone more brightly than Napoleon or Wellesley or the king of England, and maybe even my friend Thomas Jefferson.

Was I immodest? I allowed myself to be this fateful Tuesday, September 23, 1806. Will Clark and I took the corps all the way to the western sea—I tasted its brine with my own tongue and then stared at China—and back safely, a journey of eight thousand miles across an unknown land. And without loss, save for poor Floyd. Forgive me my exultation; I have done the impossible.

Those people rushing to the St. Louis levee would never know, could not even imagine, how it was. They would hear my words but not fathom the dangers, the heat and cold, the starvation, the exhaustion, the *glory*.

My men paddled steadily toward the gathering crowd, their hewn paddles drawing us through the glittering Father of Waters in our dugout canoes and the remaining pirogue toward that slippery black bank that carried the effluent of St. Louis into the river. We would return to civilization in a noisome place.

I shall not forget the moment. The air as clear as my mind; the hosannas of that crowd swelling across the lapping and thumping waters as we rounded toward that golden strand. They were cheering *us*. The rude city jostled itself along the levee, a chaos of rain-stained squared timber structures, white-washed plank mercantiles, fieldstone warehouses, all hemmed by a low bluff, upon which stood the mossy stone mansions of the French traders and prominent men, islands of elegance in a barbarous outpost. No doubt Clark and I would stay in one of those.

The men paddling the pirogue paused, marveling at our reception, which struck them like a double gill of spirits. Word of our imminent landing had arrived ahead of us, perhaps by horse from General Wilkinson's Cantonment Bellefontaine on the Missouri, where we had spent our final night. I saw Sergeant Ordway settle his dripping paddle at his feet, and lift his Harper's Ferry rifle. The others did likewise. There would be a salute.

He checked the priming and aimed his piece skyward to shoot at God; the men did likewise, and at Ordway's shout, they fired a salute, the scattered reports sharp and joyous, the popping of triumph. Men in the canoes fired as well, a ragged volley that announced our triumph to the whole world, and startled crows to flight.

Our salute occasioned a new round of cheers from the flocking crowd. I scanned the seething mass of people not for dignitaries, or people I knew, but for women. How we starved for women. How much we needed the sight of nankeen skirts and ivory lace, and cotton-covered bosoms, and porcelain faces, and glossy hair in ringlets or curls, women's hair in blue bonnets. How the sight of them there, gathered on the black and muddy bank, swelled our hearts and loins. There was no mistaking what was racing through the minds of my men. I knew them all. I could recite their private thoughts to them though they had not shared a word. They wanted women, and if need be they would spend their entire back pay to have one or a dozen.

I feared an incident.

"Sergeant Ordway, look after the men and equipment. Take them to the government house, the old Spanish stronghouse where we ran up the Stars and Stripes on the parade ground that day. That will be the armory for our rifles and gear. Give the men leave when all is secure. Tell them I'll try to get some cash for them. Be patient."

Ordway nodded. There could be no better sergeant.

"And Sergeant; look after the papers, diaries, specimens, bones—the whole collection. Especially those. The president's collection."

"In the government's house, sir?"

"General Wilkinson's, yes. It's empty now, they tell me."

I needed to say no more. My good sergeants would see to my good men, and in due course they would be paroled. It would be a merry night for them, though I doubted they would remember any of it by dawn.

I turned to the men in the pirogue with me. "I'll look after you; you can count on it. The nation owes you more than it can pay."

They paddled again, steering the small fleet toward the clamorous bank. I saw friends now; several dark-haired Chouteaus, who had been so helpful during the outfitting.

We pushed for shore as eager boys steadied our barks and caught our elkskin ropes. They swarmed us now, excited, crazed even, and I remember only one refrain: we thought you were long dead. We thought you had met your Fate. We had given up hope . . .

I clambered out, the wound in my buttocks paining me viciously, and skidded as I set foot on that vile muck. Other craft lined Leclede's landing just north; flatboats headed for New Orleans, keelboats destined for Pittsburgh.

"Ah, messieurs," Auguste Chouteau proclaimed, a vast and Gallic sweep of the arms drawing Clark and me up to dry ground. "It is a blessed miracle. You, alive! *Mon Dieu!* We starve for the news."

We pumped hands and clapped backs, and bathed ourselves in the excitement and tasted nectar. Questions flew, and we could not answer.

The mad crowd swarmed around the men and canoes, and I saw that Ordway would not succeed in executing my plans, at least not for a while.

"Has the post left?" I cried.

"This morning, for Cahokia."

"When does the post rider leave from there?"

"*Après-midi,*" Chouteau said.

"Send a messenger to hold the post. A letter to the president of the United States must go with it," I cried in a voice that brooked no quarrel.

Chouteau was no man to dither. He wheeled toward one of his servants, instructed him in short volleys of French, and I saw the man race to a bankside canoe, board it, and paddle furiously toward Cahokia, two or three miles away on the far shore of the Mississippi, in the Illinois country.

"I must write," I insisted. "I have urgent news to send my president."

I wished I hadn't used that expression. Jefferson was the

president of all these people in this vast territory of Louisiana, newly purchased from Bonaparte. But I had been his secretary; he was certainly my very own president in a way that set me above the hoi polloi.

"I ache for your news, Monsieur Chouteau, but that must wait. I abjure you, sir, show me to a quiet corner where I may draft my message."

"*Bien,* monsieur, my warehouse will answer."

But it was not to be; not just yet. There were sweaty hands to shake, fulsome greetings to absorb, compliments to blot up lasciviously, honor to be paid, and I would have to hold off with the quill for a time. The town's great men had pressed around. Will Clark had his own circle to deal with, though after a few minutes I saw him slip free and attempt to put things in order with a wave of his hand and a laconic command or two: the Harper's Ferry rifles and black cookpots and powder to the Government House, my leather-clad men breaking free of the crowd, the sweet pouty girls, and gimlet-eyed matrons hoping to discover breaches of decorum to condemn, the twitchy boys trying to be important, the silent sloe-eyed Indians, to settle our meager stores in safety.

I saw Will help Big White, She-He-Ke, the Mandan chief we had brought downriver to treat with the president, and his wife and son, out of the pirogue, and guard them. The savages stared. They had never seen a white man's city.

Leave it to Will Clark to put things right. Without him, I would not have succeeded. He deserved a reward exactly equal to my own: a captain's rank, though he was but a lieutenant; pay, bonuses, land warrants identical to what would come to me. I would see to it, fight for it.

I needed to write, not only to the president, but to my

mother and family. I needed a suit of clothes. For two years, I imagine, my body had been clad in animal skins, which formed our moccasins, our pantaloons, our hunting shirts, our capotes, our gloves. They had some advantages over cloth, being proof against wind, but they captured our salts and sweats and oils in them until they rotted off our backs.

I knew I smelled as vile as the slime of the levee, and hoped soon to have fresh smallclothes and a broadcloth suit of clothes made up by a tailor. But all in good time. We all looked like scarecrows, stank, needed to tend to our hair and bodies, and needed our wounds, and boils, and rashes attended. We looked like brigands instead of a corps of the United States Army.

I discovered myself still clutching my rifle, the instrument of my salvation; we had learned never to be without our well-cleaned, loaded piece, and our caution had saved our lives more times than I could remember.

"Will, take this," I said to Clark. "Won't need it."

Clark handed my oiled, primed, well-tended rifle to Sergeant Gass. I felt naked without it.

"*Mes amis*, what did you find? What of the beaver?" asked Jean-Pierre Chouteau.

"Beaver aplenty, a fortune in beaver."

"Ah, beaver! And Indian trouble?"

I paused. "Later, my friend," I said.

"Minerals?"

"A few, but no mountain of salt." President Jefferson had asked me to look for one.

A winsome flirty-eyed girl with brown ringlets was pressing a jug of wine upon two of my men, the Field brothers.

"Ordway," I yelled.

My sergeant broke it up. If my men imbibed spirits just

then, there would be no stopping a debauch, and all the matrons of St. Louis would be nodding their heads. I did not know whether St. Louis would dose my men with the clap, or whether my men would dose St. Louis.

I headed in a determined fashion for Chouteau's grimy warehouse, determined to announce our triumph to the world.

"Gentlemen," I said, "bear with me for but an hour: I must impart my news to the president of the United States."

They opened a path. Chouteau settled me at his own desk, fetched a quill and paper and inkpot, and I began the letter that would transform the world, secure me the gratitude of the nation, and offer indelible proof of my contributions to botany and zoology. It was high noon.

2. CLARK

Meriwether excused himself to write letters, retreating with elaborate courtesy from the crowd. I knew it was painful for him to tear himself away; he was drinking in the adulation like a man craving for spirits. But I could see that familiar taut compression of his lips that told me he was enduring delays he could scarcely bear; that reporting to Tom Jefferson came above all else, and his sole passion was to scrape his quill across foolscap and wing the great news east. He had stood there as long as he could, hearing the music of the Creoles while chafing to send the letter that would burst upon a world that had supposed us all dead.

I knew I must write some letters, too, but first there was the matter of She-He-Ke, Big White, his squaw, Yellow Corn, his boy, and the interpreter, René Jessaume, his Mandan wife and family. The Mandan chief was ill at ease, trying his stone-faced best not to show it, glancing dumfounded at the white men's structures, the whispering mob, the enameled carriages, the parasoled grandes dames in black.

The Creoles crowded around me, sharp with greed, as I oversaw the last of our debarkation. Ordway and Gass had marched the men toward Government House, freeing me to meet these calculating merchants, none of whom I knew well, for it had been Meriwether who had dealt with them all before the expedition while I erected Camp Wood across the river.

"Monsieur, Chouteau here. *Bien*, what a grand day, *oui*? It is a day always to remember!"

"Pierre Chouteau, I remember."

"Ah, Capitaine, tell me every grand thing."

I laughed. "Well, first of all, I want you to meet a friend of ours, Chief Big White of the Mandans." I spotted the translator. "Jessaume, come help us out, and bring the chief."

"It is so? This is a Mandan *sauvage*?"

"We're taking him to meet the president, and maybe put together an alliance."

"Ah! A concord."

Jessaume arrived with the chief and his family, and the translation proceeded in French, which let me out. But that was fine. I had things to do.

A short swart Spaniard I knew slightly, who had been hovering about like a bumblebee, saw his chance and approached.

"Manuel Lisa, Captain. It was a formidable journey, and we are pleased. Have you a moment?"

I nodded, reluctantly.

"Are there perhaps beaver up the Missouri?"

I laughed; that was answer enough.

"And what are the little impediments to reaching them?"

I could see where this was heading. "The Sioux," I said. "They block the river."

"Could they be pacified, or stupefied, with gifts?"

"We weren't able to, sir."

"How many would it take to break through?"

"More than you can hire, and I doubt that the government would let you."

"Are the British trading up there?"

"They certainly are. Nor'westers, mainly."

"Do they have the tribes in their possession?"

"Yes, mostly they do."

He was stroking his small jet-haired beard. "And have you a map showing the beaver streams?"

"Mister Lisa! I haven't been on shore but half an hour!"

"I shall await your instruction," he said.

I turned, discovering half a dozen men lusting after our words. St. Louis was a city built on furs; these were entrepreneurs, fur men, blotting up my every word, concupiscent for beaver that could earn them a bonanza. I grinned, perhaps cynically. I knew the sort. St. Louis was not so much celebrating our safe return as it was celebrating the opening of a Golconda. About our survival, about our reaching the Pacific, about a river route to the Pacific, about our charting an uncharted continent, they were indifferent; about the streams habited by *Castor canadensis*, they were ardent students.

"More later, gents," I said, seeing their disappointment. Fortunes, empires, monopolies, rivalries, lives of ease hung on every word I breathed, but I had no time for that. We had a guest and his family, half awed, half afraid, stiff as a plank, and needful of my comforts.

"Jessaume, tell brother Big White we're going to take them to the big chief's house and get them settled," I said.

The translator repeated that in Mandan, and soon the somber Mandan, a big, lumbering man gotten up for the occasion in his finest ceremonial leathers, and his entourage were trailing me, along with half of St. Louis, as I hiked upslope, past warehouses and then mercantile firms along the Rue Principale, on up to the decaying Spanish military post.

I found our men stacking their arms in stands, in an orderly's quarters under the supervision of Patrick Gass.

"Good," I said. "Who's in command here?"

"Don't know, Captain. They're all down to the water thinking up ways to get rich."

I took matters into my own hands, surveyed the old seat of government in Upper Louisiana erected by the Spanish, studied a dusty barracks that appeared unused, and rejected the idea of putting the Mandans in there. These savages were tribal royalty. Big White was a king. I would give my coppery brother a king's billet.

I found General Wilkinson's chambers, but no Wilkinson, made a swift decision, and put Big White and his family in them, explaining to Jessaume, who barely grasped English, that this place was the very home of the American big chief, and Big White would be his guest for now. This was high diplomacy; the navigation of the Missouri River was at stake, and the friendly Mandans would be our passport.

I liked Big White. He had a powderhorn full of courage to come down the river with us to meet his new Father, past his enemies the Arikaras, and the truculent Sioux, and there had been wailing aplenty when he stepped into our canoe. Most of his people thought they would never see him again.

Big White nodded. I hoped it would do.

"Tell him we'll feed him just as soon as we can," I said to Jessaume. "Settle yourself and stay with him."

The interpreter nodded. I didn't much trust him, and never had, since meeting him on the way out to the Pacific.

And then, for the first time since debarking, I had a moment to reflect. Where was that damned York? Never in sight when I needed him. Where would I billet myself? Probably in a tent somewhere, in my buffalo robe. What about the men? Turn them all loose?

I found Sergeant Ordway posting the corps to that empty barracks. He approached me.

"Don't know what you intend, sir. Some signed on for the trip, and should be released. Most are still regulars, and still under command," he said.

I seconded that. "Look to their mess, and let 'em loose tonight. You, too. All the sergeants, all the corps, so long as there's a guard here tonight. I'll find out who's commanding here." I grinned. "Whether or not Captain Lewis comes up with some back pay, I don't imagine you'll suffer for the want of spirits."

He nodded wryly. We understood each other. For three years we had been understanding each other.

I stepped into sunlight and found myself strangely alone, even though we had scarcely arrived. It was over. We were safe, but plentifully embroidered with boils and rashes and wounds. I had seen feet so lacerated I wondered how a man could put weight on them; men so ravaged I wondered how they could step one more time through hip-high snow. I had seen Meriwether vomit every last shred of camas root he had eaten, turn so sick I thought he'd expire; and most of the men, too. I'd been fevered and bilious more times than I could remember. I don't know how we survived, though I credit Meriwether, who learnt something from Doctor Rush, and plenty more from his mother.

Upper St. Louis was deserted and hushed. I hiked back toward the crowded levee, absorbing the city's foul stench, fetid air, the cess in the mucky lanes, the stone structures with real glass in the windows, the temporary squared log ones. Not a brick had been set to mortar in St. Louis, yet stone mansions rose upslope, and shacks jostled one another everywhere.

I wouldn't stay here long. I knew exactly where I was headed. Miss Judith required my attention. As soon as we could put matters in order here, Meriwether and I would head east, stopping at Mulberry Hill, our family home near Louisville, en route.

I remembered how she looked the last time I saw her, this cousin of mine, Julia Hancock. She was trying to deal with a disobedient horse. She was twelve, not yet a woman, a pretty thing, flat chested, in a girl's brown skirts, bright-eyed. She captured me then. I named a river for her, Judith's River, high up the Missouri. I had the same design then as now; when I got back—*if* I got back—I would head for Fincastle, Virginia, where Colonel Hancock resided, and put my designs forward.

They were affluent people, the Hancocks, landed and comfortable, but I didn't suppose I'd long be poor or unequal to their measure. Jefferson had promised me much: the captaincy had been turned down by the War Department, much to Meriwether's disgust, but as for the rest, land warrants, back pay, bonus, I'd be comfortable . . . if Judy would have me. It had been a long time, and I hadn't the faintest idea of her circumstance. I knew only my own condition, which was to make haste and claim her whilst I could. For nigh three years I had been thinking on it.

Meriwether and I had talked much of what we would do: we needed first to see the president and present him with the fruits of our labors; not merely an account of our journey, but my maps, of which I am proud because I know they are true. And the specimens, pressed and skinned and pickled by the hundreds. We plucked them up. We shot them, skinned them, preserved them, and packed their bones. We had boxes and barrels full of them, diligently described by Meriwether, less by me, though I copied out many of his pages to give ourselves a duplicate record. All of that we would soon deliver to the President's House in Washington City, or Monticello if Tom Jefferson so desired, for we had been faithful to his command, and except that our diplomacy with the tribes has to some degree failed, we had met his every objective.

But first, I would put a letter in that post bag being delayed for us at Cahokia; and soon we will be rowing and poling up the Ohio to my family home on Mulberry Hill where my older brothers George Rogers and Jonathan will be waiting.

3 LEWIS

Pierre Chouteau took Will Clark and me into his home until we could find lodging. But today we rented a room from a tavernkeeper from Kentucky to store our baggage, of which we had considerable.

I had scribbled furiously at my letter to Mr. Jefferson, and sent it off with discontent, knowing I had barely touched upon what needed saying. Ah, the impotence of words! But I took special pride in announcing that "in obedience to your orders we have penetrated the continent of North America to the Pacific Ocean, and sufficiently explored the interior of the country to affirm with confidence that we have discovered the most practicable route which does exist across the continent by means of navigable branches of the Missouri and Columbia Rivers."

I wanted the world to grasp the implications. So I emphasized the riches in furs, the commercial potential of Louisiana for the republic, and prated a little about our botanical and zoological collections and Indian vocabularies. And I did not neglect my co-commander, urging the president to make certain that Will received an equal measure of the rewards and emoluments of our perilous journey.

I had an eye to publication, and wrote not only for the

president but for the whole nation, not neglecting to tell the world what perils and hardships we had endured, and what progress we had made in charting the unknown continent upon which the republic had seated itself along one shore.

I intended to pen a reprise of our experiences, and achieved that, though I knew I could not tarry long, for I was holding the government post. I drafted a letter for Will as well, which he copied in his own hand, and we sent George Drouillard canoeing across the Mississippi with our missives. And so it was that the news winged eastward, officially proclaimed by my own hand. I knew what the effect would be. Washington City would celebrate. But I much more wanted to hear what the sage of Monticello would say when I stood at his door. Well done, good and faithful friend.

There was much to do that day, and the next days. Will and I found a half-deaf tailor who had several bolts of suitable black broadcloth, and had ourselves measured for suits of clothes and smallclothes as well, having nothing between our flesh and the public eye but the animal skins we had been reduced to wearing, and a few borrowed rags we were fitted out in until we could have some garments made up. We were both scarecrows.

I for one regretted every moment I was clad in elkskin and doeskin, though the woodsman's costume did have its effect upon the imaginations of those who beheld me, for my attire was a mark of my passage through a barbarous land. Still, I wanted my blue and white uniform, my gold thread epaulets, my lace, my well-blacked boots, my emblems of rank and honor, and felt naked without these proper ensigns of rank and position.

Will grinned at me, but he had no proper care for his person, and often it showed in his mode of dress.

"Try wooing in buckskins, and see whether you go nose to nose with your fair Judy," I said by way of retort.

He had no reply to that.

I turned that day to other matters: the men needed cash and I had to provide it. By employing my power to sign warrants upon the government, I was able to get them some coin, though little of that existed in this rude city of St. Louis; and none of it in dollars. I got them two-bit pieces, dimes, doubloons, ducats, pieces of eight, shillings, francs, and all manner of coin that the city's merchants provided by digging deep into their private hoards. Enough to help my doughty men buy what they needed, mainly pantaloons, shirts, ale, and women, for they were as reduced as I, and without means.

I turned next to a matter most delicate and private. Prior to our departure, I was greatly assisted in medical matters by the Parisian doctor Antoine François Saugrain, a royalist refugee who had settled in St. Louis and brought within his mind the most advanced knowledge of medicine available anywhere, and a mastery of science unknown outside of Philadelphia. He had provisioned me with medical supplies and also shared his medical knowledge prior to the expedition. Now I turned to him for help.

Several of my men suffered gravely from certain diseases of the flesh gotten from the savage women we had encountered along the way. This matter was so private that I made little mention of it in my public journals, but confined myself to reporting certain symptoms in some of my men, in particular Goodrich, Gibson, and MacNeal. What the enlisted men did was one matter; what the commanders did was quite another, and so I had chosen to write nothing, though in fact a certain disease had ravaged me in the autumn of 1805, and so severely that Will despaired of my health.

Thus, this twenty-fourth day of September, I excused myself from the warm ministrations of my hosts, and set out to see the eminent Doctor Saugrain with the intent of seeing to the health of the men returned from the Pacific. I did not wish to make my visit known, and thus loitered about the Rue L'Eglise until no one was watching, and then I burst into his chambers.

He welcomed me at once, this diminutive gentleman of four feet and six inches, and heard me out.

"In short, sir, we are suffering from various venereal infections gotten from the savage women, and I wish to have you consult with my men. I will write the president and ask him to appoint you as an army surgeon, thus securing your pay and achieving a desirable privacy for the corps."

Saugrain eyed me sardonically, his pointed black beard bobbing as he weighed the matter.

"My capitaine, step behind that screen and disrobe. Everything. Even the stockings. The bottoms of your feet will tell me much," he said. "And your hands, *oui*, the palms."

"Ah, I'm talking about the men. Not the officers."

His response was a small ivory finger pointed at the screen.

I surrendered. I had dreaded this moment, the shame of it, the revelation in it that I had lain with a savage woman long before. All the way up the Missouri I had ruthlessly resisted the opportunities thrown my way by eager chiefs and their eager women; but I imagined one lonely night when I was ahead of the corps, there in the Bitterroot Mountains, isolated from the world, that the Shoshones would be well insulated from this New World disease and that the chances of catching what Columbus's crew brought to Europe would escape me. I would avoid the mortification and pain that attends the discovery of such congress by friends and family and even strangers. Was I not the explorer who had been the first to reach the Pacific? I could not endure the thought that a secret vice might sicken me and ultimately expose my folly to the world.

How I rue that single night with the Shoshone woman, when I and three of my men had found Cameahwaite and his people, far in advance of Clark and the rest, who were toiling up the headwater streams east of the divide. The chief had given me a good buffalo-skin lodge and I had surrendered to my voluptuary passion, thinking myself safe enough. I was not. If I could but live my life over, I would excise that night from it. I have reproached myself a thousand times, aching with remorse and shame, but I cannot undo the bitter truth of that bitter night in the Bitterroot Mountains.

I had treated numerous of our corps with the purgative calomel, mercurous chloride mixed into a salve, directing them to apply it to any chancres on their private parts or elsewhere, and directing them to ingest my pills in considerable quantities to alleviate the burning when they passed water, and to quell the outbreaks of chancres and rashes and infections on their flesh. And I had quietly taken the same courses myself, though I made no note of it in the journal, and for some while not even Will was aware of it, though he soon figured it out.

What interested Saugrain at first was the fresh wound through my buttocks, wrought by Cruzatte's ball, which had been slow to heal and troubled me greatly, suppurating for weeks and healing improperly, so even now I could barely sit.

"Now, sit yourself on the table there, and let me see the bottoms of your feet, Capitaine."

I raised a foot, then the other.

"*Bien.* Were they sore?"

"Yes. Blisters, about the time I was so sick in the fall of eighteen and five. I had to ride a horse. I couldn't walk."

"*Bien.* Show me your hands, palms up. Those too?"

"Yes, hard liverish lumps. They went away."

"I see. That is to be expected."

From within his gloomy office, stuffed with steel instruments of torture and morocco-bound books, I could see no part of the world; his examinations were well screened from prying eyes. And yet I felt a thousand eyes upon me as he studied the evidence of my folly, the healed-over chancre on my member; the scarce-healed puss holes of a ruined flesh. He hummed, sucked breath, touched no part of me, but bade me turn this way or that, and thus he took my entire measure, his small, delicate face creasing into frowns, his small lips pursed. He spent an amazing amount of time examining my skin, the inside of my mouth, my nostrils, and the rest of me as well, often with a magnifying lens.

"*Bien,*" he said, which I took as a sign that I might restore my clothing.

"The rest, they are like this?"

"A few: I could not help Gibson; I fear for him."

"And yourself, *mon ami.*"

The way he said it shot a chill through me.

"It is far advanced, the stage *deuxième,*" he said. "You are perhaps entering the benign stage when it lurks out of sight, but the disease does not sleep, it crouches and waits. When did you, ah, acquire this badge of honor?"

I thought back to that joyous moment when we had finally found the Shoshones in the folds of the Bitterroots, and the relief I felt when I learned we might obtain horses from them; and the joy they expressed when we gave them meat that Drewyer (as I've always spelled Drouillard's name) had shot, for they were starved and intent upon going on a buffalo hunt. Oh, I remember those days and that sole night, when Will wasn't around and the main body of the corps was far below, dragging the canoes over endless shallows, and I felt free and my secret would be safe.

"Over a year past," I said. "It was the middle of August of eighteen and five."

My diminutive physician paced about, his hands decorously clasped behind his back, his black beard thrust forward like a bayonet. "You soon will enter the third and final stage, which does widespread damage to your organs. The heart and arteries especially, the brain, the system of the nerves that carry the messages of the mind to muscles."

I blanched.

"But we will try to arrest it. Monsieur le capitaine, the salt of mercury slows and arrests, but only for a while, and then the disorder gains ground again, becomes puissant, dangerous. Ah, how a man regrets his impulses then! Ah, Capitaine, what this infirmity does to the soul!"

A cold fear crawled through me.

"But there is much hope," he continued. "Many times, the disease diminishes, disappears, and it is as if nothing had ever afflicted the sufferer. I have found that perhaps a third of those who suffer it escape its effects entirely and many more are only mildly afflicted. And oftentimes years, decades, go by and nothing at all happens, as if the pox lies dead within you. I believe half of those who suffer this disorder survive it."

That heartened me. There was ample reason to hope. "Well, what shall I do?"

"We will begin a course of treatment, Capitaine. It will take some little while."

"But I *must* go to Washington! The president is expecting me. The whole world is expecting me. It's not possible."

Saugrain shrugged, a Gallic gesture that contained within it an entire argument. "Your condition prevents it. In a few weeks you will be sufficiently improved to go. You must avoid all spirits whatsoever; they accelerate the affliction. Here now, I shall mix the first batch of pills, *oui?*"

And so I knew I must tarry in St. Louis, even though I itched to head up the rivers to Philadelphia where a great reception would await me, for I had learned that I had been elected to the membership of the American Philosophical Society; to Washington and Monticello; to Locust Hill, and my family.

I paid Dr. Saugrain with a chit, for I hadn't a shilling, and arranged for him to examine my corps discreetly. I would put out the word for those suffering from the venereal, and I would charge my men with secrecy. We were heroes, and there would be no public sign of pestilence.

"I will do what I can, which is much," Saugrain said, as we parted. "Send them to me."

I stepped into the afternoon, looking both ways to see if anyone might see me emerge from the French doctor's chambers. I saw a few people down the street and a cart hitched to a mule, but no one was looking, so I slipped into the middle of the street. Not a soul in St. Louis knew where I had been, not even Will. There were things a man needed to keep entirely to himself.

Will and I would be the honored guests at a banquet at Christie's Tavern given by the leading men of St. Louis the next evening, and our great journey would be toasted and celebrated the entire night. And even before Doctor Saugrain's courses began their work, I would be violating his advice. But a man being toasted would have no choice. I would raise a glass, too.

4 CLARK

I have taken my leisure this late October Sabbath, enjoying the fine autumnal weather. I don't have much else to do. I thought we would be off for Washington City long since, but Meriwether tarries, I know not why. The president awaits us, and so does the whole republic, eager to give us the approbation that we have no doubt earned.

When I broached the matter to Meriwether, reminding him that winter is closing in swiftly, he grew short with me.

"I'm not ready. Don't press so hard, Will. I'm outfitting the whole entourage, you know. We're taking Big White and his family, and several of our men, too. The merchants don't have half of what we need. Just getting the men some money took me days. I've not gotten them a quarter of what they're owed. And not just my party, either. I've agreed to outfit Pierre Chouteau, so he can get his Osages to Washington. I'm going to auction off some of the rifles and gear, and raise something that way for the men."

It wasn't what he said that seemed testy to me but the way he said it, impatiently and shrill. I couldn't remember that metallic tone during our days on the trail.

He has been in a peculiar humor for weeks, at once drinking in draughts of acclaim along with the endless draughts of wine, but melancholic.

And so he tarries here in St. Louis. I wondered whether he wanted the word of our safe return to spread before us, thus making our passage east a sort of triumphal progress. But Meriwether is not so vain as all that. He is simply in a peculiar mood that I have not ever seen in him.

A few days ago an elderly butcher in a soiled bib approached us and shook Meriwether's hand. "I want to touch the hand of the man who walked to the Pacific," he said. "Walked to the western sea, tasted the brine, and walked back again. Now, sir, having taken that very hand in mine, I am content."

Meriwether smiled, and then reminded the old man that over twenty more had done the same thing. He is eager to share his accomplishments, and I count it a virtue in him.

But I never doubted that the command was really his, not mine, and in those cases in which I disagreed, especially about the Indians, I held my peace and found ways to be agreeable, preferring to modify his thoughts by degrees. He consulted with me frequently, usually in the confines of our tent when we still had one, or at least apart from the men, and always heard me out. But tacitly, we both knew the decisions were his to make, and he made them, and still makes them. He really gives me more credit than is due me.

He has written generous letters to the president, urging a reward for me equal to his own, including a captain's pay, and likewise he has written a commendation for almost every man in the corps, and has singled out a few for special compensation; he always was good with his men; reserved and distant, but a man to follow without question. I did follow his lead and still do, marveling in so grand a vision and keen a mind and withal, an eager quest for every scrap of knowledge that might advance science.

Time drags. I proposed a fortnight ago that I leave at once, visiting my brothers and family at Mulberry Hill until he might arrive, but he forbade it. I know exactly what I wish to do: hasten to Fincastle, Virginia, just as swiftly as foot and horse and sail can transport me, and lay siege to the castle of my dreams.

She for whom I named a crystal virgin stream.

Judy is much on my mind. She is of marriageable age now; if she will have me I intend to wed her. The vision of her sustained me during our long progress, and stayed me in moments when I might have plucked the ripe fruits being offered by tribal women. And now I am prepared to win her. My battery will consist of telling her that I named a beautiful stream for her, one that pours out of mountains and is as clear as pond ice. What woman can resist so tender an assault as that?

I think of little else. I will not be an impoverished suitor, not with three years of double back pay owing and land warrants promised me. I have already resigned my commission, having served my country well, and will begin a family, fashion a comfortable plantation in Kentucky not far from my brothers at Mulberry Hill across the Ohio, and prosper for as long as health permits. Assuming, of course, that Mr. Jefferson and the Congress keep their commitments.

Not that one can trust any government to honor its commitments. My brother is painfully aware of it. It mattered to no one, apparently, that George Rogers Clark secured the whole northwestern territory clear to the Mississippi for the republic, beating the British regulars and their savages out of it with little more than an undisciplined militia. When it came time for the commonwealth of Virginia to make good the warrants by which he equipped and provisioned his ragtag militia, the commonwealth's clerks reneged, found excuses, reproached him for the loss of receipts, and tossed him to the creditors, and so my brother was ruined save for a small amount of almost worthless land. I wonder whether that will be my fate as well. Let it be a Clark motto: put no trust in the government!

And that is why I found myself, this warm and sunny October 26, strolling the riverbank, my eyes peering across the rolling river to the east, where my heart is tugged. I am a prisoner here. I am weary of the banquets. We have been to several at Christie's Tavern where I now abide; the businessmen toast us, celebrate us—but I do not delude myself. They pump us for every scrap of knowledge about the high Missouri they can glean, knowing that their fortunes swell with such information.

The wily Spaniard Manuel Lisa makes it his business to learn everything we have to teach, and I am wary of him. Meriwether, who was almost abstemious during the expedition, has taken much to drink and at the end of such evenings needs a steadying friend to get him safely to his bed, which consists of a buffalo robe he spreads on the floor, for he cannot find sleep lying upon straw or feathers or stuffed cotton.

I strolled hard by the blue Mississippi this bright chill morn, and an hour out of town I spotted the solitary figure of a familiar and esteemed man before me, also stretching his legs. Drouillard, our Shawnee-French guide, interpreter, and hunter was the most valuable of all our men, supplying our hungry bellies with meat where none among us could find anything to shoot at. He is a dark, heavy-boned, and solitary man, preferring to roam apart from us, keeping much to himself, and yet he always had a kind word for me, and I mark him among my favorite of all those in the Corps of Discovery.

He saw me and paused.

"George, taking the air, I suppose?"

"Yes, Captain."

"How is your circumstance? Were you released?"

"Yes, sir. Captain Lewis paid me my twenty-five a month, which he got out of the merchants, and my service is over."

"You linger here, though."

"It is a place to make money, Captain. Half a dozen merchants have approached me about going upriver. Lisa, Chouteau, all of them. I may do so. I've been where they want to go, so it seems I am a man of some value."

"Along with most of the others," I said.

"A few. Most are indisposed."

"And the regulars are still under command. Who's indisposed?"

"Captain Lewis could tell you better than I."

"I thought by now most of the corps would have recovered. Better food, plenty of rest, warmth, and comfort."

Drouillard grunted.

"But maybe too much to drink, is that it?"

"There's a parade of them visiting Doctor Saugrain, Captain."

I knew of it, and knew why. "Poxed, are they? Captain Lewis told me he had appointed Saugrain an army surgeon; it would be cheaper than paying for every visit."

"Poxed, yes. Half the corps."

"But not you. You were lucky."

"No, Captain, it was not luck. I do not live by luck, but by calculation. I did not like the chances."

I thought back to all those evenings among the Mandans, Hidatsas, Shoshones, Nez Percés, Clatsops, and all the others, when men slipped away into the darkness with the laughing women. Meriwether and I had to guard our stores to keep the men from stealing a hank of ribbon or an awl or a mirror to give to the squaws. I could not remember Drouillard indulging himself. Maybe he was, like me, a careful man. We could no more stop our men than we could stop a waterfall.

That put me in mind of York. The squaws had fallen all over him, and yet he was unscathed by pox, though he had lain, I reckoned, with more Indian women than anyone else in the corps. How he fascinated them! I could not fathom it, though I would have been much vexed if he had sickened and lost his value to me. He bothers me now; the expedition taught him too much independence, and he looks at me now with a gaze I don't like, and intend to do something about.

I had Judy to think of, and a dream of a good life, and that was enough to teach me prudence. I thought it would suffice for Captain Lewis, also. Meriwether had several belles in mind, and a physician's knowledge in his head, garnered from his mother, Doctor Rush of Philadelphia, and Saugrain as well before we started. No doubt he was aware of the venereal, but maybe thought to avoid it or heal it.

He didn't. He was poxed like the rest and was dosing himself with the calomel, though no word of it entered our journals. I do not know whether he suffered the drip, or worse. I cannot name the time or place, though it was plain he was suffering by the time we descended from the Bitterroots into the Columbia drainage. I myself treated those festering eruptions on his legs and arms when we were among the Nez Percés, though he bade me do so privately in our tent, fearing discovery by our men. I kept his secret.

Though Drouillard had said nothing specific, I realized suddenly why Meriwether had not headed for Washington earlier. He would not go until Doctor Saugrain was done with him. That put a new light on things, and I pitied my co-commander. Were Drouillard and I the only two of the corps who had kept our senses—and our health?

He fell silent as we blotted up sun. Then he paused.

"You will excuse me, I trust, Captain," he said, and turned off the path. That was the way of him, to vanish from our midst after the briefest encounter.

I hiked well north of the town that day, restless and itching to get on with life, but actually still under orders. We managed to go clear to the Pacific while maintaining the fiction that we were co-commanders; but that was solely because I, Lieutenant Clark, did not press the issue when we differed. I would not press it here. It was Lewis's expedition, and he was admirably suited to the task, and to my dying day, I will view him with unbounded admiration and affection.

I returned to St. Louis with a breeze at my back.

I supped this evening with Meriwether at Christie's Tavern, as we usually do, now that the city's merchants had at last wearied of our tales of great brown bears, buffalo beyond number, tribes that subsist on salmon, and the presence of sea trader's items far up the Columbia.

I examined him with some care, it having been revealed to me why he tarries so long in St. Louis. He looked well enough; certainly better than when we had arrived. Dr. Saugrain has done him some good. As if to confirm it, he announced that we would leave for Washington City in a week or so.

He ordered porter, and then another goblet of it.

"I've had to outfit quite a party, you know. The Osages and Mandans. Chouteau's people. Several of our corps. But I imagine in a few days, Will, you'll be in the bosom of your family."

"And then Fincastle," I said, smiling.

"Ah! You are a lucky man. I have never had much luck with women, though I plan to change that," he said lightly. "Miss Randolph, for one. Miss Wood, for another. But my burdens have been so heavy, I haven't given it much thought . . . until now. Wish me luck, eh?"

There was something in the way he said it that saddened me.

I truly wished him luck.

5 LEWIS

My joy upon arriving at my Virginia home, Locust Hill, was unalloyed. I discovered my mother, Lucy Marks, my brother, Reuben, my half-brother, John Marks, and my half-sister, Mary, all present and in good health.

My mother met me on the lawn that sixteenth day of December, for word of our arrival preceded us. When I dismounted, she clasped me to her, her hands telling me how glad and grateful she was, and how proud, too.

"My very own Meriwether," she whispered. "At last my fears are behind me. And now I have a mother's pride. Ah, my son, alive and honored . . ."

I laughed, told her we would have a long visit in which I promised to reveal to her every wonder, every success, every danger. Her fingers lingered on my arm, touching the son she had thought she would never see again.

I had Big White and his family and our translators with me, and Private Frazier, who served as my aide; but Sergeants Ordway and Gass and Private Labiche, who had left St. Louis with us, had gone their separate ways. At Frankfort, on November 13, we had split up: Will had taken the trace to Fincastle, Virginia, Pierre Chouteau headed for Washington City with his Osages, and I took my party to Ivy, in Albemarle

County. Ultimately I would progress to the City of Washington.

It had been a triumphant progress, and we were greatly slowed because every hamlet along the Ohio River wished to banquet us and celebrate with grand oratory, toasts, and bonfires. Most of all they wanted to hear our stories, and we had obliged them as best we could. I am sure they were disappointed that we did not encounter mountains of rubies, fields of gold, giraffes, elephants, and pygmies.

Little girls in dimity met us with bouquets tied with yellow ribbons; raggedy barefoot boys wanted to inspect our Harper's Ferry rifles. Clerks and butchers and harnessmakers wanted to shake hands, and memorize maps, and learn if the soil out west was fertile. They all wanted souvenirs, anything at all, even a patch of cloth, that had been to the far Pacific. And everywhere, towns spread their bunting, the red, white, and blue, and hoorahed us, and told us we were as bright as the circle of stars in the flag, and men of destiny.

But at last I was home in sweet hazy Virginia; we settled Big White and his family in a spare bedroom. We were at once beset by convivial neighbors, for word of our arrival had preceded us, and in the hubbub I discovered that we would be honored at a great banquet in Charlottesville two days hence, with all the leading lights of that part of Virginia attending us.

"You look splendid," my mother said, when at last we had a moment. "I would have supposed to find you worn to a skeleton."

"That aptly describes our circumstance on more than one occasion," I replied. "We had moments so desperate I despaired of feeding my men. But somehow we survived, and we had learned the woodsman's art so well that we made meals of things civilized people scorn."

My mother, small and thin and discerning, with eyes that probed me, drew me to her and examined me, somewhat to my discomfort, for it was as if I could have no secrets from her. She was not a physician, but was much called upon for her medical knowledge, and put stock in a number of simples that were famous in the county, herbs and barks and roots she gathered in the fields each year which she decocted into teas. They said she was better than any doctor in Virginia.

"Are you well, Meriwether?" she asked velvetly, her fragile hands resting in mine.

"See for yourself," I replied. "I endured everything that harsh nature could devise for us, and yet we all got home, except for Sergeant Floyd."

I was in the very bloom of health, having benefited from the efficacy of Doctor Saugrain's courses, and I was certain that *lues venerea* was a thing of the past, and gave it no more thought.

She touched my cheek, stubbled from the neglect wrought by travel, and I was grateful that I was unshaven, for the skin eruptions of 1805 had left the faintest brand on my cheeks, small circles of obscure scar I fervently hoped she would not discover. Doctor Saugrain told me that the disease scarcely yields scar tissue, and that the healing of the skin is complete, but in my case a sharp eye might see the track of my tribulations. Under her scrutiny I had to nerve myself into the appearance of calm.

"I hope that it is so," she said softly, and I felt a great uneasiness. I did not wish for my mother to learn the nature of the vile disease that had afflicted me, and that I now had conquered; the plague of scoundrels, vagabonds, and loose women.

How swiftly our house filled. Here were laced and perfumed cousins and aunts and uncles: Lewises and Meriwethers, including my uncle Nicholas Meriwether, who had been my guardian after my father died.

And they had questions. What was it like out there? A desert worse than the Gobi? What lies beyond the Mississippi? An aching void? Did you see no white men at all for three years? Is it all barren and naked, unfit for any but savages?

For me there was no longer a mystery in it, but for them I had undertaken a journey as exotic as an exploration of darkest Africa. I may as well have been describing a probe up the Amazon, or a marooning at Juan Fernández Island.

"Louisiana," I said, "is a land so great, so rich, so filled with natural treasures, so fertile, that when it is finally settled we shall be the largest and most populous and most powerful nation on earth."

"But what of the tribes?"

"They will become our friends; I made great progress with them, except for those fiends, the Sioux, which know no fear of anything but force."

Even as I spoke, I was watching Big White and his squaw, Yellow Corn, who were wandering in sheer bewilderment through our home, marveling especially at the mounds of food hastily brought by our slaves to the dining table, along with our splendid sterling silver and Wedgwood china. Civilized life was beyond their fathoming and I was glad they were being introduced to it, because once they returned to the Mandans with their stories, the power of the American eagle would be understood within the minds of all the Missouri River savages.

Using the good offices of my translator, René Jessaume, whose own Mandan squaw was quite as dumfounded as the chief, I urged my family and neighbors to converse with this wild specimen of Louisiana mankind, which they did with great relish, along with much finger-wiggling, evoking solemn responses from the chief.

Ah, that was fun. Chouteau was on his way to Washington with the Osages, and the purpose was the same: we would over-awe them all, they would return to their huts and tell the others what they had witnessed, and that would establish permanent peace and prosperity in the unsettled country.

"Well, Meriwether," said my uncle Nicholas, "you have done a grand thing. Your fame has spread far beyond the county, and I have no doubt that your name will be celebrated even in Vermont, and Georgia."

I relished the compliment and am not shy about taking credit for the successful expedition, which I knew to be the greatest in history.

But I was keenly aware that others had contributed to our success, and was fervent in my wish to give credit where it was due. "Will Clark was my equal in all respects, sir. And we had doughty men who, after certain disciplinary troubles at the start, welded themselves into an unmatchable corps, so devoted to duty and mutual protection that it was scarcely necessary for me to drill or order them about, or even instruct by the time we began our second year. But Will Clark, with his boating and mapping skills, sir, that is what made us a match and a team."

"You share the glory generously, Meriwether."

"That is my exact purpose."

After an interval I looked after my aide, Private Frazier. He had never been in so fine a house, and he gaped his way through our white-enameled parlors, studying the oil portraits, the Hepplewhite and Sheraton pieces, and ended at last at our lengthy dining table, where cold pink beef and a succulent sugar-cured Virginia ham rested, with orange yams, brown breads, creamy sauces, and sundry other items, including an ample stock of whiskey and porter. I ate my fill, and urged him to do so also.

"This man," I explained, "has been to the Pacific Ocean with me; has seen its dashing waves and tasted its salt. We have eaten the white blubber of a whale beached there. We have subsisted on elk and buffalo, ducks, beaver, dog, salmon and bear fat. And now we go to Washington to tell Mr. Jefferson what we have seen."

I was very proud, the cynosure of much attention that hour, and I saw no reason not to enjoy it. I had done what no other mortal had done. I told them of the great humped grizzly, larger and more terrible than other bears, so great that sometimes half a dozen balls did not stop them. I told them of bearded buffalo beyond number, of the rivers we named for Mr. Gallatin, Mr. Madison, and Mr. Jefferson; of the streams Will and I named for Maria Wood and Judy Hancock; of Charbonneau's little girl-squaw, who led us toward our fateful meeting with the Shoshones and their horses.

Of many things did I speak, wonders all to these Virginia gentry for whom the great continent rolling westward was a deep mystery full of deserts and terrors. And from the bright gaze in some women's eyes, I knew myself to be an unexplored continent also.

And then I paused, addressing my mother. "And where is our cousin Maria?" I asked.

"Maria Wood? She married some while ago, Meriwether, a most blessed match, and we are pleased."

"Ah," I said, "ah . . . I named a river for her, you know. I should like to tell her. I was looking forward to it."

"I'm sure you'll soon have a chance," my mother said.

It had been fanciful of me to think she might still be available these three years. I had admired her from afar, but never had encouraged her interest before the expedition. And yet the vision of her had always sustained me. Now she was taken. I breathed deeply, eyed the clamorous horde, and knew there would be others.

Two days later they banqueted us at the Stone Tavern in Charlottesville, and there we were feted with toast after toast, and there I took pains to tell these Virginians that I had indeed succeeded: "I have discharged my duty to my country," I said. And I dwelled at length upon what Will and I had achieved on behalf of botany and zoology, for I wanted them to know that we recorded innumerable new species of plants, birds such as the magpie, and animals such as the dog of the prairie, dutifully described, sketched, pressed between pages, skinned, boned, and in some cases even returned live to Monticello.

I drank too much. Saugrain had warned me, in the severest language he could summon, against all spirits. But that was quite impossible given the hospitality I was experiencing and the fetes prepared in my honor. Should I refuse a toast? In any case, I was in fine fettle, my health was splendid, save for the endless pain wrought by the wound in my buttocks done by Cruzatte's ball high up the Missouri. And for that I had a comforting remedy: a few drops of laudanum always sufficed to ease my pain, and balm the aches of all my muscles.

They were even penning odes about us, and proposing that rivers and territories be named after me. I would not oppose the idea, for I had done what Columbus had done; what Amerigo Vespucci had done, and he had gotten his name on two continents out of it. But I count myself a seemly man, and later was relieved when Congress did not take up those suggestions.

I relished the adulation but was eager to go to Washington, and on to the nation's true capital, Philadelphia, for the acclaim I thirsted the most for would come from my president, and then from those erudite periwigged savants in the Quaker City, who had formed themselves into the premier New World organization devoted to the advancement of all branches of learning, and especially science.

The American Philosophical Society had elected me a member—I who lacked a formal education! I planned to repay them the honor, by offering them the sum total of my hard-won knowledge of the continent, including the incomparable map that Will had fashioned day by day, out of our ceaseless measurements of latitude and longitude as we ascended the great Missouri. I give him the credit for it; my own cartographic skills are no match for his.

And so, with Christmas looming, and the most remarkable Yuletide of my young life awaiting, I set off from Albemarle County for the capital, and the President's House, half-unfurnished still, to report to Mr. Jefferson, and to arrange as best I could to give Congress reason to reward all of my bold men with all the generosity a grateful nation could afford.

What better Christmas than to report my success to the governors of our new republic? And to show them my successes at diplomacy in the form of my Mandan guests? I had received word that Mr. Jefferson pined to meet Big White, even as he had rejoiced when Chouteau brought him the Osages, and the president had greeted them warmly, given them gifts and medals, and cemented relations with the savages who barred our way west.

Sometimes, in my rare moments of solitude, I was disquieted.

I was playing a new part, but I ill understood the role.

6 CLARK

I beheld the altar of my dreams, Fincastle, from a considerable distance because it lay below my vantage from the trace over Brush Mountain. Fincastle had been much on my mind, not only recently but all the way to the Pacific and back, and now my heart quickened at the knowledge that it rested in the broad valley down the long slope ahead, lost in the familiar haze of the blue ridges of Virginia. I had come a long way, and Fincastle was my lodestar.

It was the address of George Hancock's plantation, and the home of Julia, or Judy to me, his daughter and the woman of my fancies. Courting her was foremost on my mind. Let Meriwether reap the acclaim of Washington and all the leading men; all I needed was the promise I would seek from those soft lips. She would be fifteen now; the age my mother was married to my father. If Congress did its duty and ratified the promises given me, I would be eligible and with means.

We had miles to go, York and I. York walked through the December chill and led our two packhorses, while I rode along the trace we had been following across Kentucky and western Virginia, pausing at inns along the way as was the custom.

I was no longer a lieutenant, having made haste to resign my commission as soon as I reached St. Louis, desiring not to keep the subaltern commission a day longer than necessary. I wrote Secretary Dearborn a resignation letter that made it clear what I thought of the rank. I do not trust the promises of government; my brother George Rogers Clark did, and was ruined by that trust. I would not succumb to such sentiment.

"Almost there, York," I said. "Hurry now."

He nodded. York had been lost in deep silence ever since we had returned from the expedition, and I hadn't liked it.

"I will freshen up at the next stand," I said. "You will cut my hair."

"Yassuh."

"Are you sick, York?"

"Nosuh."

"Well, then answer me with respect."

I had not been barbered since St. Louis, and I would have York do it, as he often did. I had kept my auburn hair short in accordance with our republican principles. So did Meriwether. Mr. Jefferson had decreed that all army officers must abandon their queues and wear short hair, because the officer's queue was a mark of aristocracy, improper in a republican government and a citizen army. Most had. A few officers had refused and were finally pressured into cutting off their hair or resigning. Since the army's officers were largely Federalists, the change came slowly, reluctantly, and with smoldering rage. One was finally court-martialed.

But I certainly didn't mind. My queue, when I wore it, was an annoyance, needing my attention, easily dirtied. But I had known plenty of commissioned officers who wore their queues as a lordly prerogative; their mark of rank, as plain as epaulets and gold braid.

I fumed my way down the long slope, with York trailing

barefoot behind me. He had been silent for weeks, a virtual stranger in my house. It had been a mistake to tender him a certain measure of liberty on the expedition; even worse a mistake to equip him with a rifle and teach him some marksmanship. But Meriwether and I knew that every man counted, and if we could conjure a rifleman and hunter out of York, we would be that much more secure.

But now I could see that it went to his woolly head. My thoughts turned severe: he would come around or be whipped. And if he didn't, I would lend him to a master who used slaves hard, and then he would learn his lesson.

We stopped that last night at a public house at New Castle, though I was tempted to push on the last fifteen miles and awaken Judy and her family in the small hours. But I checked my impulse. At the public house I would order some hot water brought to me, freshen my suit of clothes, and make myself presentable. We would be at Fincastle by noon, a good time to discover the shine in the eyes of my beloved.

The suit the tailor had stitched up in St. Louis was ordinary black broadcloth, there being no other fabric in town. That distressed Meriwether, but I am indifferent to clothing. So long as it comforts me I care little about it.

I got an entire room at that public house but could not preserve my privacy because I was instantly recognized. Post and express riders had proclaimed my progress in every hamlet along my route.

"Captain Clark, sir, we are honored to welcome so illustrious a figure to our inn," announced the rotund proprietor, one Barteau.

"It's Mr. Clark. I'm out of the army, sir, and want no part of it."

"Captain you are, though, and a captain's billet we'll give you."

"That's fine; put me up, put my slave in your hayloft if that's suitable, and fetch me plenty of hot water. What's the tariff for three horses, myself, and the darkie?"

"For you, my esteemed sir, nothing; for the horses and the black man, a shilling apiece, including hay and feed."

"Feed them all well. I can't afford to let them sicken."

He nodded.

I had little cash; only a small purse that Meriwether had gotten from St. Louis merchants against my back pay. But it had sufficed.

We were the only guests, but I little doubted that in minutes we would not be. That was how it had been: the whole neighborhood had to poke and prod Captain Clark, wherever we stayed.

York hauled my chest and saddlebags into my upstairs room, and stared at me questioningly.

"Hay the nags, eat, and then come back and cut my hair," I said.

"Us beasts o' burden gets fed," he said insolently.

I laughed, even though I had resolved to deal sternly with him. We were old friends, York and I.

The missus arrived with a leaky oaken bucket of hot water, not much but I didn't need much. I poured it into a porcelain basin on a commode and began to scrub myself, wanting to unskunk myself sufficient not to scare off young ladies. I started with my hair, which was begrimed from days on the trail, and the application of a little lye soap restored the coppery shine to it soon enough.

By the time York was done outdoors, I was ready for him,

sitting bare-chested on a homemade bench next to the candle.

My straightedge sufficed for both my beard and my hair, and York set to work with some skill, reducing the mop of wet red hair to something that might pass muster on a parade ground.

"Make it good this time," I growled. "It's going to get looked at by female eyes."

York didn't reply.

"What's bothering you, dammit?"

York sawed off some more coppery hair. I could feel his heat. You don't live with a slave from childhood without sensing everything that passes through his mind.

"You gonna let me see my woman?"

There it was. He wanted time off to see his wife, who was owned by a tobacco man outside of Louisville.

"No, I can't spare you," I said.

"Sometime, mastuh?"

"You just mind your business and let me decide. Maybe. In a few years."

"Rest of them, on the big trip, they got pay and go fetch them a woman and catch the crabs."

"You catch yourself any crabs, and I'll put the lash to you."

He irritated me, wanting his liberty like that. I probably shouldn't have taken him west. He spent those years as free as any of the soldiers, and now I had a surly servant. Half the squaws on the Missouri had sampled his black pecker, and I didn't doubt that many a lodge contained a dusky little papoose.

No sooner had I completed my toilet than the local burghers arrived, wanting to toast me and hear the stories about grizzlies, mountains with snow on them year around, wild Indians, little prairie wolves, unknown birds, and the buffalo. I obliged them; didn't mind a bit. They raised their cups of porter, just as others had done along the route, and I accepted their homage. Why not? I would have my day in the sun, and then retreat to Kentucky with my bride, lay waste to some hardwood forest, and put in some tobacco.

The next day, Sunday the fourteenth of December, was a blustery one reminding me of how narrowly I had avoided winter travel. I dressed up in my black suit, stock, capote, and set off with York for the last lap. I hoped it would suffice. If it had been Meriwether, he would have gotten himself up in a new blue uniform with a good black tricorne hat, gold braid dripping from the shoulders, new-blacked boots, and a clanking dress sword. But I had nothing to turn the eye except maybe some land warrants and some back pay, and a reputation.

The Hancocks knew I was coming and they knew why. I had written from St. Louis. They would have heard from a hundred other sources. So I would be expected. But as I trotted my chestnut down the muddy post road, I began to rue my haste.

What if all this turned into some sort of fiasco? What if my brown-haired Judy, whose vision kept me going through cold and heat and hunger, didn't care about me, or worse, what if she wasn't anything like what I had remembered? What if she brayed instead of laughed, tittered and whickered instead of smiled, belched instead of lifting a white hand to her lips, displayed rotten yellow teeth . . .

I tormented myself clear to the portals of that imposing home erected on fertile tobacco cropland. Behind it stood several whitewashed outbuildings, a squat barn, slave quarters, summer kitchen, and sheds. One look at George Hancock's rambling house nearly did me in: my distant relative had prospered. He was a country squire, one of the first citizens of Fincastle, and here I was, an adventurer.

I gathered whatever wits I had left to me, dismounted, left my horses to York, and stiffly assaulted the front door.

She opened, and I stared at a vision of white silk, and the world stood still.

7 LEWIS

Mr. Jefferson himself welcomed me at the door of the President's House late in the evening of December 28, having heard of my arrival in Washington, and never was a mortal so gladdened as I to see my friend and mentor and commander in chief.

I had paused long enough to find lodging for my royal Mandan guests, She-He-Ke, his wife, and our interpreters. And then I hurried to that unfinished white manse to find the lanterns lit, every window lighted with tapers, and the president at the door in his slippers, gotten into a faded blue robe, his yawning stewards standing about behind him.

We shook hands heartily, Mr. Jefferson not being the sort to embrace, while the stewards saw to my chattel, especially those trunks that bore the journals and the few botanical specimens I had not earlier sent east.

"At long last!" he exclaimed, and I nodded ruefully, knowing I had been negligent about keeping him apprised of my progress and safety.

"Are you well? Hungry? Shall we talk?"

"Mr. Jefferson, let's talk if you're up to it."

"I'm certainly up to it, but are you?"

I assured him I was in the very bloom of health, and that

settled the matter. I was in fact weary, but who could surrender to Morpheus at such a momentous time? I fairly seethed with delight. I was bursting with news and observations, and at the same time aware that my arrival had caused great jubilation in Washington City; they were calling me the great explorer, celebrating our safe return, writing treatises about me.

It took but a little time for the excellent stewards to settle me upstairs in a capacious four-poster room next to one occupied by Mr. Jefferson's son-in-law, Thomas Randolph, and then escort me to the president's private chambers, where he, still in his robe and slippers, his gray-shot red hair in disarray, received me with heartfelt delight, and beckoned me to a feast of cold beef, creamy rice pudding, chocolates, and ample amounts of fine French wines, which delighted my palate.

I poured some ruby Bordeaux and plunged in, aware that my auditor was acutely absorbed, hanging on to my every word, and processing everything I had to say in that phenomenal brain of his. Mr. Jefferson was more than my president; he was a sentry patrolling the lusty frontiers of botany, zoology, commerce, art, literature, philosophy, mechanics, astronomy, architecture, ethnology, cartography, and a dozen other fields.

He did not take notes, though he was an avid note-maker, but listened so intently that I was sure he could repeat back to me, word for word, everything I told him about the course of the great Missouri, the fierce tribes along it, the falls, the headwaters, the passage across those terrible white peaks, and the descent of the Columbia to the brine of the western sea.

We talked until two, when I began to nod, and he urged me to rest myself in the bosom of the nation's gratitude, and we would pursue other matters in the morning. He stood, began extinguishing the beeswax candles with a silver snuffer until a yawning servant rushed in to complete the task, and I retreated at once.

I did meet him for breakfast, having as usual slept on my bearskin, finding beds too soft after my years of sleeping on hard ground. That grand day we examined everything in my trunks; plants he had never seen, such as the wild flax I had discovered near the great falls of the Missouri; birds, such as the sage grouse I had spotted near Maria's River and the black-billed magpies I had recorded; skins of animals new to him, such as the prairie dog; and he paused long at Will's superb map of the Missouri River, which I knew to be a masterpiece of the cartographer's art, anchored by the innumerable soundings of latitude and longitude I had taken.

When at last we had examined my specimens, he straightened up, placed a hand on my shoulder, and searched a moment for words. "Meriwether," he said at last, "you are the very embodiment of the best in this new nation. You have proven yourself in the most trying conditions, found courage when you needed it, advanced science and knowledge, acted with humane and affectionate regard for our Indian neighbors, and have shown yourself to be more than worthy of the trust I vested in you. I am proud of you; I am more proud of what you've achieved than anything else I've accomplished. You, my son, are worthy of the esteem of every citizen, and I will say so to the world."

He said it so gently and firmly and kindly that I stood transfixed. The president of the republic was saying these things of me.

"Thank you, sir," I said, fumbling for something more suited to this occasion. "I will always try to live up to your expectations for me, and give myself to a live unsullied and honorable and fruitful."

And therein had I sealed my fate.

He smiled, breaking the solemnity of the moment.

"Now, Meriwether, you must see to the publication of your journals. In fact, they belong to the government; you recorded them in pursuit of your duty. But they shall be yours. My son, they will be profitable to you, and the true reward for your courage and perseverance and fortitude. Prepare them, and swiftly, for half the naturalists in Europe, and all of them in this country, are crying to me for word of the publication, and until now I've had little to tell them."

"I will directly, sir," I replied fervently, for I would crawl a hundred miles on my knees to please this man. "I will set upon that task at once, saving only the business of looking after my men. I hope that Congress will be generous, and that my men will receive what was promised; back pay, a grant of three hundred twenty acres, and if the War Department is willing, improvements in their rank according to my commendations."

"Consider me your ally in all that," said Mr. Jefferson. "Congress meets in a few days, and we shall commence our assault upon their purse."

Ah, it was grand to be at the President's House, three and a half years after I had last seen him, my mission fulfilled and successful in every respect, for I had succeeded in every part of my instructions, save perhaps my pacification of the Sioux, which was deeply disappointing to me because they controlled that mighty river of the plains. I had not failed him.

"I fear I am keeping you all too much to myself," the president said at last. "Let your Mandan chief know that we will have a reception here for him tomorrow, along with the Osages

Chouteau brought us. You know, there's a play tonight. I imagine the red men might marvel at our theater, and get the drift of the show even if your translator—Jessaume is it?—has to interpret."

That sounded like a grand idea, and I told the president I would make the arrangements.

"Stay here as long as you wish, of course, Meriwether. We're having the usual New Year's Day open house, with many a fair lady in attendance, and I imagine half of Washington, eager to hear your stories. Have you seen the *National Intelligencer?* You will discover you are somewhere between canonization and sainthood."

I laughed, though I preferred not to.

That fine evening we loaded our savage king and queen into a carriage and made for the theater, and there before much of Washington and the diplomatic corps, we entertained the Mandans and Chouteau's Osages, who gaped and stared and giggled at the thespians, and then returned the favor by performing a frenzied pipe dance on stage, with ululating howls and horrifying screams, much to the shivering delight of the leading lights of Washington.

I sat there benignly: let them all be aware of the savage wilderness that I had penetrated, I thought. Let the howling savages, almost naked in their breechclouts, remind the civilized world where the Corps of Discovery had truly been. We had brought the menacing wilderness to Washington.

I spent the next hours preparing material to give to Benjamin Smith Barton and the American Philosophical Society in Philadelphia, my next port of call, where a banquet awaited me, and my work would be received and reviewed. That would be the crowning glory, and it would be mine alone, for I alone in the Corps of Discovery had been adequately prepared to reap the botanical and zoological harvest. I looked forward to it as keenly as I looked forward to counseling the president about Louisiana and all our western dominions.

New Year's Day, 1807, turned out to be my chance to meet the cream of Washington, who flocked in great numbers to the annual open house given by Mr. Jefferson. They came to examine my Mandans, to examine me, to discover what gaudy stories about grizzlies and savages and strange animals they could memorize to decorate their own conversations. I did not disappoint them. Most of Congress had already arrived, and I wanted to make myself available to answer their questions and at least implicitly, though it was a social occasion, to speak in behalf of my men and the awards they so richly deserved.

Ah, the women! Mr. Jefferson had mentioned them. I yearned for them. And here they all were, flocking about me with eyes aflutter. My dear cousin Maria Wood, had not waited for her wandering admirer, but married. And so I had no one, but I supposed that a young man as favored by fortune as I would not find it difficult to pluck the sweetest fruit.

So it was that I found myself in the company of a fabulously eligible Miss Cecelia, daughter of a New England senator, enjoying those glowing brown eyes, alabaster cheeks, so lovely after my long years among dusky savages, and chestnut hair in ringlets.

I smiled, but not too openly, for fear of revealing the blue-tinted gums that Dr. Saugrain's courses of mercury had given me, gums that would tell all too much to the knowing eye. That was the sole remaining evidence of my former disposition, and I hoped that the blue gums would soon vanish, just as the illness had.

"Would you favor me with an account of your trip?" she asked, over a crystal glass of Mr. Jefferson's silky red Burgundy.

"I would be honored," I replied, fending off a dozen others who wished also to glean whatever pearls of wisdom dropped from the lips of the explorer. There was but little privacy, but I steered her to a corner of that familiar manse, where I had been the president's aide for so many months, and there told her of my adventures, the great white bears, as we first called the grizzlies, the savages, the treacherous river, the dizzying mountains, now a litany so well rehearsed that it spilled easily from my tongue.

"And now I have it all in the journals and must prepare them for publication," I said. "The advancement of science and the fate of nations depends on it."

"Do you like my frock? I got it just for the occasion."

"Your gown?" I gazed at a lemon yellow silk affair, with ruffles of white lace, which sheathed a perfect young form.

"Yes, for Mr. Jefferson's open house. Father didn't approve, you know. He's a Federalist, and saw no reason to spend so many shillings on a dress to wear for an odd republican president who wanders about in his bedroom slippers."

"I see. A nice dress."

I spotted Mr. Dearborn, the secretary of war, and thought I might profitably spend a while with him. I had numerous accounts to settle, and meeting him in these auspicious beginnings of a new year might prove useful, not only to me but to my corps.

"Forgive me, Miss Cecelia, but I must say a word to Secretary Dearborn," I said.

She curtsied and turned to explore the party for other amusements, and I retreated, a little melancholic, for as usual,

I had my troubles with women. I am a serious man, and have no stomach for twitter. Still, she had enchanted me with a form that had been turned on the lathe by a master, and I reflected bitterly on my endless bachelorhood, and my frustrated plans to warm my domestic hearth.

But there would be others. I, of all men on earth, had my pick.

8 CLARK

I suppose I should thank the harsh weather for my betrothal. It kept us bound to the hearth. Give me a better clime, and I would be outside, as is my wont. I would have gotten us a picnic lunch in a hamper from the mammy and some saddle horses from the grooms and headed for the nearest green bower where I might woo that bundle of joy while slapping mosquitoes and fending off red ants.

But Julia is distracted by insects, and my ardor might well have been defeated by crawling bugs on her limbs, wasps, hornets, black horseflies, green-bellied flies, bumblebees, inchworms, caterpillars, and the whine of bloodthirsty mosquitoes for whom flesh is food and blood is drink.

So I ascribe the weather to my successful assault upon the citadel of my desire. The Hancocks left us to our own devices in a stove-warmed parlor, but there were servants hovering about, not always out of earshot, and plainly at hand to protect Julia's virtue. I take some pleasure in the discovery that she didn't entirely relish being protected, or being virtuous, for that matter. For her gaze began to swim when she surveyed me, and I saw the blush rise to her smooth cheeks, and I knew the train of her innermost thoughts.

We were not entirely decorous, for the mistletoe hung from

the chandelier, a dangling invitation perhaps the sly work of old George Hancock himself, who was scarce a decade older than I and knew well the ferment of the loins. I steered Julia under it whenever the occasion permitted, and thus discovered that she was as enthused by its magical powers as I, and for a few moments, at any rate, I wrapped that bundle in my arms and blunderbussed her, or that is the word I chose for it, being an inept man with women.

The colonel accepted my assault upon his daughter well enough; he even set aside his ardent Federalist passions to be hospitable to me. And trouble him as it might, he found the means to praise Mr. Jefferson for sending me out into the unknown.

"Cost too much, though," he said. "An engaging folly, this scheme, but you got back in one piece and I suppose the government can afford a little nonsense."

I smiled benignly. If my future father-in-law could summon a compliment for Mr. Jefferson, the courtship would not go badly. He was a great oddity in Virginia. The bastion of the Federalists was New England, and rare was the Virginian who would make common cause with the Adams family, or the late Hamilton.

"What are the western lands like?" she asked me one day, as we sipped mulled cider before the hearth.

"The air's so clear you can't imagine it, and the prairies run off to the horizon, and you can see a hundred miles, and see the future. It's a place so big it doesn't know you're walking over it."

She shuddered, and touched me. I thought to make her shudder more, and touch me more.

"Most of the savages are friendly sorts, but there's some with a look in their eye that's like a tomahawk blade, and it's pretty easy to see what's boiling inside their skulls. The proud mean ones maybe keep quiet because the chiefs make 'em, but you know what's itching them, and what they want to do."

"I don't think I would care for that!" she said, this time shuddering right up tight, and drawing her fingers over my sleeve.

I thought maybe I could shudder her into just the right mood, and get the assault over with.

"And if it isn't the savages, it's the big brown bears, so big they tower up on their hind legs and stare down at you from the treetops, almost, with their little pig eyes, and claws as long as kitchen knives, thinking how they maybe will claw you to pieces and have you for supper because you stumbled into their lair."

"Oh!" she exclaimed, this time wrapping a fastidious arm around my neck. "I hope we never go there!"

I realized the moment had come, and cleared my throat.

"Miss Julia . . . you would find Kentucky much to your liking."

"Captain Clark, I am not sure I would care for Kentucky, with all its savages."

"They're just as subdued as all the servants here, and you needn't worry about them."

She laughed.

"I am a tad older than you, but you will find that much to your advantage," I said.

"Why?"

"You will know later." That was all I could manage. "Now, it is my design to lay the proposition before your father, if you are so inclined."

She pouted a little, and I realized I had not made any declaration. Somehow I found the matter most difficult, and while I normally am plainspoken and forward, this time I was tongue-tied and flummoxed.

"Ah, my little Julia, I have had you in my mind all these years."

She frowned. "Well, I never knew it. After all, you are being presumptuous." She sipped the steaming mulled cider and eyed me levelly, being far better at the game than I. I thought hotly that I would abandon this place and head for Washington. I would be too late for Christmas but my reception there would be warmer than the chilly one here.

Then she laughed.

"Ah, Julia, the truth is, I have had naught but the vision of you in my bosom all this while; it was upon me at the very shore of the western sea. I am not a young man, being more than twice your years, and yet in all my days I never was drawn to any but you, and so I declare myself."

It was awkward, but my plain tongue had deserted me.

"I have not heard the word," she said.

"Ah, ah, it is you I love."

She smiled, and touched me again, with such gentleness that I turned to wax. "I should rather like an older man," she said, and I kissed her, servants be damned.

So it was, that Yuletide, that I formed my alliance, but first I had to take the case to her father. Since my purposes were known from the beginning, I didn't surprise him, and it no doubt had helped that the Clarks and Hancocks were well intertwined over several generations.

The colonel received me in those office chambers from which he counted his tobacco receipts and totted up the costs of the plantation. I supposed that this was a transaction like any other. He received me the afternoon of Christmas Eve, his square ruddy face surveying me with a sardonic silence. He wore his dark hair in a queue, a sign of his Federalist leanings.

"Sir, I should like Julia's hand," I said.

He smiled thinly. "And she approves?" he asked, in that thick, hoarse voice that suggested to intimate experience with the fine-leaved product of his fields.

"You might ask her," I replied cheerfully.

He gazed out upon the barren fields, half exhausted because tobacco depleted the soil. "And your age is no impediment to her?"

I shook my head. "She rather prefers a man to a boy."

"It's an impediment to me. She's barely upon her woman-hood."

"My mother married at fifteen."

He nodded. "She has grown up in pleasant surroundings," he said. "Can you assure me that it will be so in the future?"

"I am expecting considerable back pay and a land grant of some size."

"In Kentucky."

"Yes, federal lands in the west."

He opened the snuffbox and inhaled a pinch, wheezing a moment. "I never imagined she would end up with one of Jefferson's radicals," he said. "I don't suppose you'll be heading for France to lop off the heads of a few noblemen—and women."

I laughed. "I believe simply in an aristocracy of merit, not heredity."

"And not in the leadership of good families?"

"Good men, yes, that is close to my republican principles, sir. Let them elect good men."

"There are no impediments? Your health is good?"

"Excellent, sir. I know of no impediments at all."

"A soldier's life is hard." There was a question in his observation.

"I am no longer a soldier. I resigned my commission, and for good. I have no disability."

He grunted, his brown eyes glowing brightly. "Your intentions have been plain, Will, and that has given me time to ponder the matter, and discuss it as well with my wife. We are close, our families, and I am pleased by the connection, but we think it would be desirable to wait a year. She is but half a woman still, at least to us, and knows you little enough. If you should agree to that, and would postpone until January of eighteen and eight, we would welcome you most heartily into our family, and into our bosoms." He smiled. "Even if your politics are impossible."

We laughed. I shall always remember the moment, Colonel Hancock wheezing his delight; rising up and clapping me on the back, and leading me back into the great house to inform the mistress, and receive her congratulations, and then to the parlor where Miss Julia sat doing crewelwork for the seat of a dining chair.

She peered up at her parents and at me, and set aside her yarns.

"It is a very special Christmas, Julia," her father said. "Happy for us, happy for the Clarks, happy for you, I trust."

Julia smiled, uncertainly.

"If you can manage to wait a year, settle into womanhood a while, make sure of your heart, then you have our blessings to marry this big redheaded son of our kin John Clark."

Julia cried, and I took her hand and lifted her up from her chair, and we had the most sweet and sacred of Christmases.

9 LEWIS

The deplorable Sergeant Patrick Gass is forcing my hand. He has announced the forthcoming publication of his journal, even though I have expressly forbidden it. I gave permission only to Private Frazier to publish his account, but Gass has proceeded anyway, much to my annoyance.

These are unlettered men, not versed in any branch of arts or science, and likely to spread a great deal of misinformation. They have the advantage of me, hastening their small journals into print while I labor at larger tasks, not least of which has been securing the back pay of all the men in the corps, including Sergeant Gass.

This Thursday morning, the twelfth of March, 1807, I stormed into the president's office with the Gass prospectus in hand, and insisted that something be done to stop it. Gass would ruin everything.

Mr. Jefferson eyed me through those gold-rimmed spectacles of his. "It's not among my principles to stop publication of anything," he said quietly, after studying the publisher's brochure. He stared out upon the lawn. "But I do think it's going to be damaging to us. I'd suggest a warning to the public that it and any other diaries are not authorized by you, the commander, and also that they are likely to be unreliable." He smiled at me. "You wouldn't be fretting about your profit, would you?"

"Certainly not, sir. I want only for the truth to reach the public."

Jefferson laughed, which irritated me. Why couldn't the man be serious? I am not after the money; I'm concerned with the *truth,* and worried that half those note-takers among my corps will publish undisciplined, uneducated versions of events and permanently twist what Will and I so assiduously recorded.

But even the president thinks I want the bootleg journals suppressed so that I can make an additional dollar. I flatter myself that my conduct is grounded upon the highest motives of patriotism and truth, and that such base motives as private gain have no hold upon me.

We agreed that I would write the letter and he would vet it, and maybe put a stop to this bootleg publication of journals. And by afternoon that was accomplished. I wrote the *National Intelligencer* condemning these spurious publications by persons unknown to me, and cautioning readers to beware and to hold out for the true goods, the first of which I would bring out by year's end. I mentioned as well that I had authorized the publication only of Frazier's journals, but took pains to point out that the man is only a private, unlettered, unacquainted with science, and that his work must not be taken seriously. I sent it off today, and expect it to run tomorrow.

I cannot stop these pirate editions, in part because I have resigned my commission in the army and have accepted Mr. Jefferson's appointment of me as the governor of Upper Louisiana, which was affirmed by the Senate March 2. I suppose I shall have to bear the burden of these inferior tracts. Will and

I ordered the sergeants to keep journals; the more of them, the safer the record of discovery. Some of them merely copied what we had written. And now these unlettered men want to cash in, and their greed disgusts me.

I face the complex task of reducing the official journals to a coherent narrative, excising those entries not intended for the public eye, and organizing the scientific discoveries, and producing the maps we completed, and not until then will the public receive an accurate and sound depiction of all that we experienced.

Gass's brochure has put me into a funk from which I will not recover for some while. What makes it all the worse is that from the dawn of this year, Mr. Jefferson and I have been doing our utmost to extract from the public purse worthy rewards for my Corps of Discovery. We proposed to Mr. Alston of North Carolina, who chairs a special committee of the House to see into our compensation, that all my men, including those who returned from Fort Mandan with the keelboat, be given double pay and a land grant of three hundred twenty acres. And that Will Clark receive a compensation equal to my own, a recognition he richly deserves.

Alas, the War Department, in the annoying person of Mr. Dearborn, recommended less for Will Clark, a thousand acres for him as opposed to sixteen hundred for me, and a lieutenant's pay for him, and a captain's for me. But the president and I got Alston's ear, and the chairman was able to even things out somewhat: Will and I each will get sixteen hundred acres.

The president submitted my appointment as governor of the Upper Louisiana territory, and also asked Congress to raise Will Clark to a lieutenant colonel, but again the secretary of war managed to foil Mr. Jefferson, and Congress eventually agreed with him, it being the wish of the members to abide by seniority and not jump Clark over the heads of other deserving men. But I was heartened by the news that they would gladly confirm Clark in any other office within their power, and thus, at the president's behest, he will be our superintendent of Indian Affairs in St. Louis, and a brigadier of militia.

All this business consumed my days and nights this winter. It took a month of heated debate before the representatives passed even a scaled-down version of what I had asked for my doughty corps, but at least the Senate nodded it through in a trice, and I am gratified that my courageous men will benefit from a grateful republic.

Meanwhile I am the cynosure at one banquet after another. It seems all of Washington must have me at its table. The city welcomed me with a great affair January 14, in which I was the honored guest, along with Chouteau and Big White. I vaguely remember seventeen toasts. (*Vaguely* is the exact word for it.) It was at that time that Joel Barlow, powdered, periwigged, and bedizened in scarlet and periwinkle silks, first intoned his new ode, "On the Discoveries of Lewis," and I was greatly smitten by some of the bard's orotund verses:

> *With the same soaring genius thy Lewis descends,*
> *And, seizing the oars of the sun,*
> *O'er the sky-propping hills and the high waters he bends*
> *And gives the proud earth a new zone . . .*

> *Then hear the loud voice of the Nation proclaim,*
> *And all ages resound the decree:*
> *Let our Occident stream bear the young hero's name*
> *Who taught him his path to the sea.*

I fancied teaching the Columbia which way to go. And I wondered what Big White thought of all that.

There have been balls to attend, and the social life is heady. I am finding feminine company abounding, and little doubt that I shall make a proper match. I require a serious woman to match my own seriousness, and that is no simple matter, especially in Washington. There seem plenty of the fair sex making themselves pleasant to me, but I have no stomach for the twittering things.

In January Will Clark wrote me that his assault upon the fair citadel of Fincastle pulchritude was successful, and that he would capture his prize in January of next year. I rejoiced at his success, and have regretted being so busy with the president and Congress that I scarcely have found a moment to pursue the lovely and fragile beauty that appears at every prospect.

I expect him momentarily. He will head for St. Louis at once, with Private Frazier, bearing back pay for my men. He will also take our Mandan royalty, She-He-Ke, and his entourage, back to St. Louis and begin the preparations to take the chief upriver, past the hostile Arikaras, which will be a delicate business but one Will Clark can well manage.

I am glad he has delayed his journey to the capital because the President's House has been a hospital for several days. First Tom Randolph caught the catarrh; then I, and finally Mr. Jefferson. I bled the president's son-in-law considerably, and he recovers slowly.

Doctor Saugrain in St. Louis opposes bleeding, saying it weakens the patient, but he is isolated. I prefer the counsel of the eminent Benjamin Rush of Philadelphia, the finest of all physicians this side of the Atlantic, who instructed me in medical matters before I headed west. He, of course, believes with all progressive physicians that it is necessary to purge the blood of whatever bad humors evoke the disease, and the way to do it is to drain away the tainted blood and let the body generate healthier blood.

As for me, I examined myself with some concern upon taking sick, studying my mouth, my gums, my eyes, my skin, and found nothing amiss but a bilious fever, and for that I had Rush's excellent Thunderclappers, specially compounded to abate fevers, which I took to good effect, and upon this very day I am back to my usual bloom of health, and so is Mr. Jefferson, though Randolph lingers abed. I make no public or private mention of Saugrain; it is as if I have never met the man, though of course I am privately grateful to him.

I expect to wind up my business here by the end of the month and head for Philadelphia, where I will join the savants of the American Philosophical Society, and negotiate with a printer to begin work on the journals. Mr. Jefferson has been conversing with me about Upper Louisiana. We will need to pacify the tribes on the Missouri, arrange free passage of our traders, license them to deal with the tribes, keep the British out, and encourage settlement sufficient to anchor that vast territory firmly to the union of states.

Ah, Philadelphia! My pleasure in presenting the most learned men of America a bounty of new plants and animals, all carefully observed and recorded, along with accurate maps, and a firsthand account of the passage through that great mystery, the interior of North America, will, I imagine, be unparalleled and perhaps will exceed even my pleasure in reporting to Mr. Jefferson that I had fulfilled his mission in all respects.

I expect to be in Philadelphia some little while preparing the journals and discovering just what the printer needs. I am in no hurry to head for St. Louis; not with Will Clark on hand to handle our Indian diplomacy, and not with an old acquaintance, the experienced public servant Frederick Bates, brother of my old friend Tarleton Bates, heading there to be secretary, my lieutenant. I rather expect the two of them will govern excellently while I see to the maps and papers, and to that sacred duty to transmit what I have learned of the world to these men of science.

I reflect, when I am alone in my room in the President's House, how fortune has smiled upon me. It was not long ago, writing on the occasion of my thirty-first birthday in the Bitterroot Mountains—just after that moment of weakness—that I wondered whether I had given the world anything worthwhile or done anything notable during my life. Now I know I have.

But I have no desire to dwell upon memories; the future beckons. I am torn between my wish to become a man of science and a man of public affairs, and I will have to resolve the matter eventually. I am in a rare position to choose my course in life. For the moment I must set science aside and focus on the western reaches of the republic, and if I am blessed in this endeavor, perhaps I will be invited to fill larger offices, perhaps even the office held by the resident of this very house.

My public purpose, then, is to draft a paper informing Mr. Jefferson and his successors what lies to the west, and how to subdue it, and how to encourage commerce in it, and how to treat the tribes that live upon it. I will make it a first order of business to provide the government with my insights, and if my perceptions find favor, so will I.

I should like to be regarded as the new Sage of the West, publish my thoughts regularly in some news sheet, and stand up and be counted. If all that occurs as I hope, then someday my confreres in the Democratic-Republican ranks might find me worthy of higher office. And I would accept it gladly.

I have come into myself; for this was I set upon the earth. That vast Louisiana territory is mine; etched indelibly on my mind, though the world knows little of it, and won't until I publish my journals. How odd it is, during these reflective moments, that I sometimes find myself reluctant to share all that wealth of information with the public. I have little desire to publish. I would rather confide my secrets privately to men like Benjamin Smith Barton, of the philosophical society, than cast my pearls before the swine.

The Missouri country is a comely land, well watered, hilly, forested, verdant, and fertile, and I will make it my home. I am especially fond of it because it windows the world that I recently conquered. I see myself rooted in the West, settled upon a great green estate, my happy bride beside me, our children blooming. I should like to settle out there in the virgin land, my eyes upon the horizons. I should like to be a country squire, rather like Tom Jefferson, holding office, improving knowledge, and devising better ways to prosper. Every door is open.

10 LEWIS

I arrived in the City of Brotherly Love on April 10, and after settling into a room on Cherry Street rented by a Mrs. Wood, I began at once to tackle the business before me. The chestnuts were in new leaf and so was I, so happy was I to be there in that seat of learning.

I have been paid by Congress at last and am in comfortable circumstances, and can indulge my every whim if I choose. But I am a serious man, and do not indulge myself. I did, however, lay in a stock of porter, ale, and Madeira, with which to entertain guests at my lodging.

Those journals weigh heavily on my mind, along with the hundreds of specimens and drawings and pressings of plants that I have with me; not only what I had brought from the Pacific, but much that the president had kept for me, sent to him from Mandan villages in 1805.

Upon good recommendation, I chose John Conrad as my publisher and found him at his chambers at 30 Chestnut Street. I liked the man at once; a dusty, gray, scholarly gent who took his tasks seriously. His seriousness recommended him to me.

I had taken but one of the journals, and this I showed to him after we had exchanged greetings.

"I have in mind the publication of the journals in one volume, and the scientific findings, maps, and so forth, in another," I said.

He pulled on his wire-rimmed spectacles and examined what I regarded as my treasure; the daily records, mostly done by Clark, that supplied a day-by-day progress of our journey.

"Ah, I see the captain was a little loose with his spelling," Conrad said, "but that is easily remedied. I suppose you mean to condense these items, and perhaps improve them?"

"Yes . . ."

"I would recommend it. Now, what about the illustrations?"

"Well, I know little about publishing, Mr. Conrad, and perhaps you can advise me."

"What have you?"

"Field notes, including drawings; pressed plants; some feathers, pelts, bones, seeds . . . and of course the maps. Clark has some gifts, and he put them to good use. The maps are most important to all, I suppose."

"We can have them copied and I can make a plate. The drawings, Captain, are up to you. It is your project. Bring us an edited version of your journals—I'm sure a man of your experience can reduce them quite nicely. You'll need to prepare the drawings, maps, all of it, just as you wish us to produce your books."

"Have you good artists here?"

"You have come to the very place," Conrad said.

"We are in a great hurry," I said. "Mr. Jefferson is fairly demanding publication as soon as it can be arranged."

Conrad smiled for the first time. "We are honored to attend to such a project, Captain, and I assure you of our utmost cooperation. You need not complete the work before submitting it to us; in fact, the sooner you begin submitting your material, the better; I will have typesetters upon it instantly."

"Up to me, then."

"Yes, it is, sir."

"I suppose we should discuss costs."

I gave him the particulars, and he told me he would get back to me as soon as he could do the calculations.

I lost no time in contacting my old friend Doctor Benjamin Rush, from whom I had outfitted the expedition with a fine closet of medicines. He was a member of the American Philosophical Society, a signer of the Declaration of Independence, and most important for me, the nation's preeminent physician. He had charged me to make certain medical observations of the savages during the trip: time of puberty, the menses, condition of teeth and eyes, diseases of old age, and the like, and now, with utmost joy, I had the answers for him. Eagerly did I make for his home on Chestnut Street.

"Ah! The conquering captain!" the jowly old man exclaimed upon descrying my ingress into his musty brown library in the wake of a pale servant. We shook hands warmly, and the doctor promptly ordered a glass of port apiece so we might progress through our business in ample humor. "Tell me, tell me. Everything!"

"Ah, it is a joy to be back, and the pills, sir, Rush's pills, so prevailed over all manner of dispositions that I count them a universal salvation. The men, sir, called them Thunderclappers, and indeed, Doctor, they were the sovereign of all maladies. I only wish I had more with me, but I ran out of everything."

The Thunderclappers were mighty doses of calomel, which consisted of six parts of mercury to one part of chlorine, and the Mexican cathartic jalap, the pair of them a purgative that brooked no argument from any mortal bowels. I dispensed them freely, not only for bowel troubles, but as a general cathartic to purge the blood and intestine.

"I received constant petitions from them; buffalo meat especially bound them up, and I was able to end their distress with great success!"

Rush laughed. "And did you collect answers to my questions?"

"I did, sir. The customs and practices varied so much from tribe to tribe that I can scarcely recount them now, but I plan to include my entire observations in a final volume. I've engaged Conrad to do the journals, and am already at work."

Rush listened to my practiced tales of grizzly bears, the great falls of the Missouri, the sicknesses of the men, and all the rest, nodding as I spoke.

"I shall arrange a banquet directly," he said. "There are men in the society aching to hear what you have accomplished, and aching, my young friend, to pay you appropriate tribute."

Again I was awash in pleasure, and our visit proceeded with utmost joy. I could see, after the better part of an afternoon, that the grand old man was tiring, so I made haste to wind up my discourse. But one matter stayed me.

"Before I take my leave, sir, I have a matter of medicine to discuss, a delicate matter. It involves my corps, sir. Many are in St. Louis, still soldiers. During the expedition they came into intimate contact with various dusky women of the tribes, and to put matters plainly, contracted various maladies which I endeavored to heal by liberal application of mercury ointment and calomel."

"What diseases, Captain?"

"Why, they are ordinary soldiers, sir, and as one might expect they took little care. The tribes are oddly wanton and at the same time strict; a husband might offer a guest the favors of his wife, and yet if the wife engaged in such conduct on her own account, she might be severely chastised or beaten."

"Yes, yes?"

"Well, sir, I applied your remedies for what they vulgarly called 'the clap,' and of course for *lues venerea,* which many of them caught, and then caught again and again. Now, upon returning to St. Louis I contracted for their care with a French physician, a most estimable man, but of course he's isolated from the advances of science.

"I'll be returning to St. Louis soon, and thought to ask you whether there might be new remedies opened to science, known to you but not known to a physician so isolated. I have always looked after my men, sir, and continue to take their part even after the corps has been disbanded."

"Something for the men of the corps, you say?" There was a question in Rush's eyes.

"Yes, sir. For them. The captains, of course, were above such things—at least I have every right to believe that Captain Clark stayed carefully aloof. He brims with health."

Rush nodded. "Mercury is all we have," he said. "But in many cases the disease simply vanishes. Mercury in steady courses usually inhibits the disorder. Salts of arsenic or bismuth are sometimes employed, but they are dangerous and without proven effect."

"Then the St. Louis physician, Doctor Saugrain, has followed the right course?"

"I imagine," Rush said tersely.

"I am comforted that all is being done that can be. Some of them, Private Gibson especially, are sick."

I left with a new supply of Rush's Thunderclappers, and turned to other business.

But awaiting me at Mrs. Wood's boardinghouse was an issue of the *National Intelligencer* that had been forwarded to me by Mr. Jefferson himself. I made haste to discover what within its columns had occasioned the delivery to me, and found a letter from one McKeehan, of Pittsburgh, Sergeant Gass's publisher, slandering me in every sentence; declaring that my real purpose in suppressing the publication of other journals was my own profit; and much more of that bilious sort of thing. He even took the liberty of recording my very thoughts, or so he imagined!

"I'll squeeze the nation first, and then raise a heavy contribution on the citizens individually; I'll cry down those one-volume journals and frighten publishers and no man, woman or child shall read a word about *my* tour unless they enter their names on *my* lists, and pay what price I shall afterwards fix on my three volumes and map."

I was enraged, and for a while thought to challenge the man on the field of honor. My motives are as lofty as I can manage them, and I wish to produce a sound, educated, and thoroughly accurate account of the voyage of discovery, including every plant and animal we revealed to mankind, and every feature of the land we traversed. Profit doesn't even enter into it.

But the more I thought on it, the more I decided to forgo the satisfaction of honor. I contain, within my mind, a vast body of knowledge, which I alone possess, which my field notes only hint of, and not even Will Clark can imagine. The possibility that a ball from a dueling pistol might forever darken my mind, and deprive the world of the greatest body of information since the discoveries of Columbus, stayed me from that course. In the end I chose to ignore the scurrilous assault on my integrity, and proceed.

I returned to my printer, Conrad, who supplied me with an estimate: four thousand five hundred dollars to publish the journals and the scientific material and maps, and the supplement dealing with Indian glossaries and ethnographic observations. That was far more than I could afford, but Conrad had worked out some costs, and recommended that we offer subscriptions to the complete set, three volumes, published octavo, running four or five hundred pages each; the price to be thirty-one dollars. I agreed.

Worse, the entire burden of preparing drawings, engravings, the map, reducing the astronomy observations to longitude, and finally the editing, would be borne by William Clark and me, and was not included in Conrad's services. I feared we would go heavily into debt, and Will Clark would be worse off because he had been paid less.

I hired a promotions man and commenced work on a prospectus advertising "Lewis and Clark's Tour to the Pacific Ocean Through the Interior of the Continent of North America," and soon placed it in the *National Intelligencer,* where it occasioned much interest.

11 LEWIS

      I must head back to Washington to settle the accounts. The clerks keep pestering me to provide receipts for the drafts levied on the treasury; I keep telling them that they traveled all the way across a wilderness to the Pacific and back, and some got lost. But that doesn't seem to faze officials: they want paper, or else to lay the bills upon me. I am growing testy about it.

      I did not suppose I would ever weary of Philadelphia, the most civilized precinct of North America, and yet I am, and want to retreat to Locust Hill and begin work on my papers. They banqueted and toasted me here through the spring and summer, so much that my head would be turned by it all were it not for the steadiness of purpose and good character instilled in me by my mother.

      I've attended three meetings of the American Philosophical Society, and in each case was besieged by members wanting to know about the West. I am flattered by such attention, and have promised them numerous notes and papers. In May I visited the eminent Benjamin Smith Barton, head of the society, and returned to him a book about Louisiana I had carried all the way to the western sea and back. He was most delighted.

      Nor was that the least of it. Charles Willson Peale, the

eminent painter, sculptor, and museum director, has sketched me and done a facial mask. The sketch will become an oil portrait, and the mask a waxworks image of me. C.B.J. Fevret de Saint-Menim, the French artist, has done a fine likeness of me in native attire, especially the ermine coat given me by Cameahwaite. Here am I, at age thirty-three, greatly celebrated by savants and artists and poets. Peale's museum will be the repository of many of my artifacts. I have employed him as well to illustrate the journals with drawings of the animals we discovered.

I hired a fine German botanist named Frederick Pursh to plant my seeds, illustrate my books with renderings of my fieldwork, and classify my discoveries, so I have that aspect of publication well in hand. He was commended to me by a local nurseryman and botanist named McMahon, who has tenderly cultivated numerous of the Western species I managed to bring back, though so many were lost in the cache at the Great Falls of the Missouri that I am able to offer only a modest improvement in the knowledge of North American botany.

I hired the engraver James Barralet to portray the falls of the Missouri and Columbia, and employed Alexander Wilson to portray the birds. And for a hundred dollars I hired the Swiss mathematician Ferdinand Hassler to reduce my field observations to accurate longitude. Will and I had agreed to split the cost of preparing the journals but now I find myself suffering a want of funds, having laid out so much, so fast, to launch our journals.

So I have been very busy, but not so much that I could not enjoy many a night out with my old friend Mahlon Dickerson, a lawyer of great distinction and as much a man about town as a rural Virginian like me would want to know. He lightens my serious disposition, bantering about frivolous things, which I accept because he is at heart as serious as I am, and not given to triviality, which is the perdition of many a life. We have made a fine bachelor pair, roaming this venerable city, meeting the ladies at various levees, balls, musicales, and lectures, and sometimes escaping town to test our firearms against assorted stumps and toads.

It was upon one of those social evenings that I encountered the dazzling Elizabeth Burden, a young lady of such grace and fair beauty that I was instantly entranced. There she stood, in a green cotton frock, its waist gathered just under her bosom, with puffed sleeves, all of it summery and cool. I had no difficulty arranging an introduction: that occurred following an ethnology lecture at Carpenters Hall. She was in the company of her eminent father, a widowed ancient history professor at the university, and I sensed at once that here at last was the woman who combined the magnificence of form I cherished with the accomplishments that I considered absolutely essential.

I was particularly glad I had finally completed my new wardrobe. I had nothing to wear after returning from the West, and Washington was scarcely the place for a gentleman to be outfitted. So within a day of my arrival in the Quaker City, I engaged some tailors and put them to work. I certainly wanted appropriate clothing for my new and prominent life, and took pleasure in looking my finest.

This Wednesday evening, July 22, 1807, I was splendidly accoutered in cream silk knee-britches, a royal blue coat with brass buttons, white cotton stock, and a fine black bicorne, though it was perhaps too hot for such attire. I kept my coat open so that I might not sweat too much at the armpits.

I invited the Burdens to a nearby tavern and they gladly

accepted, eager to meet the explorer. I used my status shame-lessly, and why not? What better entrée into the lives of strang-ers? I bought a round of Madeira and cheese and other sundries for the gentlemen, while Professor Burden ordered lemonade with pond ice for his daughter, and I got down to the business of exploring this fair lady as if she were an unknown continent, whose rivers I was gradually ascending to their source.

"Ah, what beauteous company we share this evening. Tell me, Miss Elizabeth, about your accomplishments, quite apart from being the cynosure of all eyes."

She eyed me levelly, and I wondered whether it had been the wrong approach.

"I mean, you are here attending a lecture on Ohio River tribal ethnology."

She smiled at last, and like a sunburst. "It was my father's wish."

"I imagine you profited from it."

"I imagine," she said.

"You have been reared among books. Have you a library?"

"Governor, my particular joy lies in keeping a good house for my father, so that he may pursue his vocation. I bring him a tea tray every afternoon at four. I have a good hand. Some-times he permits me to copy things he needs, or to prepare a draft he will be sending to a printer."

"Oh? A copyist you say, familiar with unusual terms and all?"

"We have Doctor Johnson's dictionary. It doesn't always suffice."

I began to grow excited. A copyist! And I, with an enor-mous project looming over me. Not just a copyist, but one who could correct errors and spellings and put things right.

"I think you perform a most valuable labor," I said, and turned to the florid-faced professor, who wore his gray hair in a long queue. "You have a great asset, sir, in this fair maid."

"I've never thought of her as an asset, Governor." There was a certain asperity in his tone, and I retreated.

"A helpmeet, then. A daughter who is there, upon your service, doing all that is required to advance knowledge and scholarship."

He smiled. "I am the beneficiary, that is true, but I worry about my Elizabeth and her future. She is twenty-three."

Ah, I thought, the fine old gentleman is playing cupid. He's aware of what a match I would make, and what I can offer a woman. Twenty-three is older than the usual nuptial age, and she had been withering on the vine, and that only improved my chances.

Once I had properly inventoried her charms, I began at once to spin stories of my adventures.

"Mahlon has heard all these, but I always have some additional thing to tell about, and so he'll just have to listen," I said.

She smiled at Dickerson, and I began anew to relive those crucial moments in my existence when I was walking across a wilderness populated by unruly savages, dangerous beasts, hunger and cold and sickness . . . Thus I entranced her for the evening, and managed to meet several more times, always during the bright June afternoons, to take tea in the company of her aunt.

I thought surely she would succumb, but then one afternoon she declined my attentions, saying she had a headache, and after that it became more and more taxing to see her, though I found out what lectures her father was attending and sometimes caught a bright glimpse of her in those moments. She was always the soul of courtesy, but I knew that she had rejected my suit. Ah, this business of being a perpetual bachelor is woeful at times, though of course I cherish the liberty it affords me.

I knew that once again, domestic joy had eluded me, though I could not quite see how I had failed or what I had said that turned her away. St. Louis, probably. A woman so civilized and accomplished might not relish life in a raw town west of the Alleghenies. I could not find anything to fault in my own conduct, save perhaps that quality of which I am most proud, that I am a serious man and take life as a matter of much gravity.

I made light of it to my boon companion, Dickerson, and made ready to return to Washington to deal with those pesky accountants who could not grasp why I did not have duplicate or triplicate copies of every draft upon the treasury I signed during my preparation and after the corps had returned.

During this whole period I had not penned a word for Conrad. He was impatient, beseeching me to send him material so he could begin the great project, but I did not feel like doing it, and wanted to do it in a proper manner, with quiet exactitude, and not in Mrs. Wood's rooming house in a strange city. Mr. Jefferson had been beseeching me as well, saying that the scientific world awaits my journals, and he pressed me so much to begin them that I began turning aside his letters. I had scarcely gotten accustomed to life in civilization, and now I am facing impossible demands. So I am off to Washington to settle accounts, and then Virginia.

It is terribly hot. Jefferson is at Monticello, where he prefers to while away the moist summers, and I will visit Locust Hill to say goodbye to my family, and see the president there.

We have business to discuss. The Aaron Burr conspiracy trial has started, and I know he wants to brief me. I know little about the ambitious former vice president's grand scheme, having been on my great journey, but it is affecting politics in Upper Louisiana, and I will be forced to deal with the clamors of ambitious men whom Burr had recruited to sever the western territories from the republic. And the president will want to know how the publication of my journals was progressing. I could heartily assure him that work was advancing on all fronts, and I would soon begin the editing.

The heat has been troubling me; the damp air, soggy post roads, rainy weather, enervating warmth that leaves me sticky and uncomfortable and yearning for the dry high plains. And I am not feeling very well. I had some chills and diagnosed the ague and began taking an extract of cinchona bark, but the biliousness does not go away.

12 CLARK

My return to St. Louis this April of 1807 was not nearly so arduous as the eastbound trip, because I employed gravity to good effect, taking my party on a sturdy flatboat down the Ohio River. It was painful to leave Julia behind, but I was buoyed by the knowledge that soon I would return to claim my bride. And meanwhile, I had urgent business to attend.

I was charged by Mr. Jefferson to pursue several matters with utmost vigor. First would be the difficult task of returning the Mandan chief, Big White, and his party to his home, no easy matter with the hostile Arikaras blocking the Missouri River, and the Sioux sullen and questionable.

Another would be to reorganize the militia. And that would cause turmoil because I would need to purge it of numerous officers who had conspired with Aaron Burr to separate the whole territory from the republic. As brigadier, I would have to rebuild the weakened militia and prepare it for whatever might come, including war with the British, who are behaving in a deliberately provocative manner.

And finally, I would as superintendent of Indian Affairs need to effect Mr. Jefferson's policy of pacification and trade, a most arduous undertaking that would mean repealing some of the licenses General Wilkinson, the former governor, had awarded to friends, and at the same time build up government-operated trading posts, what Mr. Jefferson calls "factories," where each tribe could obtain reliable goods and pay in furs, under the watchful eye of the government.

But en route for St. Louis, I made one last stop at Fincastle to see my beloved Julia. Ah, what an occasion that was, for I had no sooner won my beloved than I must leave her.

I think back now on a moment I will not soon forget, at table with the Hancocks, the colonel at the head, ruddy and square-faced; Julia's fluttering mother at the other, and various family and guests in between, including their future son-in-law. Julia sat beside me, slim and girlish and done up in bottle green velvet for the occasion, so handsome I could scarce stop my hands from straying.

I waited until the servants had cleared off the platters and lit some fresh beeswax candles, and a pause enveloped us. I had in my brown waistcoat a small packet wrapped in tissue, and this I removed and placed before me on the white linen.

"Julia," I said, "when I was late in Washington to get instructions from Mr. Jefferson, I made known to him our attachment and received his heartiest congratulations. The very next day, though he was sick abed, he sent me this. It is a presidential gift to you, upon our betrothal."

I opened that mysterious packet, which had become the cynosure of many a Hancock gaze, and withdrew from it some jewelry, including a necklace, two bracelets, earrings, and a ring, all fashioned from pearls and topaz, a gift so astonishing that I marveled at it.

"Oh, oh!" she exclaimed.

I handed them to her, and she fingered them lovingly while

the family craned to see. Then I stood, and slid the necklace about her, taking some liberty, I imagine, as I swept her hair aside, and clasped the necklace. Then I slid the bracelets over her wrists, and tried the ring, which didn't fit.

"I am quite without words," Julia's mother breathed.

"A fine thing, a fine thing," the colonel muttered. "Topaz, is it? Pearls from the Orient. Mr. Jefferson has outdone himself."

That was quite a concession from so ardent a Federalist, and I smiled. I liked the gentleman despite the chasm between us, for I am and always will be an ardent Democratic-Republican, like my president.

I could see on Julia's face that she was transfixed, not only by the grand gift, but also by the occasion. Her bosom and wrists bore the gracious gift of a president upon them.

"Oh, Mr. Clark, my good sir, thank him for me, and thank you for these things. I shall write him myself to say it."

It pleased me that Julia could write.

Colonel Hancock addressed me. "General, your plans have changed. When last you visited us, it was my understanding that you would be settling in Kentucky or the Indiana Territory not so far that we might not see Julia, yet here you are with a new agenda."

That was George Hancock's way of asking what had happened.

"Well, sir, Mr. Jefferson proposed first of all that I be made a lieutenant colonel of infantry as a reward for our voyage, but the War Department and Congress thought better of it, and Mr. Jefferson proposed these offices instead. I had some misgivings about the regular army anyway, but none at all about these new offices."

"But St. Louis?" Mrs. Hancock exclaimed. "Such a vile place, I hear!"

I chuckled. "Not as fine as Virginia or Louisville, but Julia will be at ease."

"But it's all French! And Catholic!"

I had found the French a rascally lot and didn't want to praise them, but neither did I wish to alarm my future in-laws about Julia's safety and happiness.

"They are much like the rest of us."

"It's a turbulent city, filled with schemers and cutthroats," Hancock said. "General Wilkinson let it happen! He was a part of the Burr conspiracy until he backed out. Everyone knows it! There isn't a tawdry scheme that General Wilkinson doesn't want a piece of so long as he sniffs a profit. Imagine a city seething with traitors, eager to saw off the territory and start a new nation, and there you'll be, general of militia, the sole armed commander representing Washington against all your fellow republicans and riffraff. I fear for your safety, sir."

I smiled. It wasn't long ago that every Federalist in sight was denouncing Mr. Jefferson for buying that worthless desert called Louisiana. "I imagine I can look to my own defense, Colonel. I managed to do so for eight thousand miles."

"It is a dangerous place, and I will worry about you both."

Julia's attention had followed this exchange closely. She knew little of politics, which is the way I wanted it. I addressed her: "You shall be the queen of the city, my lovely Julia, celebrated at every ball and levee, at home in the parlors of our friends."

Her eyes thanked me, and I saw Colonel Hancock subsiding. The man had heard all the stories bursting from St. Louis; that Aaron Burr had fled to Spanish Florida but was arrested in Alabama, and now was being brought to trial before Mr. Jefferson's cousin, Chief Justice John Marshall. And there was I, taking Julia into the maelstrom. No wonder George was concerned.

"Colonel," I said, "I was not born red-haired for nothing. If anyone in St. Louis, whether its French citizens of dubious loyalty or dissident Yankees, mounts a threat to me, or my government, or my president, you will see what a Clark can do."

That mollified him, and I knew there would be little further objection to taking Julia so far from home.

I started for the trace over the Alleghenies at once. On my parting Julia wet my coat with her tears.

"I will be back in a few months, my fair lady. Be patient, and plan the matrimonial day, and you will see me before the snow flies," I said, hugging her one last time, disciplining my heart and body and hands though I never felt less disciplined in all my years. I wondered how I could wait for so long. Then I mounted up, while York held the reins, and that was the last I saw of her.

I had sent my reliable Private Frazier ahead with an important burden: he was to circulate freely in St. Louis, gather intelligence for me and for Mr. Jefferson, and report to me in private, if need be at my brother's home in Clarksville, opposite Louisville. I stopped there, of course, to see my older brother General George Rogers Clark, who was gouty and taking too much whiskey to curb his pain. They were calling him things behind his back that I didn't like; assailing the character of a great hero of the revolution, a man reduced to poverty because the government wouldn't repay him for his drafts supporting the army.

We rode the river to Mulberry Hill, in the Indiana Territory, and all the while York grew more and more agitated. He had been annoying me ever since the expedition, sometimes turning sulky, sometimes defiant.

The request came as we approached Louisville, as I knew it would. He caught me in a private moment on the flatboat, at dusk, and put it directly to me:

"Mastuh, could you be letting me see my wife a little? Get me some papers saying I can be wid her?"

His wife was owned by some Kentucky friends of my brother, who used her on their tobacco plantation near Louisville.

"No, I need you."

"I was thinking I sure do miss my woman."

"York, I said no! You will come west with me."

"I could maybe work for hire and be wid her."

"No!" I roared, and his black face crumpled. It was common enough to lease a slave and collect the proceeds of the lease, but I wouldn't allow it. I would need him in St. Louis. I had a house to buy, an office to fill, an army to raise, Big White to care for and return up the river, all on an austere budget of fifteen hundred a year, and I couldn't afford to lose a manservant, not for a moment.

He stared at me in pain, but I could do nothing about it. Maybe someday I'd give him some papers and let him visit his woman for a while. Not now.

He mumbled his way aft, and stood beside the Mandans, watching the darkly glimmering water slide by. Big White, Yellow Corn, and their son had come all this distance, absorbed the civilized wonders of the white men's world and even wore its clothing, and now were returning to their own savage society—if I could get them there.

13 CLARK

I took up quarters in the old Government House, a sorry place but it would do until I could find a home for Julia and me. It was also a military barracks, which proved to be handy for a new brigadier of militia.

Even before paying a social call on the leading lights of St. Louis, I summoned Private Frazier, my shrewd old friend from the expedition, who had been working assiduously to find out what he could about the Burr plot. It turned out he had found plenty:

"Ah, Captain, it's a pleasure to see you, sir. I guess I should call you 'general' now, eh? A general you are, and please forgive me."

I laughed. "Whatever rank suits you, my friend," I said, clasping his hand. "Now, tell me what you've found."

What he had found was that the Louisiana militia had been riddled with minor officers ready to act on Burr's behalf, merely waiting for the word that never came but might still. Traitors to the republic, the whole lot, self-aggrandizing wretches.

"I got a list, Captain. Me, I just sat in a grog shop and palavered like a Burr man, and next I knew, I had me a wee little list."

He handed me a list of militia officers, ranging from sergeants to lieutenants and one captain.

"Is that most of the militia?"

He laughed. "What militia? It's a paper army. These are border men, Captain, and not happy about being called to serve, not now, not ever, unless six thousand cutthroat redskins are descending on them. But yes, I reckon it's most of the sunshine officers. I mean them that won't show up if it rains."

I nodded. It was an old refrain. My brother George Rogers Clark had welded an effective militia and staved off the British with it, but only with harsh measures combined with generous rewards. He had shot deserters.

"What about the French?"

"Don't rely on a one of 'em. Sure, there's some loyal French, they fancy the Yank republic, but they were here before we set eyes on Louisiana, and they just want to be left alone."

"Burrists?"

"A few, them that think maybe they'll do better in the purse under Spain or even England."

"English involved?"

"With the Indians. That's how they work, lining up the Indians, buying scalps."

"The businessmen?"

"Now there's something." Frazier peered into the rosy dawn light seeping through the window. "Actually, I think the ones in the fur business like the new government; they worry more about the British snatching all the beaver than they do about what flag they serve. They may be Frogs, but they like the liberties we give 'em."

That made sense, too. Frazier had done a fine job. We conferred a while more there in the barracks, I clapped him on the shoulder and commended him, and he slid out unseen into a peach-tinted St. Louis dawn, with moisture on every leaf. Intelligence was the first priority. I needed to know who was for the government, and who wasn't.

Those of us in the old Corps of Discovery had forged bonds of steel. I would trust any of them with my life, and they would trust me. I had cash in hand, and intended to trace them all and give them their back pay and federal land warrants. Congress had awarded each of them three hundred and twenty acres of virgin land. They had dispersed, and it would not be easy to track them down.

The turbulent territory seethed with troubles, and I wasted no time putting a bayonet to the problems. At once I paid a call on the territory's secretary, and acting governor in Meriwether's absence, Frederick Bates. I thought he might be just the right man, being a Virginian, a lawyer, a Democratic-Republican like Mr. Jefferson, and a holder of numerous public offices back East.

I found an odd puffy man at the helm, his pale brow furrowed, his expression pleading, his generous brown lips pursed, and his humor rancid. He was sallow, as if the outdoors was a foreign nation to him, and his eyes were bagged with furrows that told me he did not profit from his nocturnal rest. He exuded so much dignity that I itched to step on his toe.

"Mr. Jefferson commends you, and urges upon you the importance of curbing the Burr conspiracy," I said affably as soon as we had poured ourselves a dark glass of amontillado from a decanter on his desk. "Is there still talk of a filibuster against New Orleans?"

"It's pandemonium, General," he said. "This place! You can't imagine the skulking schemers and what they want! I will be so *glad* when the governor arrives, for these matters are beyond my jurisdiction and authority, but I wish to declare, my good general, that I have proceeded resolutely anyway, in a most judicious manner, with due *prudence* and rectitude, to ameliorate these clamorous and Machiavellian uproars."

That was a mouthful.

"Mr. Bates," I said, settling back and propping my muddy boots upon his desk, which horrified him, "you just begin right at the beginning and tell me what you've done and what needs doing."

Not much, it seemed. The man had a way of papering over inaction with rhetoric, but it wasn't so much what he said as how he said it that gave me the measure of him. He put stock in words, the longer the better, and had a way with them that might spell trouble for Meriwether. Bates's brother Tarleton was an old friend of the governor, Virginians all, and that spoke well for the future.

And yet I worried. I imagined Bates loyal enough to Tom Jefferson, but doubts nagged me. His conversion to Jefferson's principles had been recent, and looked just plain opportunistic. Well, I would not confide in him, not yet anyway, but would set about putting the new command in place until I could show some strength.

My next call was to Pierre Chouteau, prominent Creole merchant in St. Louis, supplier of many goods to the expedition, trusted friend, and the man who had gone to great effort and expense to bring the Osage chiefs to Washington to meet the president, and then got them safely back to Upper Louisiana. I counted him among my best allies, sterling in his faithfulness, reliable, and eager to serve the republic.

He received me in his spacious home, a suitable domain for a young merchant prince. He had taught himself adequate English, and in that alien tongue welcomed me into his enameled green parlor during a meridian time of day when most Creoles lay dozing.

"Pierre," I said, enjoying the firm clasp of his hand. He had dark French features, and lively eyes and a mouth that suggested amusement, though he was a serious man.

I am a plainspoken man and wasted no time telling him of my mission, after we had sipped a ritual goblet of red wine from his glass decanter.

"Mr. Jefferson's commissioned me to begin certain things, and I think there might be opportunity in it for you," I began.

His eyes lit up. The Chouteaus were never known to scorn opportunity to fatten their purse.

"We are most anxious to return She-He-Ke, Big White, to his people, along with his party, and not delay his homeward journey any more. He's been away from the Mandans a long time. My first business here is to mount an expedition to take him up the river."

Chouteau listened intently, and I knew I had him well and properly hooked.

"I've detached Ensign Pryor—he was a sergeant when we recruited him for the Corps of Discovery—and will put him in command of a small detachment of troops. I've already talked to another of our corps men, George Shannon, who will go along. They've been up that mighty river, know the ropes, and have great ability."

Chouteau listened, saying nothing.

"Captain Lewis and I found that the tribes were much more tractable when goods were available, and we expended much of what we brought with us as gifts to pave our way. And that is where you come in. We want you to join the party with a trading expedition of your own; your traders and boatmen would enhance the strength of the party. The government will provide your entire party with rifles, powder, and shot, and we'll include four hundred dollars of presents. You and your fur trading party can continue upriver, trading for pelts at your leisure, once we return the Mandans to their people."

"Ah, it is formidable," he said. "Formidable."

"We had some trouble with the Sioux, who are a danger, and you might have some difficulty getting past the Arikaras because of the presence of Big White on your keelboats. But we think some gifts will smooth that over. With your group of traders, and our soldiers, you will be as large and as well armed as our Corps of Discovery. What do you say?"

"My general, we do not hesitate for one moment. I myself will go."

"Good. We're going to open up that river and license the traders and make the fur business profitable and safe. And you'll be in a good position to profit from it."

He nodded, happily. How could he refuse? I didn't doubt he would corral a small fortune from the expedition, and he would enjoy the safety of our troops as well.

I turned to other matters. "Mr. Chouteau, this territory is torn by rivalries. I am a plain man and will ask a plain question and hope for a plain answer. Are the Creoles happy with us, indifferent, unhappy, hostile?"

Chouteau did not hesitate, and as far as I could tell, he did not hedge.

"General, in the bosom of every Frenchman is the hope that the tricolor of France will fly here. But if the choice is between Spain and the new American republic, there is no choice at all. We are Americans. The Spanish, you see, have a peculiar attitude toward business. They seek to make business as difficult as possible, and at the same time, extract every possible centime for the crown. For as long as they held New Orleans, we could barely win a profit out of furs. We like your liberty. We like your equality." He shrugged, an expressive, Gallic shrug that spoke more than words ever could.

I knew then I need not worry about the French of St. Louis, and could turn to more urgent matters, including the scheming of the British, who wanted to pluck the territory from us without wasting a shot, by using the tribes as their proxies.

14 LEWIS

My struggles with the War Department exhausted me. They want receipts for everything, and I cannot provide them. I wrote numerous drafts on the treasury, every one of them to purchase essentials, wasting not a penny, and yet I was treated as if it had been my intent to skin the government. En route, I traded my officer's coat to some Indians for a canoe and wish to be reimbursed; how shall I receipt that?

I left Washington as soon as I could to escape the steamy heat, intending to improve my health at Locust Hill. The air of Albemarle County is better. It is November now but the ague still afflicts me, and just when I feel I am past it I am besieged once again with the usual chills, shakes, fever, and sweats. As soon as I arrived here, much to my delight, my mother began administering the cinchona bark extract that abates the intermittent fever, and supplemented with those simples for which she is so renowned in Albemarle County. I have in addition the services of my brother Reuben, who in my absence had completed his medical training. They have steadily nursed me back to some sort of health, though I remain oddly indisposed and afflicted with a melancholy.

She doses me every two hours with a tea decocted from the bark of yellow birch, sweet flag, thoroughwort, and tansy, boiled and then mixed with sweet wine. Her other remedy is distilled from burdock, narrow dock, yarrow, knotgrass, cleavers, blood-root, Jacob's ladder, and wormwood, boiled in rainwater. Of this I am to take all that my stomach will bear.

When I was able, I rode to Monticello and discussed Upper Louisiana with Mr. Jefferson. I promised him a paper detailing my observations about the economic potential of the territory and the nature of the tribes inhabiting it. I work on it desul-torily, every word wrenched from my brain.

Mr. Bates, the territorial secretary serving as governor until I should arrive in St. Louis, writes flattering and alarming let-ters, urging me to hasten west to my post because, he explains, the turbulent territory needs a governor's authority which he cannot provide. I will go when I can; but now I must enhance my health and vigor, and where better than in the hands of my two physicians?

Mr. Conrad petitions me for the edited journal pages, so he can begin work. I have not yet started, and do not quite know why I keep putting off the task. Mr. Jefferson presses me on every occasion, reminding me how important the publica-tion of the journals is to several branches of science. And to the nation, and I might add, to his administration. He regards the expedition as the crown jewel of his two terms, but it will require the publication of our journals to persuade his adver-saries, the Federalists, that there was much good gotten from the trip.

I have looked over Captain Clark's entries, and mine, and they bring back a host of memories, struggles and triumphs, matters that only he and I know about, things barely hinted at in the pages. I dread to touch any of it. The whole task of editing those journals is so formidable it seems worse than the trip itself. Shall I correct our field notes or leave them intact? How much should I alter the original? What should be cut out? What is not for the public eye?

All these matters swim in my head. I have tried twenty times to begin; to take the first of the bound journals and simply begin copying in an orderly manner, dates, places, times, observations, men, equipment, miles traveled, solar and weather data, plants discovered, sickness, equipment failures. All of it. I spread some foolscap before me, dip the nib of my pen into the inkpot, and then do nothing. I cannot explain it. I wish this task might be lifted from me, but the thought of that afflicts me because then I could not control what is used, what is not, and decide whether some things might best be rewritten.

At first I supposed I was troubled simply by the fierce desire to make the journals perfect; that I was simply paralyzed by the cry of soul that insists that my task must be to make the flawed flawless, the insipid fascinating, the obscure clear, the language precise and accurate. Now, after numerous attempts to start the great work, I simply don't know, and with each effort, I find myself less willing to proceed. I am disappointing Mr. Jefferson, Will Clark, the publishers, and everyone at the American Philosophical Society.

And the more I sense their disappointment, as time drags by, the worse I suffer. Captain Clark expects half the profit. The society expects a treasury of new information. The government expects maps and an understanding of the tribes and a substantiated claim upon unexplored lands.

And here I am, with more burdens pressing me that I can endure, sinking deeper into melancholia each day. I do not know what to do. Time has slowed to a halt. I am the governor of a territory several hundred miles distant, but here I languish.

Maybe in St. Louis I will do better.

My mother keeps a shrewd eye on me, but stays apart because I am not in the mood for company. She is the model of all womanhood, and I despair of finding a mate who can even approach her graces and learning and ability. I am constantly invited to balls and banquets all over Virginia, and I accept some, though my heart is not in the social life. I have been toasted and honored too many times, if such a thing is possible. I attend these affairs, so that the world might see the explorer in the flesh, and drink their toasts, and return to Locust Hill all the more melancholic.

At Captain Clark's behest, I traveled to Fincastle, near Roanoke, to visit Julia Hancock and to meet some of the young women he thought I might find attractive. I have met more women in the past months than I can count, but they all fall short one way or another. I am fussy. If an eligible young woman is not serious, and cannot address me on the terms of my own thinking, then I find little of interest in her, and she drifts into the arms of someone else.

At Fincastle, while a guest of Colonel Hancock, I finally discovered a young woman who filled the bill, so far as I could see. Certainly Letitia Breckenridge is a comely damsel, of exceptional beauty and quickness. I met her and her sister Elizabeth by design, for Will had paved the way. They are daughters of General James Breckenridge, and thus well suited to my social requirements.

I well remember when we met; the nankeen dress, the subdued intelligent gaze from hazel eyes, the seriousness she displayed, unlike her more boisterous sister. She did not then know that I would court her; the whole had been artfully arranged by Colonel Hancock so as to appear to be a Sabbath stroll, taking the air while the weather held.

By then they were calling me "your excellency," or "governor," and all that, so I had the advantage, and made haste to pace beside her on a stroll along a shady lane that led into the hazy hills, and thus engaged, made inquiry into her nature. She did not measure up in terms of education, but no woman does, and I assumed that she would be too busy rearing a family to pursue scholarship further. She had a sublime form, which the shifting gold muslin, a lovely autumnal color that complemented her bold beauty, sometimes revealed to me as we strolled.

"Your Excellency, when you are quit of St. Louis, what will you do?" she asked.

"I am thinking of high office," I replied. "Often I ask myself the same thing. Just now, I wrestle with a paper that distills everything I have learned of the Western country for the edification of Mr. Jefferson and future presidents. But that's just the beginning, you know. Here I am, at thirty-five, and known from top to bottom. I am thinking that the Democratic-Republicans may call upon me, and so I regard my tenure in office as a sampler, Miss Letitia."

"Call upon you?"

"I am a simple man, much given to philosophy, and my predilection is to return and look after my mother, and care for Locust Hill. But if duty calls, I will be ready."

"I see," she said.

I inquired of course into her political views, and found them appropriately republican, at least as someone in her female estate might grasp the term. I discerned that she was exploring me, as well, inquiring into my plans, how long I should reside in distant St. Louis, and whether I had slaves. I confessed that I had none as personal property, but I oversaw the estate of my mother, who possessed many, and was therefore familiar with the handling of them.

I found myself coming to life at last, after so long a hibernation, and when we returned to the Hancock home I raised a toast to her and the happy future, and then several more. She flushed, and this time her gaze was averted. I could not tell how I was affecting her, but knew that I would pursue her.

I had seen a President's House devoid of its mistress, and while the vivacious Dolley Madison, wife of dapper James Madison, served admirably for Mr. Jefferson, the president's society wanted that domestic touch. I eyed the lady beside me with that in mind, and I fancied that Letitia understood the matter.

Her father collected her in time to drive his carriage home after an afternoon's repast, and I raised a last toast to her, her sister, and her illustrious father before settling them in their carriage. I spent the next days in a reverie. Here was a woman I might propose to; in most respects suitable, and one to stir my blood. I had been smitten many times since returning from the West, but in the end, all of those damsels were unsuitable. Letitia was suitable. I proposed to call on her in a day or two.

But Fate intervened. When I did ride to the Breckenridge estate, some miles distant, I discovered that Miss Letitia had gone to Richmond with her father and would be away for some while. I grieved, and then put it out of mind. I never should have confided my ambition to her. But I am too serious a man to waste feeling on a disappointment of the heart. I considered Elizabeth, but set it aside. She was not adequately serious.

I languished unwell in Ivy this autumn, uncertain what was eroding my health. My discerning mother eyed me sharply from time to time, and once even inquired if I was well. I assured her I was, and yet I was much fatigued and in a distemper. I resolved to see my friend and companion of the trail General Clark married in Fincastle in January, and then be on my way west, though I would be traveling in winter. The general would honeymoon and then join me in St. Louis, where by arrangement I would board with them.

I completed my lengthy treatise on the West, which I presumed would form the foundation of Indian and fur-trade policy for the next twenty years, and fell into one of my moods again. I do not know why I was able to write ten thousand words with fierce discipline, yet am stymied every time I open my journals. Is it because the journals are mostly Will's? Or is it because the whole world awaits their publication?

It was then, nearing the end of November, that Mrs. Marks, the legendary healer of Albemarle County, called me into her drawing room, and into the aura of the tile-clad stove.

"You are still unwell," she said. "Indisposed. Fevers."

"It is only the ague."

"Yes, the ague," she said. "But the weather has turned."

"I am in perfect health; just a little of the intermittent fever now and then."

"You wander the plantation, doing nothing, writing nothing. Are you troubled, Meriwether?"

"Not a bit!"

"Thirty-five and a bachelor."

Her candor shocked me. "I simply am unlucky," I replied testily. I did not want her sympathy. Letitia Breckenridge had fled, for whatever reason, and I hadn't met another I cared about more than a day or two.

"When are you going to St. Louis?" she asked.

"When I am ready!"

"You were appointed in March; now the year has passed."

"I have things to do here."

She asked me to draw close, and ran her experienced hand over my face and neck, discovered some gummy thickening of the flesh on my forehead, and along the jawline, lumps so subtle I had not been aware of them myself until her fingers found them.

"Let me see your arms and hands, Meriwether."

I undid my sleeves, and pushed them up. She examined my arms, her gaze pausing at the arciform red-stained scars there.

"Your hands?"

I extended them to her, filled with a nameless and terrible dread, a pit of horror whose jaws were opening wider and wider as the minutes fled by.

She studied the palms, turned them over and examined the backs. I saw nothing amiss with them. But she traced her finger over a discolored area.

"There, you see? I am fit as a fiddle."

"Meriwether," she said, "I am here only to help, not judge a son whose life has taken him so far from the comforts of civilization and religion. It is necessary to begin a course of mercury immediately, and I have some simples, my wandering Meriwether, that will relieve you. The venereal is far advanced."

15 CLARK

Tomorrow, January 8, 1808, will be my wedding day. I await that holy event with scarce-concealed anticipation. Tomorrow, before the Episcopalian parson from Roanoke, the Reverend Mr. Smith, my Julia and I will recite the vows. The colonel has turned his spacious home into a virtual hostelry, so many are the guests.

I arrived here in Fincastle, Virginia, from St. Louis in ample time for the Yuletide, and spent a most joyous Christmas at the hearth of my in-laws, who have treated me with grace and affection. There is merriment in their eyes. They permit me a while alone each day with Julia, and make much reference to the mistletoe once again hanging from the cut-glass chandelier in the parlor.

She has met me each day, her face flushed and bright, her lips soft and welcoming. She has been full of questions about St. Louis, and wild Indians, and the ruffians of the border, and the army. I assure her things will be terrible; we will live in a dirt-floor log cabin, she will slave at the hearth and garden and spinning wheel, I will shoot marauding redskins through the loopholes of our fortress house every hour or so, and we will lack beds, tables, chairs, windows, and privacy, and sleep on bearskin robes.

She laughs, but uneasily. I tell her that I am a general of the militia, and command an entire army of bedbugs. She thinks that is very merry, and I see panic in her eyes and kiss it away, enjoying the moment.

Guests are arriving at every hour; my brothers and sister and assorted relatives are staying with friends in the area. Colonel Hancock has put me in one of the bedrooms, and York out with the darkies, and that offends him. I will let him taste the whip if he remains in such a mood for long.

Ah, tomorrow! For too long have I dreamed of this. I will sweep my bride away to a bower that is prepared for us, and there we shall know each other in tenderness and joy. It is for this heaven that I have returned from St. Louis; it was for this heaven that I sustained my courage and resolution on that long journey into the unknown West. A wedding is a little like a voyage of exploration. We do not know what land we are piercing, or what we may find there; but I do not doubt it will be full of wonders and sunshine.

Soon after my arrival I met with Meriwether about the condition of the territory he governs, and found him in a peculiar mood, taut and irritable but papering it over with vast bonhomie. Something is troubling him.

He ventured here from Ivy a few days after I had arrived, knowing how much I wished to be with Julia. I greeted him, noted that he seemed unsettled as we exchanged news, and then we closeted ourselves in the front room to discuss affairs of state.

"Secretary Bates begs for you," I said. "You are certainly needed."

"What sort of man is he?"

"An able one, I think, but a handwringer."

Meriwether laughed, a brittle, strange cackle that was entirely new to me. "Not used to command, I take it."

"No, and brimming with anxieties."

"That is not a kind assessment."

I sighed. "I am a plainspoken man," I replied, and let it stand. Frederick Bates had rubbed me wrong, and I could not fathom why Thomas Jefferson had entrusted him with so weighty a position.

"What about the militia? And Burr?"

There I was on better ground. "I inherited a paper militia that could not muster a hundred true men. It was shot through with Burrite officers, too. Frazier got me a list of them. I did some interviewing and cashiered most of 'em. Now I'm rebuilding. It's hard to turn border men into a force, and the only hold I have on 'em is Indian dangers. I've been working with some loyal noncoms, good stouthearted men, and building around them rather than the officers, who are mostly sunshine soldiers. When I get a militia I can trust, we'll have a grip on the territory."

Lewis nodded. "You got Big White back to the Mandans?"

"What? I thought you knew!" I said.

He shook his head. I had sent the news by post, but that was a slow and unreliable means, often two months between St. Louis and Washington this time of year.

I told him about Ensign Pryor's trip up the Missouri to take the Mandan chief home, in the company of Pierre Chouteau and twenty-two trappers. It had come a cropper at the Arikara villages, where the tribe we supposed to be our friends savagely assaulted the party on September ninth, killing three of Chouteau's traders, wounding ten men including our old friend from the Corps of Discovery, Private Shannon, whose leg had to be amputated. Pryor had fled down the river, reaching St. Louis not long before I headed east. She-He-Ke, Big White, and his family remained in St. Louis, his way home barred by the suddenly ferocious Rees.

Meriwether absorbed that, his gaze darting about, his brow furrowed. "We will have to try again with a stronger party. The president will be distressed. He takes it as an obligation of honor to get Big White safely back . . . and now this."

"We'll try again," I said. "A stronger party. Meriwether, I can't properly govern, and Secretary Bates is, well, ineffectual, and Upper Louisiana can't be governed from Virginia. We need you."

He glared at me, as if I had affronted him. "I will come when I am ready. I am pursuing important matters here."

"The editing?"

"The work is proceeding. Pursh is drawing the plants. Hassler's astronomy calculations are almost done. Peale is sketching the animals. I have an artist on the birds."

"Soon, then. You promised the first edition by year's end."

He looked horrified. "Well, not so immediately."

"I would welcome the profit, Meriwether. The burdens of marriage and office tax me and the salary of an Indian superintendent doesn't cover."

"Well, I can help you. When are you returning to St. Louis?"

"We will honeymoon a few weeks in Virginia, visiting relatives. I hope to be in St. Louis early in the spring."

"Count on the army," Lewis said. "I will move you."

That sounded like a good offer, and I chuckled. "I think you ought to find some lady and follow suit."

He laughed almost boisterously. "I'm just an old bachelor, too fusty and musty for 'em," he said.

"No, Meriwether, you are the most eligible man in the United States."

He cackled happily. "Then they'll give me a good chase," he said. "I will let one catch me."

His laugh was as brittle as old parchment. He was hiding his sorrows, and I knew at once that his disappointment at the hands of Letitia Breckenridge had afflicted his spirits.

"Governor, let me tell you, in St. Louis the belles will flock to the balls, and if you know a few words of French, such as *oui, oui, oui,* you will captivate more hearts than you'll ever know."

He wheezed out a laugh, and it was like hearing old paper crumple.

"You look to be in good health, Meriwether."

"I'm in perfect health, brimming with life, ready to advance my fortunes in St. Louis. But I've been wrestling with the ague. It comes and goes, you know, but as soon as my dear mother gives the word, I'll head down the river."

That sounded fine to me. We spent an hour talking about the politics of the territory, the innumerable trading licenses General Wilkinson had granted to cronies before he departed, the smoldering embers of the Burr conspiracy to peel the whole area away from the republic and build a new nation out of scoundrels and traitors. Lewis brought me up to date on a myriad of things; the Burr trial and acquittal in Richmond, Jefferson's struggles with the British, who were boldly provoking war by pressing American seamen and engaging in other calculated affronts. That worried me.

"Meriwether, if there is war, I command a hopeless rabble.

Half don't have rifles. We need some steel—cannon, rifles, everything—and I'll count on you to apply for it from Congress."

He nodded, unhappily. Again I had the deepening impression that Lewis was a troubled man, insecure, in pain of some sort.

That was the last I saw of him until today. He arrived for the wedding, looking fit and strong, and acting more like his old self, gorgeously accoutred in his gold braid and blue. I had little time other than to greet him and see to his quarters.

York greeted the old captain effusively. "Massah Lewis, Captain, is mighty nice you come to this heah wedding," he exclaimed.

But Meriwether ignored the darkie, as if York had not traveled with us clear to the western sea. I watched York closely, worried that the man's insolence would get the better of him, but York held his peace.

Lewis is much the center of attention today; men, women, children all press him to spin his anecdotes once again, but he does so reluctantly and by rote. He's worn down by the attention. There is a banquet tonight, and a ball tomorrow, and Colonel Hancock has kept the punch bowl filled for days.

Meriwether hangs about the punch, downing cup after cup along with port and porter and whatever other spirits the Hancocks provide.

It has been a long while since we returned from the West, and yet that expedition affects us both even now, and Lewis especially. I see it in the face of everyone I talk to; they see the explorer, and not the Clark. I am eager to turn a new leaf.

Tonight they will hide Julia from me and I will not see her until the sacred rites, when she will be an angel on the arm of her father. I will be waiting there, in the green parlor, when she waltzes down the stairs in rustling white silk and ivory lace, her hair aglow, her lips ruby, her eyes shining upon me like little suns . . . or slides down the banister with a whoop, if I know my Julia. I will be there, and so will the preacher, and so will a hundred guests, my brothers and their spouses, my sister and hers, assorted cousins and friends. And I will take my beloved to my bosom there, pledge myself to her there, hear her pledge herself to me there, and that will be the beginning, as well as an end.

16 LEWIS

I tarried this January of 1808 in the frail warmth of Locust Hill, but my heart is cold. Many were the dreams that had sustained me during my eventful life. I had dreamed of honor. I had dreamed of love. I had dreamed of devotion to our infant republic, that we might prove to the whole world that men may live free and equal. I had dreamed of accomplishment. I had wanted to make my widowed mother proud. I wanted the name Lewis to shine for a thousand years. I had hoped for children. I had hoped for an illustrious name that would echo through the generations, a name unstained and blameless.

Now, by terrible mischance—or was it my own folly?—everything that I dreamed of, everything that I was, everything that I might still be, lay in ruin, blackened by a shameful disease that evoked the loathing of the world, a disease whose name was not uttered.

I could not talk to my mother about it; not Lucy Marks, who had borne me, raised me up, educated me, and quietly nurtured me through the vicissitudes of youth. I could barely talk to my physician brother Reuben, either, but held it all in, mortified, desolated by the scourge that rotted my parts as well as my very soul. I told Reuben very little; only a date: August of 1805. He had remarked the speed at which the disorder had devastated my body, faster than usual. I had no reply other than that we were famished, eating poorly, and suffering the want of many necessaries in our diet, and maybe that had advanced the plague within me, which rolled like a black tide through my flesh and blood.

He held out a little hope, and I clung to it.

"Meriwether, often the pox passes by, and leaves the victim unscathed. It is the common thing," he told me.

"But what of the others? Half the corps has it."

"We'll never know how they fare. It's a disease that mimics several others. It attacks different parts in different people, choosing the weakest portion. In some, it savages the heart and veins and arteries. In others it assaults the mind and nerves. In others it aggrieves the flesh, muscle, bone. I see none of that in you."

He was holding out hope to a mortified, mortifying man, and I clung to it desperately. He put me on mercury courses while Lucy Marks boiled her simples, and fed me this or that extract or broth. She brewed a tea of cuckold (or beggar-ticks as it is sometimes named), especially sovereign against venereal complaints, but also ginseng, fitroot, slippery elm, and burdock, which purifies the blood. She favors blue flag steeped in gin, which is also effective against venereals. She did not probe, but Reuben sometimes did. He wanted to know everything, as if my telling of those August nights in 1805 would somehow be my catharsis. But I knew he was merely curious.

I will always keep those nights to myself. No one on earth knows of them, not even Drouillard, Shields, and MacNeal, the only men with me as we probed the east flanks of the Bitter-roots looking for the Shoshones. Clark and the rest of the Corps of Discovery were far behind, toiling up the Jefferson River.

We spotted a native boy; then some women, all of them shy as bats in daylight. But finally we did connect with the chief, Cameahwaite, and his band, and we rejoiced. They were starving and we got them meat. They promised to sell us horses. We went through tense times waiting for Clark to show up with what few items we had left to trade them for horses. But thanks to the sign-talker, Drouillard, we parleyed with the young chieftain, assured him of our friendship and demonstrated that we wished no ill upon them.

By the firelight they danced for us in those mountain meadows, and got my two privates and Drouillard dancing, and persuaded me to dance as well. Their women were sinuous and comely and honey-fleshed, and their eyes glowed in the firelight. The chieftain offered us our choice; it being a great honor among their women to embrace an honored guest. It took little effort to persuade the soldiers, but I designed to tarry long after they had vanished into the buffalo-hide lodges that soft autumnal evening.

I wrestled long with my own temptation: both Will Clark and I had steadfastly refused the offers of other tribes along the Missouri, though the men partook of all that savage hospitality, and paid a price for it in the drips and other venereals, all of which I treated with mercury salve and calomel. Sometimes the chiefs had taken great offense at our reluctance, thinking that we were disdainful of them and their women. I can't speak for Will Clark, but I was merely being prudent. And he had his Judy to think of.

I feared that Cameahwaite might take similar offense; he who could provide us with horses and spare the whole discovery expedition from disaster. And so I reasoned my way forward.

This one time, far from the corps, far even from the eyes of my three companions, far from civilization, far from white men's diseases in this remote corner of the mountains, far out upon a sea of wilderness, I might quickly enjoy the great embrace.

I had, indeed, my eye upon a glowing young woman with come-hither eyes, lithe and sinuous, with strong cheekbones and smooth, tawny flesh; a woman with a bold assessing glance that spoke to me in ancient ways, beyond what words could convey.

I smiled at her; she returned the compliment tenfold. We drifted off into the pine-scented darkness, far beyond the camp-fire and its dancing light, into a starlit void, and finally into an arbor paved with thick robes. And there I threw my life away, all unwitting, all with the purpose of avoiding offense to these savage people.

Or so I tell myself. At other times, I am more honest. She had awakened in me a lust that had slept restlessly in my loins for more months than I could remember.

Oh, if only that night had never happened! I have cursed my fate ever since, choked on my own desolation and shame. I prowl the hills, thinking of nothing else. I meet young women, and shy from them: can they see? Do they know? Has word about me filtered out insidiously, whispered from lip to ear, a blackening pool of horror about the explorer?

I walk the lonely paths beyond the barren fields, thinking of Letitia, of the others, of the women I cannot have. If I am an honorable man I must not even taste the pleasures of an unsuspecting wanton, much less a woman of virtue. But all that is dead in me except for the dread of being discovered. It mad-dens me, the thought of whispers, the pursed lips, the side glance, the turned head. Did Letitia Breckenridge flee because she read something in me, something that I did not yet know about myself? Ah, God, what is left of my dwindling life? And how long will it run before my vile secret is made public?

I tried to rejoice at Will's wedding, but my heart was all ash. I bantered with him about women. I told him I would find mine. I made great sport of the chase and the conquest. And all the while my soul was shriveling inside of my parched and fevered body. I made a great show of merriment at the punch bowls, but I did not feel it, and any close observer of Meriwether Lewis must have seen my dissimulation and wondered at it. What did Will think? Or was he too much absorbed in his own good fortune to notice?

My mother and brother have improved my health, and my indisposition wanes, and as it does my hopes prosper. Most survive! In many the plague vanishes! And yet I cannot put the horror of my condition out of mind. It is there, stalking me, my very shadow, whenever I take some porter at the public house and talk to my neighbors; whenever there is a quadrille or minuet or a hunt.

Reuben warns me to avoid spirits; but if I were suddenly to stop, the world would study me too closely and wonder why. I cannot change my conduct in the slightest for fear of discovery. They may not know, but I do, and I cannot walk the lane without this grim ghost stalking behind me, my bleak shadow, my shame waiting to ruin me.

I have not written a word. My journals are untouched. A thousand times I have opened the morocco covers, and plucked up a quill, only to slump in my chair, watch the rain drip from the eaves, and close the journal.

My publisher, Conrad, presses me for pages. The president of the United States sends me letters in that fine hand of his, courteous, affectionate, but between the words is an edge, and I see it, and he means for me to see it. The unpublished journals reflect on his administration. I had promised the first volume before year's end. It is not even begun. This is maddening. For the life of me I do not know why I avoid that great task.

I hear from Secretary Bates, who says the territory is in an uproar and he is dealing with scoundrels, and that his word lacks the authority that mine must have. But his excellency Governor Lewis does not come, and Bates is growing desperate. I draw a governor's salary from the federal treasury, but I languish a thousand miles from the seat of government.

I cannot go. Not until my brother and mother finish the courses with which they treat me. I probably slow their progress, sipping as much as I do, and yet I will not stop. Reuben warned me; Dr. Saugrain warned me. My mother didn't, but I see the disapproval in her eyes every time I sip some port.

I tell them nothing of the laudanum I sometimes use for sleep, when my worries lie too heavy upon me and I can get no rest. Six drops in a tumbler of water puts me into a peaceful sleep, and I awaken refreshed, unlike so many nights when I lie abed swimming in my bitter fate.

Reuben tells me I am much better and can leave in a fortnight if the weather permits. That would put me in St. Louis in March. I am eager to go. At moments a heady optimism lifts my spirits; I shall be one of those who has conquered the venereal! I shall put all this behind me, govern that unruly province with a firm and fair hand, deal sternly with traitors and opportunists.

I will treat with the Indians, assuring them of the items they need, such as kettles and iron implements, in exchange for their good conduct. I will restore order to the fur business, get my Mandan chief, who still languishes there, back to his people, deal with those treacherous Rees, subdue the haughty Sioux, and return after a few years in triumph. Never let it be said that I lack determination.

PART II

17 LEWIS

I arrived in this raw, secretive, scheming city of St. Louis on the eighth of March, 1808, after an overland journey in which I paused in Kentucky to make sure the family's land claims, some of them won by my father for service in the revolution, were in good order. That meant examining the tracts for encroachment, checking the stakes, making sure of the records. Reuben accompanied me that far and then sailed with my equipage down the Ohio and up the Mississippi, while I continued by land. He reached St. Louis a fortnight ahead of me.

I am in robust health, never felt better, and am eager to begin governing this unruly province. For months I have been receiving a dire correspondence from Territorial Secretary Frederick Bates, describing the anarchy prevailing here, especially as regards Indian policy. I will deal with all that soon—if it really exists. St. Louis is tranquil, greening, and brimming with spring warmth.

I paid a courtesy call at once upon Bates, who greeted me effusively, apparently relieved not to have to cope with the ambitions of various factions who want the government to stay out of Indian affairs altogether so that ruthless traders may have their dubious way with the tribes, virtually ruling them with their trinkets. I will see about that.

Mr. Bates is a sallow and bag-eyed sort of man, mellifluent with words, an attorney given to much rhetoric but also bending with the wind. I very nearly drowned in his compliments. He was telling me all at once what villainous parties roam the territory; how treacherous are the Indians, British, Spanish, French, and other dubious sorts; how wisely he has governed, with shrewd appointments and policies intended to quiet the clamor and placate the cutthroat traders. I listened much, said little, and took the measure of the secretary. I sympathized: he had been the sole federal official for many months, with General Clark getting married and I at Locust Hill.

"Now, Your Excellency," he said, "General Wilkinson issued the trading licenses promiscuously, the *congés* as the Creoles call them, and to the benefit of his own pocket. I suffered great opposition when I attempted to repeal them, it being my design to limit the licenses one to a tribe, so that rivals wouldn't demoralize the savages . . ."

"That's not our policy. Mr. Jefferson and I believe that the government should establish forts with trading stores in them, open to all tribes equally, to keep the peace and win their allegiance, and license traders only above the Mandan villages."

"Very good, Your Excellency, but you would be advised to consider the weight of my experience here, and consult me about the difficulties you will encounter among these avaricious Frenchmen, and other rascals. I will, Your Most Esteemed Excellency, save you infinite grief. I am, of course, at your service."

I saw at once that he was unhappy. "I am grateful for your counsel, Mr. Bates."

"You must grasp, sir, that this is a territory rife with anarchy. Trading parties head up the river without the slightest approbation of the government, much less a proper trading license. They bargain for furs with whatever tribes they encounter, and set the savages against their rivals. I cannot stop the scoundrels. They buy a load of trade goods and are off."

"I'll be putting a stop to it. General Clark and I plan some fortified posts commanding the river."

"Command the river? With what? Your Excellency, General Clark has done wonders with the militia, but take it from an experienced man, sir; the Creoles cannot be trusted. Their loyalties are highly suspect. My instinct is to show them some muscle, and compel them to serve, and if they don't, deny them licenses . . ."

"I have found the French to be eager to cooperate with us, Mr. Bates. Mr. Chouteau brought the Osages clear to Washington to meet Mr. Jefferson, and then took them safely back here. We have good militia officers in Lorimier and Delaunay."

He paused, as if to regroup. "Yes, of course, Your Excellency, some small fraction of them will cooperate, but I recommend, upon long observation, that they bend with the wind. You would wisely exclude them from command—"

I refused to let him impugn loyal Creoles. "Mr. Bates, they are good men. What have you done about the land titles? The lead mines especially?"

"Why, sir, it is a very cauldron of troubles. First Spanish, then French, and now American grants of title. And is the measure in arpents or acres? The older settlers show dubious title to the mines; little was recorded, you know. So I have encouraged the American claimants. They stake their claims, and we describe them in acres. It is good business, Your Excellency. The government has collected numerous patent fees from the mining claims, and I count it one of my small but shining triumphs."

"But what of the Creoles? Does any one of them think his title is secure? Mr. Bates, I want you to affirm the original titles at once. It is not the policy of the Jefferson administration to dispossess any of the original owners."

"But Governor! Ah, yes." He smiled suddenly, with a great contortion of his facial muscles. "That involves a radical change from settled practice, but if it is your wish, count me your loyal and obedient underling."

"What of the Spanish, Mr. Bates?"

"They connive to peel the tribes away from us; the Osages in particular, Your Excellency. My recommendation, sir, is that you employ agents along our southwest frontiers, and keep ever vigilant, even as I have done these months when duty devolved upon me in Your Excellency's absence. I believe you will find my labors on that account most satisfactory."

"Yes, General Clark and I have something like that in mind."

"I fear you trust too much. General Wilkinson, sir, might be the commander of our armies, but he is a treacherous and unscrupled man, and up to his elbows in Colonel Burr's schemes, Your Excellency. The trouble is, there's no *proof*. He covers his tracks." He leaned forward to add a note, sotto voce. "But I can tell you, a ring of his cohorts flourishes in St. Louis, meaning to weaken your regime until all of Louisiana can be tied to England or Spain."

"And how do you know this?"

"Spies, sir. Men come and whisper in my ear, and I take heed. You and the president and the secretary of war have all been apprised by my correspondence, you know."

"Who are they?"

"Why, sir, I hesitate to *name names*."

"Who, Mr. Bates?"

"I will prepare a list of suspects, sir."

I nodded.

It was an odd interview, with Bates acting, in turn, obsequious, welcoming, delighted at my arrival, but at the same time resentful of my presence, secretive, distressed by the slightest change from his practice, and eager to charge me with how little I knew of territorial politics and strife. The message was clear: let him continue to govern and propose and issue permits, and I would put the official seal upon his policies, and take my leisure. He wanted me to be a figurehead, he the éminence grise employing my legitimate authority, and he must have supposed that my limited experience fitted me to be nothing more.

"What a beneficent moment this is, sir," he said. "At last! We shall elevate the government to its proper majesty, and you may count me your trusted advisor and the *executor* of your design."

"Very good," I said. "I'll get settled and assume my responsibilities directly. I am grateful for your professions of allegiance."

Oddly, he grimaced.

I sensed that I would run into the classic bureaucratic obstructionist, resisting me whenever he felt my policies didn't agree with him. Perhaps it was a family matter. His brother, Tarleton, had hoped to become the president's personal secretary, and when the president appointed me instead, I fear the seeds of bitterness may have been sown.

I would be patient with Mr. Bates, and magnanimous, and complimentary, and hope I might yet fashion a good relationship with my second in command.

I spent the next days hunting down a home. Rents were appalling in that burgeoning city. Most suitable houses went for five hundred a year. Will Clark agreed to let me board with him, the bachelor at their table, and toward that end I hunted an establishment adequate for us all.

I finally found one on South Main and Spruce Streets for two hundred fifty a year, four rooms, a summer kitchen, and an attic for slaves, and hastened to engage the place from the landlord, who fawned over me as if I had the blood of kings in me. It was substantial for St. Louis, but nothing compared to the great, comfortable stone mansions erected by the Creole gentry, stuffed with fine furniture, the best imported wallpapers, and fireplaces in every room.

I sent a card to my friend Moses Austin, thus announcing my arrival, and joined with Reuben on a tour of St. Louis. It was, by any measure, a gray, filthy, and disgusting city, teeming with new arrivals, dangerous to life and health, raw and gross, except for those heights well above the reeking waterfront where the Creole merchants lived in spacious mansions, sipping the finest coffee brought up from New Orleans, attending each others' soirees and balls in imported silks and satins. But that is not where we headed.

I showed my brother the levee, swarming with rough rivermen and slaves unloading keelboats and flatboats, swart odorous men who spoke strange tongues. I showed Reuben the sprawl of Creole buildings, their squared timbers set vertically in the French manner, that served for dwellings; the mucky streets that bred mosquitoes in every puddle, the flats along the river suffocating in foetid air, redolent with sweat and other, ranker, odors.

"Here is where the furs arrive from high up the Mississippi, in that vast wild around Prairie du Chien," I said. "Here is where the boats are outfitted, and the crews hired, and brave men push and pole and pull these keelboats up the Missouri, day after day, far beyond the world of white men, into a lonely land of savages, seas of grass, countless buffalo, and innumerable beaver."

"I want to go up there," he said.

I feared I had talked too much, too enticingly, of the voyage of discovery. "I need you here," I said.

"No, Meriwether, you need your very own brother in whatever fur company you invest in, to keep an eye on your investment and keep the crew in good health."

I could not object to that. But I had hoped he would remain in St. Louis as my aide and confidential assistant . . . and private physician. But he was a free man, not bound by any promise or agreement, and I could only wish him his heart's desire. He had healed me of that unspeakable disease, but I wanted him close in case the ague or other indispositions might arise in this moist and unhealthy place.

We had talked much of investing in the fur business. I had acquired some experience with it, and knew who was competent and who wasn't. I imagined I could triple my investment in a year. I certainly wished to profit from it, and from the rising prices of land about St. Louis, where happy investors doubled their money in a year. I would see about that, too, if I could borrow enough to purchase some tracts. I wanted a share of everything: the mines, the land, but especially the fur trade, the one field I understood perfectly.

Reuben agreed to stay with me until the Clarks should arrive, and together we settled the house on Main Street, the Rue Principale, and moved in.

A youth found us there, unpacking crates, and handed me an envelope. Within it was an invitation from Pierre Chouteau to sup with him that very evening, and to let the boy know.

"Yes, tell him we'll be there, with great pleasure," I said.

The boy nodded and hurried upslope. This evening would mark the beginning of many things, including the landholdings and fortunes of Meriwether Lewis.

18 CLARK

We arrived in St. Louis yesterday, June 30, by keelboat, having made good time from Louisville because Meriwether had detached Ensign Pryor and a squad from the regular army and sent them to our assistance. I had, aboard, an entire household in one keelboat, and in the other, trade goods, a grist mill, blacksmithing equipment, and other items for the government Indian posts we intended to establish along the lower Missouri River.

Meriwether met us at the levee, having gotten word of our slow progress up the Mississippi. Even as the boatmen were securing our keelboats, he was pacing the muddy bank, bursting with energy, handsome in his royal blue coat and white silk stock, which he wore even on this steamiest day of the summer when it was so close it was hard to draw breath.

"Ah! How good to see you at last! How beauteous is the new Mrs. Clark! How ravishing is Miss Anderson," he exclaimed gallantly, barely after we had set foot on the mud. Alice Anderson is my sister's daughter, a comely and marriageable young lady who will be a part of my household for a while. "Why, Miss Anderson, every bachelor in St. Louis will toast you, and rejoice at your presence, and I expect there will be duels and jousts among the bachelors. You will slay the whole unmarried class of males with that smile."

My chestnut-haired niece colored up at all that, but only smiled at such effusive greetings. She was not accustomed to such gallantry in the Clark household.

We all greeted Meriwether warmly. Even York trumpeted his pleasure, though I thought it was unseemly. Julia curtsied shyly in her white cotton frock. She wasn't much used to being in the company of governors; she wasn't even used to being in the company of generals, though I have been giving her lessons. I have so far persuaded her that a general is less formidable than a lieutenant, but when she met my brother George a few weeks ago, a respectful silence fell over her. George Rogers Clark is an old man, but with a certain august presence, and she has yet to celebrate seventeen years. I fear she might be ill at ease in a household that includes the governor.

"Come, let me show you your house," Lewis said, clapping an arm around my shoulder. "I put some effort into finding just the right place. You'll like it."

I nodded to York and the two black women, Julia's house-maids and cooks, to follow, and we proceeded through a torpid afternoon when sensible people should be under roof, to Main and Spruce Streets, not far from the riverfront. There indeed stood a comfortable, mortared stone house with a rain-stained verandah on its east and south façades.

"I hope you like it; I've reserved a bedroom for myself, but if that should not be convenient, I'll board elsewhere. The Chouteaus have already offered me a room. But you're my old tent mate and it seemed so natural just to continue being mess-mates," he said. "Together, we'll bring good order here."

I glanced at Julia, who was looking less than happy, and wiping her brow where sweat had already accumulated from our brief passage from the steaming levee. I had my doubts about such an arrangement but thought to say nothing for the time being.

Julia kept glancing at the governor who was suddenly intruding upon our happy lives, a stranger in our first home, and I could almost hear the objections forming in her mind. The house proved to be a suitable one for my purposes; it had four rooms downstairs, two bedrooms, a parlor that opened on a dining room; a pair of rude attic rooms suitable for the slaves; a detached kitchen with good stone fireplaces; a carriage barn; but only a noisome, small outhouse that fouled the air of the rear yard, and would be inadequate for our purposes. I would need to do something about that, and would set York to work.

"How is this? Perfect, I'll wager," the governor said. "See, everything's right. Room for the slaves up there."

I studied the two attic rooms: the women would go on one side; York on the other. The rafters were exposed, there were small grimy windows at either gable, and a narrow precipitous stair wound down to the back of the first floor. They would have to sleep on the planks, but I had a few old buffalo robes for them. I understood slaves. If they were tired from lack of sleep they wouldn't work as hard, so it paid to offer some comforts.

The governor had taken the sunlit corner bedroom for himself; that left one for Julia and me, and none for my niece. However, we could convert the dining room, and eat at the commodious table in the detached kitchen. It was far from a perfect place for us as long as the governor was present.

"This will serve, Meriwether," I said, not very certain that it would. But I did not wish to spoil the moment of our reunion.

Julia looked downcast. Ever since leaving Virginia, she had been discovering the hardships of the frontier, and I had bolstered her spirits daily with reports that St. Louis was the very cradle of civilization. She had not been assured by the rough-timbered buildings, boatmen's shacks, foul muck on the streets, or the hard men who watched us pass by with calculating stares. My promises weren't worth much just then.

"All right, York," I said. "Sergeant—ah, Ensign Pryor is getting drays, and you'll move our household goods here. You'll move in upstairs, and so will the women. I want supper by six."

"Yas, mastuh," York said dismissively. Damn him! He was becoming less and less valuable to me, and I glared at him. Sweat had beaded on his sooty brow, and collected under his armpits, staining his loose blue shirt.

He herded the slaves back toward the waterfront. The women as well as the men would be toting and hauling for two or three days. But I wanted that kitchen functioning in time for supper.

Lewis was addressing the ladies: "You'll enjoy St. Louis. The Creoles throw a ball for every occasion. There's a fiddle in every household. Wait until you see the great homes, the finery that rivals anything in Paris, the pianofortes, the harps, the libraries, the Paris wallpapers, the fruit trees, the spacious grounds. Ah, you'll see the real St. Louis soon!"

I wiped beads of sweat off my brow and lips. "I think the ladies may wish to retire and freshen," I said, responding to the pleading in Julia's eyes.

"Use my room; there's a commode," the governor said.

Julia nodded, curtsied, and led my niece to that haven. The door to the governor's bedroom closed firmly.

"What a lovely beauty your niece is," Lewis said. "A Grecian beauty! Alabaster flesh! She'll drive the bachelors mad. Ah, youth! I've lost it. I'm such a fusty old man that I won't even make my bid, but of course I'm busy with this territory. But I wager you won't be lacking suitors at our door."

"I'd thought maybe my niece might be a good match for you, Meriwether."

"Ah, Will, my heart's not in it. Letitia's gone! Married. And a good match, too. Maria gone, married. No, my friend, I know my fate. I'm doomed to bachelorhood by a broken heart."

"Meriwether, you old gallant, you could beckon to any damsel in St. Louis with your pinky and end up with a wife."

He sighed unhappily. "No, no, they'd just turn me down, like Letitia. That's how it is with me, Will. I'll dance a few waltzes, dance a few quadrilles, and sigh a few sighs."

That struck me as a sharp retreat from his gallantry of the past. I had the strangest sense that something was amiss. What was that undertone in his voice? Was this the Meriwether I remembered? Maybe it was. Which startled me.

"Alice wanted to sample St. Louis life," I said, "but I don't know how long she'll stay. Perhaps you'll give her a reason." He grinned at me crookedly, so I changed the subject. "Well, now, old friend. Is there news?"

"Yes, always, and I am having my difficulties, mostly Indian troubles, the Great Osage and Little Osage, and the problem of Big White. He's here, put up by the Chouteaus. How will we get him back? It will take an army! His presence is embarrassing the president. How is it that a big nation of white men has been stymied by a handful of dusky savages? That's one problem. But my main problem is Bates. How did you find him?"

I smiled, and then proceeded recklessly. "A man on every side of every issue. A pessimist, who thought my every effort was futile."

"That's my impression also. Ah, Will, it is so good to see you. There's so much to discuss. We're cocaptains again! This place will make us rich! I've already bought land, two farms from the Chouteaus, over a thousand arpents, they're eighty-five hundredths of an acre, and I plan to buy much more. I'm in over a thousand dollars. I've already leased my farms out, and I'm a dairy farmer now. It's all going up.

"That's just the beginning. I'll buy shares of companies in the fur business. You can't help but prosper, Will, and half the French in St. Louis are eager to put us properly into business. This is the best place in the country to gain wealth, for any man with money or slaves."

I grunted. Meriwether had always been the plunger, sometimes acting rashly, and now he was at it again. A thousand dollars! On a modest governor's salary. Tom Jefferson had cautioned him before the expedition about that trait of his, and as long as we were in the field he contained it, but now I could see that Meriwether was losing the discipline he had imposed on himself, and it worried me.

I could see that this was not the day to begin boarding Meriwether, as I had agreed to do, so I suggested that he dine for a day or two at a tavern until we could put the house together. He agreed instantly, having a sensitive regard for my wife and household. He said he would return only to sleep, and if that bothered us, he would find other quarters. And with that he strode into the lowering and motionless air, which plastered our clothing on us like soaked rags and made every move miserable.

Julia emerged from the bedroom, peered about, and relaxed. "He's gone?"

"Until this evening."

"General Clark? I fear to trouble you. I . . . know I am being selfish. But please . . . would you do something for me?" She looked at me so plaintively that I knew her mind.

"If you mean evict him, no. He's my friend, my cocaptain, my commander, and now my governor. I also owe my success to him."

But Julia had a steely will and a mind of her own, as I soon found out after we had exchanged vows. "I know that," she said. "But this house is too small. It wants comforts. I have no proper closet to bathe. The slaves are right above us and can hear our every word. *Everything we do.* There's no room for Alice. It would all work out if the governor would leave this house to us."

On principle, I couldn't let a wife whittle at me like that, substituting her will for mine, so I shook my head. A man has to resist women and slaves and come to his own judgments, or he's not a man. But I thought the world of her, loved her, knew she had started a child in her womb, and I didn't like disappointing her, and truth be known, she had a valid point.

"Give it two months," I said, wanting Meriwether to see the difficulty himself.

She smiled resolutely, and then the first furniture arrived, and she was herself commanding the sweating army.

19 LEWIS

I opened the confidential letter from the president eagerly, knowing the great esteem he held for me. It had been some while since I had heard from him, so I relished the wax-sealed missive that arrived in the posts this day, Friday, August 19, and unfolded the thick vellum.

It was dated July 17.

"Since I parted with you in Albemarle in September last, I have never had a line from you," it began.

I paused, my brain swarming with objections. How could I write him before I had sorted things out?

The president went on to say that perhaps a letter from me was en route, that he would have written sooner but for his belief that something from me was coming.

It wasn't. In truth, I didn't really want to have him or Secretary of War Dearborn looking over my shoulder overly much, especially during my first months when I was making crucial decisions. They were seven hundred miles away, and could not easily be consulted. They had delegated power to me to govern in St. Louis, and I was doing just that.

Mr. Jefferson, always courteous, said he was writing to put aside this mutual silence, and to ask for a report.

He went on to say that it was not until February that he

had learned of Ensign Pryor's defeat by the Arikaras and his flight down the river. He stressed again the necessity of returning the chief of the Mandans, Big White, to his home. "We consider the good faith and the reputation of the nation as pledged to accomplish this." He added that he wanted Big White returned, at whatever reasonable expense.

Well, that was an authorization to spend, and I would have to do just that to get the Mandan home.

There was more. He told me of a great company being formed by John Jacob Astor to harvest furs in the West. He wrote about the deteriorating relationship with the British, and how badly he wanted to avoid war even in the face of deliberate British provocations at sea.

And he ended with a sentence that evoked such a conflagration of feelings in me that I have no words for them:

"We have no tidings yet of the forwardness of your printer. I hope the first part will not be delayed much longer."

I read the letter again, in a sinking mood. It was as close to a rebuke as President Jefferson ever came. The publisher and I had promised the first volume would appear in November last, but I had not prepared one line for typesetting. The president was so eager to see the journals in print that I knew he was containing himself, teaching himself patience. And I was failing him, failing my president.

I set the letter aside, my mind in turmoil. I could not fathom my own conduct. The stark reality is that I wished to be left alone with my projects, without officialdom looking over my shoulder and questioning my every move. Someday soon I would write Secretary Dearborn and tell him the Territory of Upper Louisiana was secure. I had penned three detailed letters to him since I arrived; was that not enough?

I had worked in a perfect fury ever since I landed here, and now Will Clark and I were succeeding. For one thing, we had brought the dangerous Osage tribes under control. The Osages live no great distance west of St. Louis, along the Osage River, and are the source of constant friction with settlers. They are an unruly and sullen lot, horse thieves and raiders. Will Clark promised them a mill, blacksmith shop, and trading post in exchange for a treaty, and he has been delivering on his promise.

We will end up treating with two bands separately, the Great Osage and Little Osage, but we will have our treaties, with a line demarcating the settled country from Osage lands. I sent Pierre Chouteau, who has great influence with them, to get the terms I want. When I have a satisfactory treaty I can submit to Congress for ratification, and settlers there are safe, I will inform the president about it. But now I fear I will have to report it prematurely, and there will be backbiting. I've had Will Clark appoint Reuben subagent for the Osages, which will not only profit my brother, but help me keep an eye on those obstreperous savages.

Secretary Dearborn has already rebuked me for my silence. His letters irritate me with their petty complaints. How can I tell them that I have barely begun? They have no idea just what I face here, and how governing so immense a territory consumes all my energy.

I will write him in response to his rebukes, saying that it is my utmost concern to administer the territory in accord with United States policy, and I will be more diligent in my correspondence, but I will also ask him to take into account the six weeks it takes for a letter to travel between us.

I am glad Will Clark is on hand. He is a man of such

solidity that I trust everything he does. Already, he is hard at work on a new fort overlooking the Missouri River, named Osage, which will have some cannon with which to command the Missouri, and will bring illicit traffic to a halt. He is also building trading posts and government forts at other points, to pacify the savages and supply them with the means to become yeoman farmers and acquire civilized ways.

It took the counsel of a wise friend, Moses Austin, to help me make sense of the strife in St. Louis and I have privately dined or sipped porter with him numerous times. Austin knows men, and knows who is loyal and who isn't. There are those who want licenses to trade upriver because they have none; others who have trading licenses and want to exclude competition so they can enjoy a monopoly.

There are agents of the British, seeking licenses to trade upriver even while undermining the tribes' allegiance to the republic. They succeeded in gulling Frederick Bates, who granted them trading privileges on United States territory even while swallowing their pious protestations. The British trader Robert Dickson is such a man, a soft-talking provocateur whose lullabies lulled Secretary Bates. The Scot James Aird is another, both of them bent upon ruining our grip on Louisiana and fomenting Indians against us.

Austin has steered me well. He has given me the measure of several troublesome men, most of them Bates appointees, and I have removed one from office and am watching others. But the most troublesome of all is Secretary Bates himself who spreads his discontents across St. Louis. I resolved this day to confront the man and if possible win his cooperation, for without my secretary I am ineffectual.

This afternoon I approached him in his Government House

office. He keeps regular hours, and is actually punctilious about his duties, and I knew I would find him there, in the brown and tan rooms vacated by General Wilkinson.

He glanced up as I entered, a bland mask dropping over those puffy features.

"What is it, Mr. Bates, that troubles you?" I asked abruptly, for I wanted to catch him unprepared.

"Why!" He started up from his chair, and stood across the waxed desk, exhaling much air. "Why, Your Excellency, it is true that perhaps I don't always agree with your decisions, but you may count me among your most admiring colleagues."

"I hear otherwise, Mr. Bates. I hear that you can barely mention my name without casting aspersions upon it."

"I'm sure the gossipers are giving you spurious information, Your Excellency."

"I hear that you oppose my appointments."

"Well, now I concede that now and then, without the experience that only long residency can bring to you, some unfortunate appointments—"

"Who? Daniel Boone?"

"Why, sir, I would not wish to delve into names."

"Word comes to me that you find my decisions unsatisfactory. Now is your chance to tell me to my face."

To my face. All of it had been behind my back. Fortunately I have friends, like Moses Austin, who listen carefully, and make note.

"You are a most admirable man, sir, and a great explorer, and the territory is honored by your august presence. On occasion your behavior is a bit, ah, uninformed. If you would call on me to instruct you before you act precipitously, you might thereby save yourself the inevitable grief of a mistake, as well as spare the government a great sum of money." He continued, peaceably. "I know that Secretary Dearborn is much vexed, sir, at your inability to convey to him on a *regular basis* the state of affairs here, and I know that this silence is something that needs your close attention."

Bates always spoke like that to me, often in windy tropes. But I wanted particulars this time, and intended to press him.

"Mr. Bates, I have it on good authority that you are telling people my public approbation here has waned. Have you said it?"

"Why, I cannot recollect it. You see, this is a treacherous place where words are twisted—"

"Is it perhaps because I proclaimed the land to the west of us an Indian Territory in April, and informed those settlers west of the line, who were squatting on Indian lands to which we have no title, to abandon their homesteads?"

"Well, Your Excellency, I hear much anger about it. You are siding with the savages against our own white settlers."

"I'm favoring the fur trade as well as the tribes. And now the paradox, Mr. Bates. Have you also told people that my Indian policies are too harsh and that I will bring down war upon St. Louis?"

He shook his head sadly, even as his eyes blinked and blinked.

"That my celebrity as an explorer has gone to my head? That I have been spoiled, as you put it, by the flattery and caresses of the high and the mighty?"

"I have not publicly said anything of that sort, Your Excellency; only that you want experience."

"Then privately, if not publicly?"

"I can't imagine where such gossip rises from, sir. This is a city of wagging tongues."

"And does yours wag?"

"I try always to be the soul of discretion, Governor."

"I am told that you feel I have no ability to govern and that my military habits make me inflexible, that I don't take advice, and that my acts are harsh. That you resent my partnership with General Clark, and that you feel left out."

Bates blanched. "Really, Your Excellency, this is scarcely the time or place to hash out such matters—"

"What better time, Mr. Bates? Let us put matters on the table. If you have aught against me, tell me first. If you oppose my policies, tell me first. You are a conscientious public servant. You've organized and published the legal codes of the territory, and been of great service to me, and I will make a point of thanking you for your attentions to duty. If you are unhappy and want to hold this office, say so to our superiors, and to me. If you are not content as secretary, then make the proper decision based on your circumstances. I am offering you the hand of friendship now."

I extended my hand. He grasped it and pumped vigorously. I hoped it might lead to peace, but my instincts told me it wouldn't.

20 CLARK

Julia has been pressing me for relief from the crowded conditions here. She braced me in our bedroom the other night, just before we snuffed the candle, saying that she needed more space and privacy. The baby is due in the spring and she wants room to lave and cradle it. My niece lives a half-public life in the makeshift bedroom we have supplied her and is talking of returning to Kentucky. I would rather she stayed to make company for Julia.

I could see the fear in Julia when she asked me the question she had obviously been working toward for weeks: would I ask Meriwether to find other quarters? I listened carefully, keeping my own wishes hidden, and reluctantly agreed. In fact, the governor's presence in our household allows us to proceed seamlessly in public affairs, because we hash things through at supper each evening, and come to a meeting of minds.

But Julia has a point, and as loath as I am to change the arrangement, I know I must.

There is something more about this that has concerned me. My young bride does not like Meriwether. She has not told me so and never will, but it is plain to me. She curtsies when he enters the house, addresses him stiffly, turns from an effusive and chattering young woman into a starchy one at the table, and avoids him whenever possible, pleading the press of household duties.

I have watched this odd behavior for months and last night, when she again broached the subject of evicting our boarder, I questioned her gently about it.

"Is there something about Meriwether that troubles you, Julia?" I asked.

"General, he is a most esteemed man."

I laughed, spotting the evasion. I took her hands and clasped them. "I think you are not at ease with him."

She stared at me a moment, like a doe caught in lamplight. "The very opposite, General. He is not at ease with me. His voice rises, and he becomes, well, very strange and polite. So I am not at ease with him. He is not comfortable with anyone of my sex, sir."

"You don't say!"

She wouldn't say more, just shook her head, even though I probed further. I did not want discord in my household and knew I would be forced to act.

"Very well, Julia, I'll ask the governor to find other quarters. But I will urge him to partake of our suppers, as always, because we have much to discuss. It is an arrangement very satisfactory to me."

"Oh, would you?" She beamed at me as if I had conferred a great honor upon her. "Alice will be so happy! And once we have the bedroom back, I'll . . ."

I chuckled heartily. I enjoy pleasing her whenever I can.

"Oh! I'll have a place to wash the baby and change the diapers," she said. "Oh, General!" She clasped me to her bosom and gave me a great hug, so tenderly that the clocks stopped.

She was so ecstatic over that small change in our lives that

I marveled. And yet I should not have marveled at all.

Julia's conduct affirmed something that was becoming more and more obvious to me: Meriwether has an oddly negative effect on women. Alice Anderson flees him just as much as Julia does, and he has made no headway with her. Something about him falters at the doorstep of the fair sex. I am too dumb in that department to fathom why. But it is plain to me. I have watched it at balls and banquets. I have seen it in his banter: he rattles on about women almost obsessively, as if he was trying to make a point. Of his manhood I have no doubt at all, but his defeats have disarrayed him and women flee from him.

"You will need another laundress, maybe two," I said, alluding to the burden of diapers, in addition to the bed and table linens and towels and clothing the household dirtied in abundance.

"Yes, General, I will."

"I will send to Kentucky for some of my slaves," I said. "I need one myself. How about Khaki, Truman, and Mousy? I've leased them to my brother, and I can get them back. This is October fourth; we should have them before Christmas."

"Oh! I'd feel pampered!"

"Consider it done."

I had not seen Julia so happy since we arrived here. She beamed, pressed her hands to her stomach, and sighed.

I will have my slaves shipped from Kentucky. I need another houseboy. Public service requires every moment of my time and I cannot devote it to the mundane management of my dwelling. I am beset by impending war with Great Britain, and war with the Sauks, Fox, Potawatomis, Sioux, Osages, and maybe other tribes, and I've a half-trained, half-armed militia.

So I will put them all under York's supervision, and make

space in the attic. It will be crowded up there, but they should be grateful to be out of the cold. The alternative would be to build a slave shack in the back lot, next to the slaves' privy.

This evening I will tell Meriwether our family is growing and we need the space. He will understand, being a sensitive man and affectionate friend. He has already told me that he can have a room with Chouteau until he finds rooms.

I hunted for York, and found him carrying stove wood into the parlor, his black muscles rippling.

"You lookin' for me, mastuh?"

"I'm bringing three more slaves into this household, and placing them under you. Two laundresses and a houseboy."

He settled the wood carefully, unsmiling. I had thought he might enjoy having more of the darkies around.

"You gonna stick them up the attic, too?" he asked.

"There's room enough."

"Room enough, yassuh, so there is, lying side by side."

"You have objections?"

He fidgeted a moment, his yellow eyes peering at the floor. "I've been meaning to ask, boss. You maybe hire me out in Louisville for some little while? You gets the money for me workin'?"

"Why?"

"Ah sure wanna see my wife, mastuh."

"No, I need you here," I said.

He looked so crestfallen that I regretted my tone. "Maybe a visit. I can send you back there for a few weeks, but not now. Next year."

His cheerfulness deserted him entirely. "You mind if I ask something? You let me speak some?"

I nodded. He was my old friend. We had grown up together

from childhood and he had been my personal servant for as long as I could remember.

"I goes out on that big trip, and I's as good as any man you got there. I cooks the food just as good, and I hunts good, and I lifts and totes just as good, and I paddles hard, and I guards you like a soldier. I gets just as hungry as them white men, and I gets colder because I's the last to get some skins to wear. But I never do no complaining, not like some white men. You nevah hear a word of anger out of me all them days. You pay them, but you don't pay me because you own me."

He was raising my bile but I pushed it back. I knew where this was heading and didn't like it. He was virtually a free man out West, welcomed into the company of my men. He had the same liberty as they; wooed the dusky maidens as they did. Carried a rifle and hunted, dressed the meat, cooked and walked and paddled and starved. It was like schooling. Once they learn their ABCs, they're ruined. You can't make a slave out of them if they get their learning, and the only use is to sell them for field hands and let them taste the whip. Now, suddenly, York is remembering how it was, and he's little good around here anymore.

"Get it out of your head, and don't ever let me hear it again," I said. "I'm not going to let you go. I'm not going to let you buy your way out, either. You're worth fifteen hundred dollars, and I can't afford to replace you. You are going to keep on right here, and do it cheerfully, or I'll sell you to someone who's a lot harsher than I am. Count yourself lucky."

He seemed to pull deep into himself.

"You can see your woman next spring," I said, intending to soften the decision a little.

He said nothing, but he lifted his gaze from the floor, and

stared directly into my face, and I could see those yellow-brown eyes examine me, as if I was on trial. He radiated pain, a hurt so strong and dark that I almost recoiled.

"Yes, General," was all he said.

I stalked away, itching to whip him for his insolence. But I am a man of slow temper and I checked myself. I do not fathom why he irked me almost beyond my limits.

This evening, while Meriwether and I sipped some New Orleans amontillado while we waited for the mammies to finish cooking the supper, I braced him.

"We've a child coming, Meriwether, and my wife would like to commandeer the rest of the house." I smiled. "She is a woman of great determination, and has taken to ordering the general of militia around."

"A child! I might have guessed! Congratulations, old friend!" Lewis exclaimed, the brittleness of it odd in him. I had never heard this tone during the whole expedition.

"I shall be the gallant and remove myself forthwith," he said.

"Meriwether, I salvaged a little from her onslaught: we hope you'll continue to sup with us."

"General, how can I resist, with so fair a young lady as Miss Anderson to grace our table?"

There it was again, this banter about women. "We always have certain matters to discuss, and it seems a very good time to do it," I said.

"I fear we just bore your beauteous niece with our business," he said.

I had no answer to that.

21 LEWIS

Almost every day I open the journals and read them. Most entries are in Will's hand, and are brief. He was faithful to the task, and recorded the day's events without fail, save only for a brief hunting trip, and even then summarized what had happened during that one lapse.

I planned to keep a full journal myself, but found myself otherwise occupied, so that I did not live up to my good intentions. I wish to excel in everything I do. But it had been a matter of indifference to me whether the events of a dull day were recorded. I always had a higher task in mind, which was to record anything of *importance*: plants, animals, geographical features, oddities, weather, and always, the savages. This I did as faithfully as steady old Will kept the daily accounts of mundane matters.

It is a matter of temperament, that's all. I am inclined to scribble endlessly about a *new species*; he is content in his phlegmatic way to record the miles we traveled, the latitude and longitude, and the condition of the troops.

I room now with Pierre Chouteau in a spacious, sunny manse delicately appointed in all the latest fashion, with fabrics and furniture sometimes brought clear from Paris or England. The place suits me, though I will not abide here long for fear of their hospitality wearing thin. I am looking for rooms. I have rented an office not far from Will's house, to which I still repair after a day's toil to sup with him and his blossoming Julia. She seems more at ease now that I no longer intrude upon her nest.

The journals cast a spell over me and I cannot escape it. They seem heavy in my hand, like pigs of lead, crushing my fingers under their weight. And yet it is all illusion. The cold weight, really, is the expectations of the world and the growing impatience of Thomas Jefferson and the eagerness with which my colleagues in the American Philosophical Society await the detailed account of our great voyage. Here it is, mid-October of 1808, and I have not yet started.

Each day I open them intending to begin an edited version for my publisher, Conrad. Each day I read the entries and they release a flood of memories in me. Here Will describes the time Charbonneau almost sank the pirogue. There I describe the magical moment when I beheld the falls of the Missouri. And here is where we finally found the Shoshones, shy as mice, and with them and their horses, our *salvation* . . .

I page through them: Will's hand is as familiar to me as my own. His want of learning shows; my schooling shows whenever I put nib to paper. His entries are strong, honest, and prosaic; mine extend beyond the ordinary realm, soaring into feeling, speculation, observation—especially observation, for I pride myself on a keen eye, and with that eye I discovered more new species of plant and bird and beast than I can name.

It is an odd thing, opening those journals and swiftly returning to that bright sweet land, never before seen by white men, the shining sun-baked prairies, the gloomy snow-mantled mountains, the wary savages thinking unfathomable thoughts, the rolling river, the salt-scented breeze off the western sea.

This flood of images trumps my best intentions. Why do I pen letters and long treatises on policy, but never put nib to paper when it comes to these journals? It is maddening.

I don't suppose mere words can adequately describe our great journey, the sight of men toiling up the river, the fear and pleasure as we set ashore at the Sioux or Arikara or Mandan villages, the dread with which I first sliced a gray morsel of roast dog and put it in my mouth, the rejoicing when we tasted the brine of the western sea. No, these are too private, too vivid, to convey to the world.

But my president grows restless. And underlying that restlessness is the simple fact that these journals are not really mine or Will's; they belong to the government. We recorded events as officers in the army, as a part of our public mission, expressly for the government.

Mr. Jefferson has graciously given us the priceless opportunity to profit from them, a gift so much larger than anything else he or Congress did for us that it chastens me. There is a large profit to be had from it. Will and I have invested most of what we received in back pay from the voyage of discovery in the project, but after publication there will be money enough to keep us in fine style for years to come. And yet I have not begun. And daily, Tom Jefferson's disappointment in me deepens.

I tax myself with it. Why have I delayed? It is now two years since we set foot in St. Louis. I am stopped! My mind recoils! In the East I proceeded at once toward publication, getting an education in the printer's arts in the process. I hired various artists, even Charles Willson Peale; put a fine mathematician to work on our celestial observations, put draftsmen to work on the maps, got out an attractive prospectus, and all the rest. They have all been busy working with my drawings and specimens: Frederick Pursh, the botanist, has rendered the plants exquisitely. Everything progresses except me.

I offer myself excuses. I was ill and privately closeted at Locust Hill, I'm pressured by the chaotic territory with its catalogues of troubles, I am in great demand as a speaker and guest and civic leader, which consumes most every evening. My Masonic lodge consumes my time. But they all seem lame to me. I know only that each day I fail to write, I feel further squeezed by a terrible vise, and now I contemplate these journals with quiet desperation.

I have been fitful this autumn, suffering the ague twice, and conquering it with the familiar extract of cinchona bark called quinine that is commonly available here for the malady, as well as some calomel. My body aches; I believe the privations of our long overland journey taxed it and I have been slow to recover. I am increasingly excitable, a humor I ascribe to the pressures I labor under.

To curb my restlessness I sip spirits during the day, porter, wine, and sometimes whiskey. In the evenings, I sample whatever my hosts and hostesses place in hand, and am calmed. My sleep has been restless, but I have found a good remedy in the drops of laudanum I drink before bed.

Pierre Chouteau is the soul of hospitality, and includes me in the bright evening society of the Creoles. I take breakfast with him, and for all this he scarcely charges me anything, which is just as well because my accounts are strained to the utmost.

I have made progress on all but one matter: our Mandan guest, Big White, remains in St. Louis, and I am charged with getting him home. Indeed, Mr. Jefferson considers it the highest of my priorities, believing rightly that our entire Indian diplomacy in the West depends on our success.

She-He-Ke, his wife and son, and the interpreter Jessaume, had been settled at Cantonment Bellefontaine, under the watchful eye of the army, but the chief grew restless and insisted on coming here. Chouteau is good with Indians and I have put our guests in Chouteau's care.

Big White has gotten but a few English words, and I cannot communicate with him, but I gather from Jessaume that he regards himself as a brother of the president, that is, a chief of state very like Mr. Jefferson, and wants to be wined and dined as such. And so we do, at the expense of the territory.

Jessaume and his Mandan wife and son have been cooperative. I've taken a liking to the boy, and see some potential in him and have offered to school the boy if Jessaume wishes it. I have in mind making him a factor in the fur trade someday; maybe putting him in charge of one of the government posts we are erecting. In all this I am borrowing a leaf from Will, who offered to settle our interpreter Charbonneau and his Shoshone squaw hereabouts and raise and educate their son, Pomp. It's my fancy to do much the same.

Meanwhile our savage guest has gotten himself up in a fine broadcloth outfit, along with his wife, and they parade through St. Louis daily, delighting the citizens with their affable greetings, their wonderment at all the devices of white civilization, and their prodigious appetites, for no plate is large enough to placate She-He-Ke's appetite.

Meanwhile I brood about the task before me. With the Arikaras so violently opposed to our passage because of an imagined insult, the whole might of the United States is checked, and the British are playing havoc. The Rees, as most men call them, suppose one of their sachems was murdered by us while visiting here, though in fact disease took him off, and on that misunderstanding rests our difficulties.

The regular army cannot help me. I made application to them and was rebuffed. They are understaffed and desperately trying to prepare for war with England. It's going to be up to our militia to do the job, but I have been thinking there might be ways to engage enough men to get past the Arikaras.

Thanks to the good offices of Chouteau, we are well advanced on a plan. The idea now is to form a company, the St. Louis Missouri Fur Company, subscribed by leading men here, to equip a formidable force that can return our guests to their home. Chouteau has lined up Will Clark as a partner, along with my brother Reuben, though I will not participate because this is to be a mixed government and private enterprise.

The partners will include Auguste Chouteau, the wily Spaniard Manuel Lisa, that knowledgeable Creole merchant Sylvestre Labbadie, Pierre Menard, William Morrison, and the merchant Benjamin Wilkinson, who is a brother of the conniving general, which worries me. Most of these are merchants. Reuben brings medicine and youth to the enterprise, and preserves our family interest in the venture.

They are working on articles of agreement now, though I have carefully stayed out of it. But my plan is to pay them a considerable sum of public money to take Big White home; a sum that will, with their own capital added, permit them to raise a formidable army of trappers and traders. I shall, of course, impose strict conditions, and require their departure as early next spring as possible.

It seems the best way to get Big White back, given our lack of resources. I can only hope that Secretary Dearborn cooperates and approves. It is a matter most vexing to have to explain the realities of life on the far western borders to men back East; and the secretary has often proven to be obtuse. He will raise stern objections to my proposal to arm these private citizens, and supply them with trading goods with which to ease their way past the numerous tribes along the river.

Shall the government endow a favored few who are thus enabled to make a great profit? Actually, it saves the government great expense. Persuading him of the merit of this plan is crucial, and failure to explain the necessity will be the death of me, I suspect.

22 CLARK

I fear I will end up in debtor's prison unless the new company earns me a good return. For some reason beyond my ken, Meriwether had done nothing about the journals, and with each passing day my hope of gain for the heavy investment I have shouldered to prepare them for publication seems to retreat.

I had put my back pay into them; my stipend as superintendent of Indian Affairs and as a brigadier doesn't stretch far enough to cover my large household, much less get me out of financial peril. I have land in Kentucky, but could scarcely give it away just now. I have household slaves but they don't earn their keep, unlike field slaves who produce marketable crops. Here it is December, over a year after publication was promised, but I have said nothing to Meriwether about the endless delay. Whatever is bothering him, it is afflicting my purse.

Meriwether must be even worse off, because he continually borrows small sums from me, an incontinence that surprises me, but that I indulge. He is spending considerable in taverns and seems to be arrayed with medicines, but I don't ascribe his straits to that but to his speculations in land. He is purchasing thousands of arpents of farmland, most of it from the Chouteaus, almost entirely on credit. I privately question his wisdom.

He had not been so injudicious on the expedition, and now his conduct puzzles me.

The new fur company revives my hope of gain. The principal merchants of St. Louis have been gathering regularly in Pierre Chouteau's parlor to contrive an agreement. Meriwether was on hand at every meeting, and in fact we could not launch the St. Louis Missouri Fur Company without his support.

We have a sense of possibility and optimism. Manuel Lisa and his partners returned from the upper Missouri with a fine harvest of beaver pelts and buffalo robes. They had gotten past the Arikaras. Now the three of them, Lisa, Menard, and Morrison, are forming the core of the new outfit. They want me in the organization for several reasons, in part because I can license them, in part because of my knowledge of the upper Missouri, and in part because I have been involved in marketing the government's pelts acquired through our factory trading system, and know how to get the best prices.

So we gathered this chill evening to fashion an agreement, after much discussion. Chouteau had a fine blaze going in his fireplace, and treated us to black cheroots and a lusty red port. The Cuban cigars wrought a pungent haze in the candlelight, and put us all in a good humor.

The governor, who had plainly done some thinking, offered us his terms, pacing the parlor with an energy that startled me, as if he contained within something that would burst him wide open unless he released it.

"The government places utmost importance upon returning Big White to the Mandans. Mr. Jefferson requires it of me and has authorized any reasonable expenditure. We lack the armed strength to do it, and must rely on you. I will pay you seven thousand dollars for the safe delivery of Big White. With this money you will equip your own militia of at least a hundred twenty-five men, and will supply them with rifles and powder and lead, as well as other necessaries.

"I will supply a departure date in the spring; you will need to leave before then or forfeit. I'll put that in the contract. We will provide you with trading licenses and whatever other assistance you require."

Meriwether spelled out a great many details, almost as if they were rolling out of some articles of agreement already fashioned in his mind, while the partners—I should say future partners because no such articles of agreement have been completed—listened and smoked.

I knew they would agree to it, without a murmur.

There were men sitting in that parlor I did not trust. Lisa for one, the crafty Spaniard who had overcharged Captain Lewis for the goods he got us on the eve of the expedition. And Benjamin Wilkinson, brother of the conniving general. But such was my fever to conquer the upper Missouri that I resolved to stomach the opportunists.

The British are up there, flagrantly and openly trading with the Mandans, Sioux, and Hidatsas, and other tribes in Upper Louisiana, and setting them against us. It is a part of their undeclared war, this nibbling at our sovereignty and our commerce.

If war does break out, we might well face a massive Indian uprising, orchestrated by the North West Company in Canada and intended to sever the whole territory from our grasp. To stop that, I would make alliance with the devil. The very word *Briton* is enough to put me in a bilious humor.

But these merchants are not devils, merely opportunists,

and one way to secure their loyalty, and procure the allegiance of the tribes, is to let them profit.

"Mes amis," said Pierre Chouteau, "we have heard the governor. Are we to form the company or not?"

We agreed to form one, a partnership in which we all would put in an equal share, as we had already discussed at length. I didn't know where I'd find the means, but I would, somehow. I had land to trade. Andrew Henry was as strapped as I, but had made enough from his lead mines to invest. About Reuben Lewis I didn't know, but he seemed as ready as the rest.

We spent the remainder of that evening hammering out the articles, while Meriwether sat silently by. Quite possibly he was a silent partner, with Reuben as his proxy, but none of us would ever know. Given his position, he was judiciously staying apart. Most of the partners would go up the river themselves; I was exempted because of my office. They made me the accountant and offered me a small salary to handle all the receipts, expenditures, and disbursements. Given what I knew of the fur markets, I thought I could do a good job of it.

The agreement had still to be drafted, copies made and signed, but we walked out of that meeting with a capitalized company. My fortunes would ride on its success. The government's Indian diplomacy would ride on our ability to restore She-He-Ke and his family to his people. If we did that, and showed our muscle, we would hold the Missouri River.

I started downslope that night with my cape drawn tightly about me, my mood as blustery as the wind. I rather hoped to encounter a pair of footpads, just so I could bang their skulls together. But no one molested me.

I knew what was roiling me: I ached to go upriver. The talk in Chouteau's parlor had unleashed a flood of memories, of breezy prairies under an infinite sky, of the river dancing in sunlight, of iridescent black-and-white magpies darting ahead of us and making as much commotion as they could, of standing on a bluff overlooking the sweet land, the sea of wilderness, seeing the bright snowy mountains on the farthest horizon, the backbone of the continent, and feeling more at home than at any hearth back in civilization. I wanted to go. The westering itch had nipped me. But I had a bride now, and a child on the way, and an army at my command, and a president looking over my shoulder.

An icy gale banged me into my house, and I pulled off my cloak and stood a moment in the darkness. York materialized out of the gloom, but the candles were out.

"You have a good meeting, mastuh?" he asked, taking my cloak and hanging it.

"The partners are saying yes," I replied.

"Goin' up de river?"

"Beaver pelts and robes and maybe chasing the British back to Canada."

"Lots of men goin' upriver, get past them Rees?"

"Two hundred anyway, including a hundred twenty-five armed." I grinned. "We'll get Big White home this time."

"They leaving in the spring?"

"May at the latest."

"You want anything, mastuh?"

"No, York, I'll go to bed."

"The mistress, she done gone an hour ago."

I nodded.

"You mind I ask a question, mastuh?"

I stood, waiting.

"I's wanting to go up the river. You sell my services, you

make plenty money, and I go work my way with them that goes to the mountains."

I stared at him. He stood in the shadows, his hands wringing, his cat-eyes soft upon me.

"Mastuh? I been up that river. I knows the ropes. I's experienced. I's good with a gun. I's a good cook. I's a man can skin a hide off any critter. I's a man been there and back . . ."

He wanted to go up there plenty. I could see it in him. I could sell his labor, profit from him, two hundred dollars in my pocket and I wouldn't have to feed or clothe him. He'd be an asset to them. He'd be one of a handful who had been over every inch, who knew every trick.

"No, and don't ask me again," I said, a steely tone in my voice.

"Mastuh?"

"I said no! No! You've got an eye for those savage women, and you can just forget that."

"That ain't it, mastuh."

I knew that wasn't it. Up in the mountains he would be a free man for a few months. He would do better than most of the whites, especially the greenhorns.

"York, go to bed. You will do as I say, when I say, and without objection."

I heard a moan, an exhalation, a collapsing of his lungs, and watched him shuffle off through bleak shadows.

"York! You can go to Louisville and see your woman for a few weeks."

"Thank you, mastuh."

I heard him shuffle up the narrow stairs.

Anger percolated through me. The trip west had sabotaged a good slave. But I pitied him, too, old York. I knew exactly what he was hoping for. Just before the wind blew me into my house, I was thinking of the shining mountains, and longing for the boundless land. York was longing for it, too, but for different reasons.

Well, damn him. I'd whip him if he asked me again, damn his black hide. Old York, my friend from childhood.

A great weariness afflicts me. The more I achieve, the more rebuff I encounter. Now it is Bates again. Let me decide on a course of action or appoint a man to any office, and he will take the opposite tack or complain that I have selected the wrong man.

I gave him some advice, hoping to slow down the galloping gossip floating around St. Louis: "When we meet in public, let us at least address each other with cordiality," I said.

He seemed to accept the prescription.

I thought I had patched things up. He promised to bring his objections to me privately, where we could discuss them frankly, but that scarcely lasted a week. He fumes and fulminates and complains and imagines rebuffs and insults in such number that I am baffled. The effect of all this is to make my burdens heavier and impede my progress.

And now about the ball. It is the December social season, and these affairs occur almost nightly and will continue until well into the new year. It is de rigueur to invite the governor, and I go to as many as I can, enjoying the company, and the belles.

But there Bates was, self-important and dour, at the punch bowl, discussing affairs of state with a guest, and staring daggers at me as I approached. I had no wish to offend, nor did I wish to speak or suffer yet another altercation so I simply sat nearby and began conversing with a Creole dowager who knew a little English.

Ah, that was my mistake! I had ventured in public too close to his person!

A great quiet settled over the hall. Bates had proclaimed far and wide in Missouri that he would meet me only officially, and never socially, and here we were, only a few yards apart. The gossips were watching.

With an affronted mien, the secretary of the territory abandoned the punch bowl and walked as far from me as he could, an obvious and blatant insult.

That offended me more than any other of Bates's malicious acts. The ball was over, at least for me, and I stalked into the cold night, boiling at the man, thinking to meet him on the field of honor, outraged at his infinite capacity to cause trouble. I have never been so angry.

This time, I sent my new mulatto manservant, John Pernia, to Clark, thinking I needed a second. Clark hastened to my office, where I met him in the cold darkness, without lighting a lamp, and there I told him I had had my fill of the obnoxious secretary, and that his conduct was intolerable, and I would seek redress. I would not let it pass.

The general calmed me down. "I'll talk to him, Meriwether, and see whether I can win an apology."

"Do it now."

"No, not now. I'm going to let him cool down."

"He gave deadly insult. I'm ready for what comes!"

Will eyed me quietly. "One Aaron Burr is too many."

I thought of Tom Jefferson's embarrassments and how I

might add to them out of rashness, and subsided. Vice President Burr had fallen into disgrace after killing Alexander Hamilton in a duel; he had dabbled with empire building out here, inviting the British and then the Spanish to help him detach Louisiana from the republic.

He had been acquitted of treason for want of firm evidence, and had fled to Europe in voluntary exile. His lovely daughter, Theodosia Burr Alston, wife of a Carolina governor, was an acquaintance of mine. The gossips had linked us, but there never was a thing to it. I had watched the Burr trial in Richmond as the president's observer, and that was as close as I ever wanted to get to Aaron Burr.

The image of that hollow-eyed, haunted, and bitter man, sitting in the dock, flooded through me, and I realized that my old friend Will was steering me away from the dock in his own gentle way. It was not the first time I felt a flood of gratitude toward my old comrade.

But Will was not done with me. "Governor, it behooves you to consider what you have said or done that maddens Frederick Bates," he said.

The heat boiled up in me. "Are you accusing me?"

Will grinned. "Just that sometimes we don't see what we do to others."

"I have treated him with perfect civility."

"And so you have, old friend. Why then, do you set him off?"

"I haven't the faintest idea," I said sharply, my tone telling Clark I had no wish to pursue the matter further.

"Do you seek his opinions? Counsel with him?"

"His views aren't worth my attention."

Will started to say something, and then obviously checked

himself. "I get along with him all right," he said at last.

"You're not the governor! He was the acting governor until I arrived, and he can't forget it."

Clark clapped me on the back. "Guess he can't," he said cheerfully. "Guess you can't, either."

That last lanced through me, and it was all I could do to stop the black mood that surged through me. Was he telling me the fault was mine? What *was* he telling me? Was he my friend, or had he turned on me, too?

"Let's go home," he said gently.

I parted with him in the dark street, my thoughts riding furiously in all directions. Will was settled and happy; a baby was coming soon. He enjoyed St. Louis. I had never heard a whisper of malice directed toward him. What had Fate given him that Fate denied me? I watched him vanish into the closeness of a starless foggy night, and turned toward my rooms, my mind still churning.

Would anyone ever honor me for all that I had accomplished in Louisiana? Not even Will knew what I had done. As I walked, I took refuge in my accomplishments.

I had made great progress, started a road to Ste. Genevieve and New Madrid, published the territorial codes, proclaimed an Indian territory, promulgated a law allowing villages to incorporate, curbed promiscuous licensing of traders, put up forts on the Osage and Des Moines Rivers that helped check the British, appointed good men to various offices, put out a spy network to keep an eye on the Spanish along our southwest border, put Nicholas Boilvin, my best man with the Indians, to work dealing with the Sauk and Fox tribes up north, and bringing to justice some murderers they were harboring.

And with Will's help I had dealt with the Osages and submitted a treaty to the Senate, cashiered the disloyal and lazy elements from the militia and put good men in command, settled some of the bold stakery, or the claim disputes, over the Ste. Genevieve lead mines, started work on a shot tower, won over the wary Creoles to the republic, and now, at long last, was closing in on the hardest and most urgent of all tasks, getting Big White back to the Mandan villages.

I should have been proud. Instead, I was weary in a strange way that seemed to rise from my very bones. Secretary Dearborn had become more and more abrupt and demanding, and also more obtuse about the dangers here; and Mr. Jefferson, a man I regarded as my father, had written sharply to me about my failure to correspond, and to put the journals in order.

And as great as my accomplishments were, the combined dissatisfaction of the president, Secretary Dearborn, and the territorial secretary, who loathed my very presence, weighed more on me than everything I had achieved. They were hovering over my shoulder like ghosts, wanting to undo my decisions.

Governing was harder than I had ever imagined. I had expected to make enemies as well as friends; I hadn't expected the backbiting, gossip, malice, and secret machinations intended to undo my every act, and drive me from office.

I am feeling indisposed again, and fear another bout of ague is coming. But these come and go, and I am in the pink of health, except for an odd and inexplicable malaise, like a crouched wolf within me. I do not call on Reuben for treatment, and have not seen a physician on my own account since I arrived here. Such remedies as I need for the ague, such as cinchona bark extract called quinine, I can get easily enough from the Creole apothecaries in town.

There is a bright spot. Through my solicitation, I have gotten a newspaper into the territory, the Missouri *Gazette,* and by it I am broadcasting my ideas and publishing my laws and regulations. Though I am consumed by territorial business, I still find time to pen my thoughts, which are duly published under the nom de plume Clatsop. What better means could there be to shape the opinions of my citizens? I much prefer penning my thoughts for publication than writing to all those in Washington who demand things of me. My own father died when I was a boy; it is painful for me to correspond with those who presume to govern my conduct.

I have not neglected my own fortunes, either. I have written my mother to tell her that I am putting the family estate at Ivy up for sale to finance my purchases here. It is my intent to bring her and the rest of my family here and settle them on the generous and fruitful farmlands I have acquired from the Chouteaus. I have already paid three thousand for these lands, and owe two more large payments next May and the following May. And then the Lewis and Marks families will be handsomely established here in the West.

But until I effect that sale in Virginia, I will be pressed to the limit. Just the other day, I borrowed $49.50 from Will for two barrels of whiskey. I have had to borrow from him, from the Chouteaus, and others, mostly for ordinary medicines and spirits, and the care of my manservant, Pernia. I have a few dozen small notes about town, which I will redeem as soon as I can.

There is no margin of error: I have put every cent into real estate and fur trade interests, which should profit me handsomely and secure a comfortable income for my family. But such is the rising value of land here that I can scarcely go astray, and I am deeply indebted to the Chouteaus who have made such rich farmland available to me.

I live in great expectation, sensing that everything for which I was put upon the earth is coming to fulfillment.

24 CLARK

This Wednesday, December 7, 1808, I shipped York to Louisville on a keelboat and gave him four dollars to feed himself. I told him to be back here before the end of May. I supplied him with papers and had him carry a letter to my brother in which I said that if York should prove refractory, he should be sent to the auction in New Orleans and sold.

I am glad to have him out of the house. He was a sullen presence here, full of the notion that he should be freed because of his service during the expedition. He's not fit to be a free man, though he thinks he is. He will visit his wife while hiring out for her master, and if that doesn't cure him I will ship him south to the slave auction myself.

This aggravates me. He was a faithful friend and servant until he got back from the West. Now he is hardly worth the auction price of an aged male. Let him find out what life as a field hand is like, if he continues to spread his malcontent in my household. I blame myself: I never should have taken him with me. He got notions out there that will never go away.

I am having a bad time with the slaves. They don't like their attic quarters, and I am growing impatient with them. Maybe a taste of the whip will cure them. Meriwether tells me to contain myself. I think he has an eye to the national acclaim we share, and doesn't want my dealings with York to intrude upon our celebrity. He is kind to York, but that is only because he doesn't own York or face his daily insolence.

The holidays are upon us, and my household is greatly improved by the absence of discord. My niece, Alice, left a fortnight ago, having had her fill of St. Louis. Suddenly we have room and privacy. Julia has not yet closeted herself, but will soon. She is suffering from a variety of ailments, including nausea in the mornings. She is feeling ungainly but when she thinks of the child she brightens, and her eyes glow. She takes my hand and presses it to her swollen middle, and I marvel at the life that is blossoming there.

We still have Meriwether for supper each night, and he joins us in our dining room to discuss the state of the territory. He is a gifted man, and yet I worry about him. Why does he provoke Frederick Bates almost beyond reason? I have no trouble with Bates, apart from considering him a windbag and a vain man. But Meriwether turns Bates into a rabid dog.

I visited Bates in his office a week or two after the great public contretemps, and told the secretary that I was acting as an intermediary and peacemaker, and I regarded him a friend.

"Frederick, maybe it is time to reconcile with the governor," I said, after we had gingerly visited a bit. "You might find him eager to accommodate you if you were to stop by and see him."

Bates would have none of it. He sprang to his feet, in a huff, and began shouting.

"No! The governor has *injured* me and he must *undo* the injury or I shall succeed in fixing the stigma where it ought to rest. You come as *my* friend, but I cannot separate you from Governor Lewis. You have trodden the ups and downs of life with him and it appears to me that these proposals are made solely for his convenience."

I nodded, for there was nothing more to say, and retreated.

Once out the door of that meticulously disciplined office, where not a pin is out of place and every paper is nested in its proper folder, I smiled. The secretary evokes that in me.

But Bates's conduct opened certain avenues of thought that perplexed me deeply. The man has trouble getting along with anyone, and routinely ruptures relations with men all over the territory. And yet, and yet . . . why is he doubly venomous toward Meriwether? And is there blame on both parts? Mr. Jefferson and Secretary of War Henry Dearborn have confidence in Bates, and that says something.

If Bates has succumbed to an excess of feeling, so has Meriwether, and this new quality in my old friend puzzles me. If it had existed on the expedition, he had checked it so thoroughly that I never imagined him to be turbulent. But Meriwether is increasingly troubled here, just when he should be quiet of heart.

I took Bates's obdurate response back to the governor, who simply shook his head. His heat about Bates has left him, and he queried me about other things, not least the health of my expectant bride.

"She's aglow, Governor. But she's wallowing about like a walrus and wishing it was over. I will tell you something. If it is a boy, we will name him Meriwether Lewis Clark."

The governor paused, his blue gaze gentle upon me, registering that. "I wish I could do the same for you," he said. Then he brightened. "Why, what a thing to do! I hope the little rascal is bright as a button!"

He beamed at me, and I saw a flash of the old Meriwether shining for a moment.

But then he clouded again, and I saw something haunted in his face. "I'm just a musty old bachelor," he said. "I'll never have children, though it has been my deepest desire for as long as I can remember. I'm getting old and set in my ways, and there's not a woman who would want such a man."

I meant to put a stop to such melancholia, but instead it seemed to drive him deeper into gloom.

"Governor, every time I see you at a party, half the women have eyes for you, and the other half wish they weren't married," I said.

He turned to me with such seriousness, with such pain in those blue eyes, that I supposed I had accidentally stepped on his most tender humor, and I pulled back at once.

"Old friend," I said, "the right woman will come along and then you'll know the bliss of marriage, an estate that I find suitable to my temperament."

He brightened. "I have an eye for the ladies, and maybe I'll go wooing," he said, but with that odd brittleness in his voice again.

I sensed he wouldn't. I sensed that woman was an unscalable alp for Meriwether, but I am dumb about such matters, and didn't even hazard a guess why.

"Thank you anyway," he said softly. "I never have had a child named for me. Ah, Will . . ." He sighed.

I do not know why I worry so about the governor.

The new year approaches. We have just received word that Mr. Madison probably will be our next president, though they were still counting rural precincts and nothing was official. He is an intelligent bantam with a bright new wife named Dolley, a Virginian like Thomas Jefferson, but not a quarter the man. I worry about whether he grasps how close we are to war with England and what the Canadians are regularly doing across our western frontier.

I would like to travel to Washington to take the measure of the man, and also to brief him about our parlous defenses here. I could use a few tons of powder, a thousand muskets, and a few dozen artillery pieces, not to mention a shipment of uniforms, boots, gloves, hats, and mess kits, but that won't happen unless James Madison's secretary of war is a man of vision. The new president's appointments will tell the tale.

My ears have already picked up a scandalous rumor, spread by Bates of course, that Meriwether will be replaced shortly. I don't doubt that the secretary of the territory is doing everything in his power to cause it to happen. He is a veteran letter-writer, and a facile one, and I cannot help but believe that the man whom Mr. Jefferson regarded virtually as a son will be the target of abundant criticism now that Meriwether's patron is leaving office. I would not want to be in the governor's shoes.

His future is bleak. He was orphaned during the revolution, and now he may be orphaned again, in a different but equally grave manner. But he is a grown man, inured to hardship, and surely he will ride any storms. The new men in Washington will honor him as an explorer, but whether they will honor him as a governor remains to be seen. He scarcely knows any of them. They don't know me, either, and I intend to go east next year to make sure that there is some acquaintance among us.

This evening at supper with Julia, I quite unwittingly provoked in Meriwether the first petulance he has ever directed toward me. It came so suddenly I scarcely was girded for it, and came on the wings of a question so innocent of malice that I had to take stock a moment.

I said, simply, "How are the journals coming?"

He shook his head and swallowed some of the pureed potatoes before him.

"I suppose you're about finished," I said.

He flared up. "I will write at my leisure, and do a proper job, and correct the innumerable errors, and if that doesn't suit you . . ." He left the rest unsaid.

I sat, astonished. Not in all the three years we toiled side by side on the expedition had he raised his voice to me.

I did not quite let go of the subject.

"We have a lot invested in it. The artwork is done; the astronomical calculations are done; the maps are complete. I would like to see the first edition. Money has become a pressing matter with me."

Meriwether glowered. "You have no idea the work that goes into the task," he said. "It requires education and intelligence and abundant time."

I still had no answer. I did not know whether one page or a thousand had been organized and transcribed for Mr. Conrad.

"You could hire it done. I imagine five hundred dollars would pay for an editor."

He continued upon his biliousness, first dabbing his face with a napkin.

"First of all, I don't have five hundred. Secondly, I am the only one who can do it. I alone have been there, know what we saw, and have the schooling to set it down properly."

I grinned at him, and the governor reddened, and mopped up our gravy in silence.

25 LEWIS

I have been sick abed this entire wassail season and am uncommonly slow to recover. It is the ague again. I have dosed myself with the extract of cinchona bark over and over, but it has little effect. The chills were not present this time, either. Usually, a few hours of chills and shakes precede my fevers, and I am puzzled by the lack this time.

I purged myself with one of Doctor Rush's Thunderclappers, and that seemed to avail me somewhat, but the remedy cramps my belly.

I have second-floor rooms on the Rue L'Eglise now, a parlor and chambers for myself and my manservant. This Monday morning, the second day of January, 1809, Pierre Chouteau stopped in to greet me and found me abed.

"Ah, it is the *maladie*. Shall I summon Reuben, my friend?"

"No, no, I know as much as he does," I said. "We're a medical family."

"*Bien*, if you need a physician, let me know, then, *mon ami*."

"I have not only the proper remedy but a knowledge of my mother's simples, which I used effectively during the entire expedition. I have just taken some ginseng and goldenseal."

He pursed his lips a moment. "I know of an excellent physician, a royalist refugee from Paris, who practices the most advanced medicine anywhere—"

"Doctor Saugrain," I said. "I know him."

"Your Excellency, he is the man to consult."

"Yes. I've had dealings with him. I engaged him as an army surgeon to look after my men when we came back from the West. Some were sick, others wounded, and all half starved. He did an excellent job."

"Ah! Then you know of his prowess. A great treasure in St. Louis! I can send a boy and have him here in no time."

"No!" I said sharply.

Chouteau shrugged, that Gallic signal of resignation. "Very well, *mon ami*. I keep account of your men; their health matters to me. We wish to employ them to go up the river with the new company. Ah, the experience they have! They would be invaluable, knowing every mile, every danger. And so I keep track. They are all well, save one."

"Who is that, Pierre?"

"The private called John Shields."

"He's sick? I hadn't heard."

"*Oui*, yes, *très malade*, very sick. The good doctor Saugrain cares for him."

"I am tired. Thank you for your concern," I said abruptly.

I must have addressed him brusquely because he apologized and hastened out the door. I did not mean to be so abrupt with my friend, who was only trying to help. I must curb this uncivil habit; too often I have seen people retreat from me after an exchange. I am under pressure, and sometimes that rules me.

The news of Shields's sickness troubled me. He was one of those who accompanied me in search of the Shoshones that summer of 1805. Shields, MacNeal, and Drouillard and I had gone ahead of the corps to find the Shoshones and their horses.

Poor Drouillard. He went to work for Lisa, was sent to find a deserter named Antoine Bissonnette and bring him back dead or alive, and he brought him back lifeless. The man's relatives demanded that Drouillard be tried for murder. He was acquitted, but the stain is upon him and he has fled upriver. My best man, who saved the whole corps with his brilliant hunting, being tried for murder. It puts me in the bleakest humor.

Shields in poor health, Shannon a cripple after having a leg amputated; who of the old corps will be next? I am most worried about Shields and think I might go to Antoine Saugrain and inquire privately about the matter when I am up again. I want to know the nature of his illness, just for my own information.

So I lie here, in my rented upper rooms on the Rue L'Eglise, with a view overlooking the levee and the great gray river, mending while the business of the territory languishes. Will has come by regularly, and on him rather than Secretary Bates the good order of the territory depends.

Will tells me the baby is coming soon; that Julia is strong and healthy but so burdened with child that she barely can navigate. She depends now on the slaves to bring her meals to her. Even before she was well along, she preferred to retire to her room for her supper, leaving the dining table to Will and me.

My manservant John Pernia attends me daily even though I have little use for him during my illness, and this time I had a request for him apart from fetching my meals, which I purchase at the Old Tavern.

"Bring me Doctor Saugrain," I said.

Pernia, a capable man, nodded and left, and I waited but

a short while for the little Frenchman to make his appearance at my chambers.

He bustled in, eyed me, and pulled up a walnut chair beside my bed. Even as he perched on that chair, his slender face rose barely above my head. He had changed none at all since I had engaged him to look after my corps. The black suit, ivory face, pince-nez, coal eyes, spade beard that jutted cockily outward, the flowing salt-and-pepper hair that was gathered at the nape of his neck with a purple ribbon, all comforted me somehow.

"Ah, monsieur, Your Excellency, the governor," he said with a lavish and Gallic sweep of the hand. "You are indisposed?"

"No, I'm getting well, a bit of ague, but it is almost behind me now."

"Ah, the ague, an intermittent fever that torments its victims. We shall look at it."

"No, no, I just want to ask you about my old Corps of Discovery private, John Shields. He is under your care, I believe."

"I cannot talk about the ailments of others in my care, Your Excellency, so forgive me a thousand times—"

"I think you can talk to the governor," I said, "and to the commander who arranged with you for the medical care of my men."

He considered a moment, all the while reconnoitering me with his practiced eye. At last he sighed, frowned, and proceeded.

"*Monsieur le capitaine*," he said, thus revealing the military grounds by which he would breach a confidence, "it is so. The private Fields suffers from *lues venerea* in the third stage, afflicting his heart and arteries, and my treatments no longer avail. I would give him maybe a few months at the most."

It could not be! "But Doctor, so short a time!"

He shrugged amply, his small arms spread Christ-like upon a phantom cross. "The disease takes its own form in each victim," he said. "In some it advances slowly; in others it is like a rampage of evil and consumes the victim in a few years. In some it disappears and does not emerge until many years later, and then it is often fatal."

"Are you sure?"

"A classic case, Your Excellency. Fast, yes, but as you yourself pointed out to me, your men were weakened by starvation and hardship and the gates of the body were wide open. It was not hard for a disease to enter the door and conquer."

"But the disease mimics several others! You might be mistaken!"

"I might. There is always that."

"What are Shields's symptoms?"

"The disease assaults his heart and arteries. Already there have been hemorrhages. His pulse is erratic. He may fail from an aneurysm. His nerves fail him. He walks on feet that flop about, as if severed from his brain."

I felt a great weight lift from me. I laughed. "What other symptoms of the third stage do you observe?"

"Why, my capitaine, unexplained intermittent fevers, the gummas, or thickenings, especially around the face, destruction of the throat, usually with craters in the middle of them, scars from lesions, copper-colored nodules, hoarseness, an aortic murmur, the femoral pistol-shot sound and double murmur known as Duroziez's sign, aneurysm, strokes, advancing paraplegia . . ."

"When do these appear?"

"Usually it takes a few years. Who knows exactly?"

I laughed again. His brows shot up.

"It depends, my capitaine. The *lues venerea* attacks the weakest system in the victim. So each case is different. In the most tragic cases, it attacks the system of nerves and the brain, and in time induces paresis, or madness, or deterioration of the mind, of thought, of rationality, of feeling, and the worst of it is that the victim knows exactly why his mind is failing and why his feelings are tempestuous; the unspeakable disease is rendering him into a blundering idiot.

"He can read the signs. He remains mostly rational until the last. There may be seizures. Loss of short- and long-term memory. Flawed judgment, loss of language ability and vocabulary, strange moods, irritability, anger, delusion, hallucination, apathy, weakness of muscles . . .

"He can share his grief with no one. He hides it from the world. He closets himself. He prays, in his saner moments, that no one will ever discover that his madness was caused by a moment of illicit pleasure and that he got from it the most shameful of all sicknesses. Ah, monsieur, that is the worst case."

I laughed, for none of that had anything to do with me.

"Is there any cure?" I asked.

"None. The salt of mercury, it is less and less sovereign as time goes by, and by the third stage, it does little good at all, and only briefly. It might delay, but it cannot conquer."

"My mother has simples for everything."

He lifted those little ivory hands again. "Then I shall gladly learn from her," he said gallantly.

"You'll have the chance. I plan to bring her and my family here shortly."

"Now that I am here, do you wish an examination, Your Excellency?"

"No, I'm recovering from the ague, and have dosed myself."

"Ah, I see. The bark, oui?"

"Yes, and some calomel."

"Ah, I see. Shall I listen to your chest?"

I had no wish to be examined, but as long as he was here, I supposed it might not be a bad idea.

He was already opening his bag and extracting his black lacquered listening horn, so I lay back and waited, knowing I shouldn't submit because I have no way to pay him in the immediate future.

"Ah, now, Your Excellency, we shall see," he said.

26 LEWIS

In this disquieting manner did the year eighteen and nine begin for me. The Lilliputian poked and probed my anatomy, including the bottoms of my feet, employing his listening horn to hear the rumble of my vitals, and his magnifying glass to examine assorted skin rashes. I was amused, though too feverish to enjoy it all.

"Extract of cinchona bark five times daily," I said. "Five drops of laudanum in water, as needed."

He harrumphed and smiled.

A hard sun low in the heavens bit brightly into the room. At last he ceased, and carefully placed his horn and magnifier into his black bag. He turned to the window, his jutty beard poking at the sun, his small body arched to make it an inch taller than it usually was.

I awaited his verdict with rare humor.

"Have you been irritable, my governor?" he asked.

"Uncommonly."

"Impatient?"

"Of course. If you had to deal with what I deal with—"

"What is my baptismal name?"

"Ah . . ." I paused, trying to dredge up a name I had not used in years.

"It is Antoine François."

I was embarrassed. "Why do you ask?"

"Medical reasons."

That seemed most peculiar. I grunted.

"When you posted me as an army surgeon in 1806 to treat your men, you recollected it readily enough after three years in the West, without prompting, Your Excellency."

"I am sorry I am not measuring up to your expectations," I said tartly. "It's been a while. Send me your bill."

He raised a tiny alabaster hand. "It is not about your social aptitude that I am concerned."

"Well? I have the ague. A fevered mind doesn't serve as well as a healthier one."

He paced sternly about the small bright room. "Are you living within your salary?"

"That is not a matter I wish to discuss. I will pay you for your services as soon as possible. Now, if you are done—"

He smiled brightly for the smallest moment.

"*Ah, non, mon ami.* There is more. I have subscribed to your journals, thirty-five dollars to the publisher, Conrad. For this I apply myself to the English. How soon may I expect them?"

"Ah . . . I've been busy."

He peered at me with those black marble eyes. "I am a great admirer of yours. To make that unspeakable journey into the unknown. Ah! What a grand feat! Your Excellency, I await with the great, ah, great eagerness to read of the voyage, and your gifts to science, the new species of the plants and the animals."

He was making me miserable. "It will be some while," I said.

He turned again, frowning. "Is it that the work seems formidable, ah, difficult?"

I nodded.

"Is it that the words don't come?"

"No, I've just been busy."

"Is it that you are, ah, uncertain? How shall I attack this beast and conquer it?"

I smiled. "I suppose you want to help me. You have a background in science. But I alone am qualified. No one can help me."

"Ah, no, monsieur, it is all part of my diagnosis."

I was weary, feeling out of sorts and feverish. I didn't have the energy for social banter. "I am tired, Doctor, and—"

He perched on the edge of my bed, his miniature body birdlike above me.

"It is the venereal," he said.

I smiled. "You have that on your mind. It is an intermittent fever, common to southern latitudes."

He shook his head. "*Lues venerea* lurks like a vampire in the body, silently eating the parts it attacks, invisible to all but the experienced eye, such as mine."

"No, my friend, it isn't." I knew medicine and I knew that I had an intermittent fever, not the venereal. I brightened, making a joke of it. "You Frenchmen, that is all you think of."

He allowed himself the slightest smile. "A little bit of mercury, not a lot. And avoid spirits. That is what I will prescribe. Too much mercury chloride ruins you faster than the venereal. It poisons the brain and ruins the bowels."

"Ah, so now you think I am mad." I glared at him. "Too many of Doctor Rush's Thunderclappers. That's what you're driving at."

He hesitated. "No, not now," he said. I knew there was more he intended to say, even if he wasn't saying it just then.

He stood, his dignity towering much higher than his small frame, his mien grave and sad.

"In some people the disease arrests naturally. In others it progresses, furtively, a secret enemy, an insidious mole tunneling through the body, fouling it. In some, it attacks the heart and arteries, and in others, it commits its sacrilege upon the brain—"

"Doctor Saugrain, that's a fine description of the venereal, but I haven't a sign of it. You are inflicting pain upon me for no good reason."

"I am sorry. I do not wish to inflict pain upon anyone. My oath and dedication are to relieve pain, not inflict it, Your Excellency. A bleak diagnosis is painful. Perhaps some other time, when you are ready to talk to me, I will be found in my chambers."

He pulled his thick black cape about him, and lifted a shining beaver hat to his head, which increased his height dramatically.

"I am sorry," he said, and left. I heard some indistinct commotion as Pernia saw the doctor to the door.

Fevered or not, I sprang up in my nightshirt and examined myself before the looking glass. Was I not Meriwether Lewis, conqueror of a continent, celebrated explorer and naturalist and soldier and governor? Was I not a man of intelligence and learning, a quick study, a man of many parts? Was I not a man of great repute, admired across the whole republic, friend and secretary of a president, and a man with high office in his own future?

I saw all that in the mirror, and something else. I was fevered, and my face was drawn and flushed with heat.

I had had many of these bouts. The ague strikes mostly in warm weather, when the miasmas rise from the swamps, but it recurs anytime, and that was my trouble.

Venereal, indeed! Those French think of nothing else.

I had a bottle of the quinine on my commode, and from this I poured a generous dose into a tumbler of water. I would dose myself more rigorously with the extract of the miraculous bark from South America until I was past this misery, and then return to my tasks.

I gulped down the bitter stuff; nothing is quite so sharp on the tongue as quinine. Immediately I felt better. I would be up and about in a day or two. I regretted engaging Saugrain; I could afford neither his bill nor his misdiagnosis.

I ached, so I uncorked the blue bottle of laudanum and poured a few drops into the tumbler. Actually, eight or ten drops, more than I had intended. But the tincture of opium always put me at peace; it was a stalwart friend in a shifting world, a remedy I could always count on. I drank it, and then crawled under the gray coverlet, waiting for its beneficial effects to steal through me.

It was not always available in St. Louis, because every drop of it had to be shipped up from New Orleans, and I lived in constant dread of running out of it. I have often abjured the apothecaries to hold back some for me, the governor, no matter what the case, but sometimes they lacked a supply. If worse came to worse, there was always Dover's powder. My injuries, especially the shot through the buttocks when we were near the confluence of the Missouri and Yellowstone, pain me and require relief.

Within a few minutes I began to feel just fine. Maybe this

very hour I would rise and set to work on my journals. It was a simple task, transcribing and correcting them. All I had to do was dip the quill and begin. The sun seemed terribly bright, and I thought to ask Pernia to close the draperies, but instead I rolled away from the blinding light and closed my eyes.

There was so much to do, but I didn't feel like doing it. There would be a new president in a few days, and I intended to write James Madison, as well as the new secretary of war, and let them know what I am about. I intended to write Thomas Jefferson and explain why I had not been a good correspondent. But I decided not to do that; he would only inquire once again about the journals, and I wouldn't want to stir up that line of thought.

My indisposition slows me, and loosens my mind, so that it is hard to collect thoughts and send them to the new men. I am going to have to concentrate my mind. I have met Mr. Madison many times; he has been a part of the Jefferson administration. I never cared much for him. He is not a bright man; I fear I will have to explain things to him that Mr. Jefferson grasped instantly. Nor have I seen in the new man the slightest interest in science, and only a minimal interest in commerce. It will be up to me to school him, and his new war secretary, whoever that may be.

I lay back on my pillow and thought of the little Frenchman, Saugrain, fussing about his governor and finding overly much wrong with him. I smiled. He is an eminent physician, and thus always on his mettle, looking for the unseen, spotting the disease that eludes all else. But he missed the obvious in me: malarial fever, and nothing worse.

Tomorrow I would be up and about, and I would return to my tasks.

27 CLARK

The midwives banished me from my own bedroom a few days ago. I sat helplessly in the parlor while servants bustled in and out of there carrying towels and hot water. I didn't like the sound of it, the groaning that pierced even closed doors, the low murmur of worry, the grim looks of the black women who filtered in and out on mysterious errands. But at last, after waiting through a day and half a night, I heard a new sound, a wail, coughing, outrage at being alive, and quiet sobbing. A half hour later they let me in.

The tapers were all lit. It was much too hot even though a March wind howled outside, thundering against the sides of the house and driving tentacles of air through every crack. They had cleaned everything up. Julia lay abed, pale and sweaty in a fresh white nightdress, her hair matted, her features gaunt, her eyes huge. But she was aglow, and on her bosom lay a little boy wrapped in swaddling clothes, my firstborn, my son.

"He is perfect," she whispered, as if to answer one question.

I stood beside the bed, my hands clumsy.

"It was hard," she said, answering the other question. This was her first child, pushing his way through untraveled country, little explorer that he was.

I beheld a son, with downy blond hair glinting redly in the

wavering light of the beeswax candles. The infant was asleep upon the damp cotton over her bosom.

"I am glad," I said. "For you, for the son. I am blessed."

She smiled wanly, and I knew she wanted only to fall into slumber, a sweet oblivion that would begin the healing.

The midwife, Mrs. Perrigault, stood quietly nearby, candlelight glinting from a great silver crucifix upon her black dress. "Is Julia all right?" I asked.

"She is torn."

"Badly?"

"I will need to watch closely. And so will you."

I ran a hand through my coppery hair, and nodded.

Julia opened her eyes again. "Meriwether Lewis Clark," she said, and closed them.

It had been a disappointment to her. She wanted Hancock in the boy's name.

Her hands fondled the child. I studied its tiny mouth and mottled pink face and thought it was the plainest son ever born, plainer even than I am. I shouldn't have named it after handsome Meriwether.

"*Bien,*" said the midwife, gesturing me out. I knew who was the real commander in that room. In that company, I was the private.

But I would gladly leave all that to the women. I had supplied Julia with enough house servants to keep the baby in diapers, to take care of the infant, a wet nurse to suckle it if need be, to guard it and clean it and to ease every burden of motherhood. I was glad I had the household slaves to do it.

A son! Like little Jean Baptiste, or Pomp as I called him, born of Charbonneau and the squaw Sacajewea way back in 1805. I had taken a shine to that little lad, and now I had one of my own, named Meriwether, too. Maybe Pomp and my boy would meet someday. Long ago I had invited Charbonneau and the squaw to settle here, and promised I would look after Pomp's schooling. But I had not heard a word filtering down the river. Somewhere, Pomp would be growing into a fine boy. Like Meriwether Lewis Clark.

I notified Meriwether and invited him to see his namesake, but for some reason he delayed, at least until this Wednesday, the Ides of March. He promised to be here for supper, and we would visit Julia together. My wife remains mostly abed, having exhausted herself in this hard labor.

Meriwether is taut as a bowstring these days, and I ascribe it to the burdens of office. He walks catlike, as if afraid to put down a foot; a strange conduct after walking across a continent. He has often pleaded illness and no longer sups with us and I miss his lively company.

This evening he arrived in his blue uniform, gold braid shining, boots freshly blacked. He has often worn it since resigning his commission. He looks dashing in it, though it hangs loosely around him.

I greeted him in the parlor upon being notified of his arrival by my houseboy.

"Ah! Meriwether!"

"I've come to see the little gentleman," he said.

"High time," I replied. "You are got up for the occasion."

He eyed me. "Let my namesake see a captain, not a governor. Let him follow the beat of drums, not the beat of politics."

That puzzled me, but so did a lot of things about Meriwether in recent months.

I excused myself to see whether Julia was up and about.

She greeted me in her pink wrapper, sitting in her oak rocking chair.

"The governor's here to see the boy," I said.

"Oh, pray wait until I make myself ready."

Some lengthy time later—I cannot fathom why women consume the better part of an hour to make themselves ready—I ushered Meriwether into our chamber, where Julia held the infant in her lap.

"Ah, madame, it is so good to see you up and well!" he said.

She nodded demurely. "The same might be said of you, Your Excellency."

"And here's the tyke!"

Meriwether circled about, as if he were examining an eaglet in its nest. "Like the sire, like the sire," he said. "Yes, a Clark clear through."

"Would you like to hold him?" Julia asked.

Meriwether fell back at once. "No, no, I would drop him," he said, discovering that ten feet was safe enough distance from the ogre in Julia's lap. "Babies and captains have different humors."

I laughed, but I didn't fail to note Meriwether's edginess.

"You are a lucky man," he said. "I am just a musty old bachelor, and will never have a child of my own."

"Why, of course you will, Meriwether. A woman is easier to conquer than the Bitterroot Mountains, and you conquered the snowy Bitterroots twice."

He didn't laugh as I thought he might. He just shook his head and then smiled brightly, his lips crooked. Then he remembered the graces: "I'm honored to have this boy named for me. May he be blessed. May he grow up strong and true."

He bowed grandly before the boy and his mother.

Julia's face softened. She had not lost her reserve around the governor.

We repaired to the parlor for a glass of amontillado, and Meriwether hastily downed three before he settled into the horsehair settee opposite.

"A fine boy, a compliment to you and your mistress," he said grandly.

I had not heard of an infant described as a compliment before. But then, Meriwether was acting in a most peculiar manner. I poured him a fourth drink from the cut glass decanter, but this time he only sipped.

"Will," he said, "I'm pressed. Mostly medical bills. This ague, you know. Could you spare a few dollars again? It'll all be returned with the next voucher from Washington."

"How much, Meriwether?"

"Twenty? I need to apply ten to the doctor, and my manservant needs something . . ." His voice trailed off.

I nodded, and dug into my purse for some national bank notes, Hamilton's work. I was hurting badly myself, but I would refuse my colleague and captain nothing. He had borrowed other small sums, still unpaid, but no mortal was more honest and I knew it would all be settled eventually. I only hoped I could hang on, myself.

He nodded and tucked it into his pocket. "It won't be long; I promise," he said.

"I can wait. How is the editing coming?"

I had asked the wrong question. He looked like a rat trapped on a sinking ship, and shook his head. "No time," he said.

There had been time aplenty. I remembered the balls and

card parties and Masonic lodge meetings he had attended. Reluctantly, I put aside all hope of seeing any immediate gain from the journals, or my investment in their preparation. I checked a tide of irritation that sloshed through me unbidden.

He must have sensed my distress. "My investments are going well. Three farms, over four thousand arpents. I have them rented out. Some city lots, too. I've put the family estate at Ivy up for sale, and I'll move my mother out here just as soon as I can. We'll be together here. But it's been a struggle, finding the means. I owe Chouteau another sixteen hundred in May, and a like sum in May of 1810. And then . . ." He left the rest unsaid, his mind elsewhere.

He was leaving much unsaid these days. I had noticed it, the incomplete thoughts. He either supposed his auditors knew what he would say, or else he was groping for words. I never imagined I would see the day when Meriwether groped for words.

I nodded, not wishing to express my true feelings. What was the governor doing, borrowing small sums from me, from the Chouteaus, and others, while engaging in grandiose land schemes to ride what might be merely a bubble?

Was this the competent, prudent man who had governed his mother's estate at Ivy for so many years?

Would those farms really appreciate? We were on the brink of war with England. Mr. Jefferson's embargo had bottled up the traffic in furs to Europe. The economy of St. Louis was faltering because peltries were heaping up in warehouses. He knew all that, and yet had plunged every shred of income into Missouri farmland.

We were soon at supper. The servants brought Meriwether's

favorite dish, curried lamb, and he beamed brightly as they set the plate before him.

"Ah!" he exclaimed, all starchy blue and gold braid, across from me. He dug into his tunic, extracted a small phial, and poured several drops of something into his tumbler of water. This he downed before corking the phial and returning it to its nest upon his bosom.

His countenance changed dramatically in the next moments.

"Now," he said peacefully, "tell me about the fur company. Are you gentlemen going to get Big White home at long last?"

Opium, I thought. Opium has got him.

Bates again. He stormed into my office in a fit, ruining a spring morning. He had in hand a fair copy of the contract I executed with the St. Louis Missouri Fur Company. He glared down at me, his woolly eyebrows arching and falling, his milky eyes bulging with antagonism for whatever reason I soon would know.

"Yes, Mr. Bates?"

"This contract, sir, is an abomination!"

I settled back to receive the rodomontade, knowing I would not be spared by this uncivil man.

"You have named General Clark as your agent in your absence. But I am your second. When you are absent, I am the acting governor. That is the law. You had no business violating the law of the land—"

I raised a hand. "Mr. Secretary, this contract governs Indian affairs entirely. Will Clark is our Indian superintendent. He's a partner in the company, fully aware of its difficulties. Who better to appoint than the one public official who is empowered to deal with Indian matters?"

Bates didn't subside. "You have offended me once again, sir. You and your coterie of *privileged* men. But things will change. There's a new administration, and you're no longer in the same position. You grasp that, sir? You are no longer *protected* by Mr. Jefferson. He's retired from office, and a good thing if I may say so."

"I'm well aware of it, Mr. Bates."

"And I've written Secretary Eustis about your expenditures, and this abominable contract, which puts public funds into the hands of your cronies. Yes! Your cronies. You are mulcting the government."

"It's the only way, Mr. Bates. The army can't spare the troops to take Big White safely home. It is a matter of highest concern to the government to do just that."

"Hah! No one cares about that savage, save for you and those profiteers who will pillage the public treasury to do it. I shall, sir, let the entire world know. I will see you put out of office, sir, like a cur put out on the streets to starve."

I rose swiftly.

That was a dismissal, but he ignored it. "This contract creates a monopoly. Who but your cronies will profit? No one! You will gouge the treasury, feed on public funds."

I stood, not feeling well, and motioned him toward the door.

"Just remember, you no longer have Jefferson to bail you out of trouble!" he snapped.

I quieted myself. "Mr. Bates, though you array yourself against me, let us at least maintain some civility in public. Pray you, confine your disputes to these private meetings."

He nodded curtly, which I took to be agreement.

I watched the wretched man stalk away, marveled that he could work up such a temper about so little, but I counted him a danger to everything I had worked for so long and hard.

I knew also I could not placate him. I could grant his every wish, cave in to his every demand, flatter him, publicly praise him, and that would only excite him to further assaults upon my person. I was puzzled. I had no idea what I had done or failed to do that excited such a violent passion in him.

I knew for certain that his letters, which he had been mailing to Washington at the rate of one or two a week, would have their effect, and that I would be forced to return to that seat of government ere long to deal with the accusations. He had been bragging about town of his correspondence with two or three secretaries and Mr. Madison. I would have to go back there, as much as I dreaded it.

I wanted to meet William Eustis, Madison's new pinch-penny war secretary. I thought I could allay the suspicion and Bates's wild accusations if we could but meet and if I could sit down with the secretary and the president and explain matters. Some things can't be resolved through correspondence.

It would take an armed force to deliver the Mandan chief to his village, past the hostile Arikaras. I offered the St. Louis Missouri Fur Company seven thousand dollars to do it, thirty-five hundred payable at the start, when they were properly organized and ready to go. But my terms were strict and if they failed to be properly prepared and off by May tenth they should forfeit three thousand dollars. The risk was all theirs.

My contract with them required a hundred twenty-five armed Americans in their entourage, including forty riflemen, all in addition to the trappers and traders they wished to take along. They would be traveling in an armada that would carry over two hundred armed men, a force strong enough to compel the respect of the Arikaras.

How better to do it, as long as the army was unable to help me? The public funds were indeed the foundation for the whole business, but all of the partners were risking most of what they owned in the hope of reward. The company would have a monopoly on the fur business only above the Mandan villages; the government would show the Plains tribes that it could overwhelm any of them, and was not to be obstructed in its purposes. Out of it would come commerce and peace, and the firm hand of the republic ruling the new territory.

Lisa and Chouteau had been working furiously to put the venture together, hire the entire company of men, supply the expedition, and obtain the keelboats to take them up the Missouri. Every partner was busy preparing. Reuben was collecting his medicines; Ben Wilkinson was purchasing supplies or providing them from his store; Will Clark was looking after the finances, along with Auguste Chouteau. Lisa was out on the levee, hiring the best rivermen, trappers, riflemen, cooks, translators, and traders in St. Louis, and finding more takers than anyone had imagined.

I was busy, especially because I had lost so much time to my sickbed. I authorized payment of the translation of a court record into French, knowing Bates would object on narrow legal grounds, and sent the voucher off to Washington. He was objecting to everything, and perhaps that was all to the good. They would see him for the embittered man he was.

Lisa visited me this afternoon.

"Yes, Manuel?"

"Ah, Your Excellency, I am glad to see you up and about. You look the very picture of health."

The man was prevaricating, but I ignored that. "How are you coming? Will you be off by May tenth?"

He shook his head. "It is a worrisome thing, Governor. I come to talk about the diplomacy, yes?"

"With the tribes?"

"Since this is a government expedition, we think you should provide the gifts, the little items of honor, to give to the headmen and chiefs, to win their undying allegiance to the government of the republic, yes?"

"That should come out of your funds."

He shook his head. "Every cent is committed. We will not have enough, even with the payment you have promised us."

"I've written Washington that I've committed seven thousand to this. I can't go further."

He shrugged. "Then we go without the gifts. We have nothing to trade for food, for canoes, for what is necessary."

I remembered how valuable our small stock of trade items was during the great trip west and how I yearned for just a few more blue beads, or hatchets, or iron arrow points, to win the perfidious chiefs. Time after time, en route home, we had come to the brink of disaster because we lacked things to trade for food. Even so, I was reluctant.

"You are going to have to provide those yourselves. The contract we signed is generous."

He shrugged. "And the risks are generous, too!"

I rose and paced my office. With Bates howling about every cent, I couldn't help much. And yet, I felt that I had to. I could not fail to return Big White to his people. That was Tom Jefferson's mandate and it was written in a tone that brooked no failure.

"What is the absolute minimum you need?" I asked.

"Two thousand dollars for the purchase of gifts, beads, metal items, knives, awls."

"Two thousand dollars!"

He nodded. But I knew the crafty Spaniard. He probably wanted five hundred and knew how to turn the screws.

I was weary of being importuned for money. Half the people entering my office begged money from the government.

"What exactly would you spend it on?" I asked.

Lisa shrugged. "You have told us many times what the Corps of Discovery needed and lacked. I would follow your wisdom, Your Excellency."

Blue beads.

I nodded. At my desk I lifted a quill, sharpened the point with my blade, and dipped it into the inkpot. I scratched out a voucher on the United States Treasury, on the account of the secretary of war, for one thousand five hundred dollars, payable to Pierre Chouteau because I didn't trust Lisa, to be employed in the purchase of public gifts to be given to the tribes as needed to insure their allegiance. I spilled ink on two occasions, my hand being unruly these days for some reason, blotted up the ink spots, and handed it to Lisa.

"Wait," I said. "I want to inform Will Clark of this."

I penned a second note for Will, letting him know I was adding trade items from the public purse to foster amity and help preserve the company's passage.

"Give this to the general, please."

Lisa took the note, nodded, and smiled. Was it slyly? Had he gulled me? Was this the crafty Spaniard's way of enlarging the profit at the expense of the public purse?

I exhaled, and watched him go. He didn't linger about for social amenities, and I wondered if the Spaniard was a friend of anyone, or loyal to anything other than himself.

I made a notation to put the draft on record. Bates would

cause more trouble. I felt unwell, and settled into my chair, my mind climbing the skies like a hawk.

Oh, to go with them! Oh, to walk those golden prairies, and see the eagles own the sky! Oh, to be young and strong and filled with life again! Oh, to dream great dreams!

Secretary Bates sprang upon me moments after I arrived at my office, and he was in a wrathy mood. I had scarcely hung my cape over the antler coatrack in the corner and opened the casements to let in some April breezes when he burst in, fires glittering in those milkstone eyes.

"General, sir, I have come for a *confidential* talk about certain matters pertaining to the lawful governance of the territory!" he exclaimed.

I said nothing and made no assurances about confidentiality. I have made it a lifetime habit to listen attentively, and keep my counsel, by which means I get along with all manner of men, and even a man so fiddle-strung as Secretary Bates.

I could tell at a glance that he had rehearsed this moment all night, and perhaps for days.

I gestured him to a seat, but he declined, preferring to pace about like an advocate before the bar, making his case with a multitude of theatrical gestures and postures.

"I know, General, that you are a *close* companion of the governor, the partner in a long journey, and therefore my views are likely to be instantly dismissed. But I am compelled by the *law* and *justice* and *propriety* to make the case before the only other official in the territory whose conduct *influences* the affairs of Upper Louisiana."

I nodded. This was going to take some time. Bates often talked like that, using twice the words he needed to. He paced again, his hands clasped behind him, his kinked dark hair drawn tight into a disciplined queue without a strand out of place. I wondered how a man of such unruly feeling could rule his hair with such total sovereignty.

"By appointing you his agent in his absence, in the matter of the St. Louis Missouri Fur Company, General, he violates the law. The code is explicit. The territorial secretary shall act as governor in the absence of the governor. He is *wilfully and wantonly* offending the government, offending me, and insulting me by demonstrating his lack of confidence in me."

I thought it would be this. I had hoped he would let it pass. I said nothing, as was my wont, but nodded.

"This is a dangerous and unlawful precedent," he said. "I have written Secretary Eustis about it, intending that the authorities should know at once. I fear, General, that the tides that will wash over the governor will wash against your shore, also."

"I see," I said.

He took that for encouragement. "The man is behaving in a most improper manner. He signs warrants for any *small* expense, expecting Washington to pay. Why, sir, without any authority he had a public notice translated into the French and printed in French, though there is no provision for it. I sent it along to the treasury secretary as directed, but *over my protest.*"

I wanted to tell Bates that if some official matter is made public in Louisiana it must be made so in two tongues and the government must shoulder the cost. But I get more from listening than I do from debating, so I simply nodded.

Bates stopped pacing suddenly, and faced me. "All this will come down upon his head. I will make sure of it. He cannot govern improperly without the eyes of *responsible* men observing his misconduct and taking the necessary steps."

He was proclaiming he was the tattletale, which interested me. I nodded.

"He borrows money right and left, General. From you, I know, from Chouteau, even from *me*. Why, he had the audacity to press me for twenty dollars a day or two ago, knowing that a mere *servant* and *underling* cannot refuse his governor, and so I lent it. I have eyes and ears in this town, sir, and I get wind of how he spends all this money. It is upon draughts and pills."

He leaned close, his air confidential. "I happen to know that he consumes large numbers of one-gram pills of opium. One gram! Several times daily. It is a frightful habit. Where will it end? In madness? Do you know what that does to his judgment? He is falling into grievous error, General, because his mind is clouded by *opium*."

I hadn't known it was so bad, but I suspected it was true. Bates had an amazing intelligence network feeding him dirt. I wondered what he knew about me, or thought he knew.

I nodded.

He liked my attentiveness; it encouraged him. "And that's not all, General. He doses himself with cinchona, calomel, and other powders. But it is not for the ague or intermittent fever. Not for bilious fever. Not for consumption. Have you seen his gums, General? Blue! The *Mark of Cain*."

I knew what he was talking about.

I hadn't noticed, and the accusation worried me. Perhaps I had been too close to Meriwether to see him clearly. Then again, maybe Bates was merely imagining things. I had not seen any such mark of mercury poisoning upon the governor. But it was possible. He had borrowed, he said, to pay medical bills.

"Mark my words, General. The time of protection, when our heroic governor was *untouchable* because he was harbored in the esteem of a president, has passed. Now he will be scrutinized with care and integrity, and by men who are less impressed with Meriwether Lewis than he is impressed with himself."

That was the unkindest cut but I wanted to let Bates run with his indictment. I was learning fast.

He continued in that vein a while more, and when he finally wound down I knew that Lewis had a genuine enemy in Bates, a man who itched to depose the governor and rule the territory himself. I felt certain also that Bates could do considerable damage to Lewis with those letters; that Bates did have a certain punctilio about the law on his side, and that his sort of songs would find receptive ears among a certain class of lesser clerks in the warrens of the government.

"Well?" said Bates, having emptied himself.

"Mr. Bates, I would like to offer my good offices toward reconciling you and the governor," I said.

"No, you will only take the governor's part," he retorted.

"I will follow my own counsel, I assure you. It is an offer set before you. Perhaps I can help you work out some common ground."

"I do not wish to share any ground with that cur, that dog," Bates said. "Look at me! I am here *complaining*! Yes, *complaining* about another mortal, and thus demeaning myself before your very eyes. You know what the world thinks of complainers! But I have no recourse, sir. I must complain because that is the only avenue open to me, even though it besmirches me to speak so ill of another."

"What do you want of me?" I asked.

"I came to warn you that you are under scrutiny as well, sir. And that you might properly distance yourself from the governor."

I grinned. "Mr. Lewis is my friend and I hope you can be also, Mr. Bates. You are a skillful man and needed here."

He puffed up. "I should hope so," he said. "I mean no man harm who has done me none."

That's how it ended. Like a steam kettle breathing its last vapor into the atmosphere. I saw him off, and settled into my chair, running over the accusations and threats, and finding little in them but wind. Still, a man wrapped in such passion could be nettlesome, and I resolved to brace Meriwether about Bates, as I had several times in the past.

The danger lay in Bates's objections to various expenditures, including those for the St. Louis Missouri Fur Company for the delivery of Big White safely home. I resolved then and there that I must head for Washington before the travel season ended, and talk to Eustis and the president myself. If money was the bone of contention, then I would contend about it.

I settled back in my desk chair, remembering Captain Lewis of the Corps of Discovery. He had been occasionally severe, especially in the way he meted out punishment for military infractions. And yet, no man of the corps, not the lowest private, had grounds to loathe Lewis, and in fact he inspired in them a great devotion and a yearning to excel.

Without Meriwether's skills in dealing with our men the corps might have faltered; might even have died, to the last man. They loved him, love him still. They admired him in the field, and admire him still. He has seen to their back pay, their pensions, their honors, their retirement, their medical needs.

He nursed them through desperate times and brought them safely home, as only a great man will.

He preferred to walk the banks of the rivers while the rest of us poled or rowed or pulled ourselves upstream. He walked in perfect grace, his lithe footsteps keeping pace with us, even though he took the time to examine every plant and animal that caught his eye. His great mind is what mesmerized us all. There was something grand in everything he did, as if he could see over horizons, anticipate the next crisis or triumph. He had no Frederick Bates along to whittle him down.

I have little stomach for politics, for backbiting, for the snares some men lay to trip others. I debated there, in the April sun, while breezes wafted across my desk and rattled my papers, whether even to bring this latest bout of Bates distemper to Meriwether.

Blue gums. I didn't believe it. The Mark of Cain was not upon Governor Lewis. But next time I saw him, I would see for myself. It was something I had to know.

Dover's powder helps. I take one-gram tablets and find they clarify the mind and help me to see keenly into the mysteries of the world. The powder not only sweeps away confusions so that I see all of life with burning clarity, but produces a fine sweat that keeps my occasional fever under control. In spite of the great burdens of office, I find I can proceed calmly and even with some degree of equanimity. I am able even to cope with Frederick Bates day by day.

I have a standing order with the apothecary, Marcel Rolland, to fill my phial once a fortnight, and I require him to keep some back so that the governor might be supplied as needed. The supply of Dover's powder from New Orleans is tenuous and seasonal. He is admirable in his eagerness to serve me. The powder has an unfortunate tendency to bind me, but Rush's Thunderclappers never fail to relieve my distress, and I count the calomel in them as a good weapon against the fevers that afflict me more and more. My ague is more severe than most, and often leaves me weak and dehydrated.

The St. Louis Missouri Fur Company is engaged in a last-minute frenzy to set off for the high Missouri, and I have turned most of my energies to making sure the partners are well equipped and ready for anything. Big White at last is going home, and the Mandan chief's eyes light up at the prospect. He struts the levee, a dandy now in black frock coat, red shirt, beaver hat, blackened boots, and white breeches, along with his bedizened wife and son, his shrewd savage eye upon the river men loading the keelboats for the great haul into the wilds. I shall be relieved to get him back to his home; nothing burdens me more.

I would love to be present when he regales his brethren in the Mandan villages about what he saw here and in Virginia and in Washington. I hope he is up to it; if not, I fear they will think him a big liar. Toward the end of making him credible to his people, I have showered gifts upon him, all of them calculated to display the magic of the white man. He grins broadly at each item; the compass, the book, the various weapons, the silks, and all the rest.

Some advance elements of the company have already started up the river; most of the rest must be under way this Wednesday, May 17, 1809, or forfeit three thousand dollars to the government. My contract sets severe penalties for nonperformance, which is one reason I am mystified at the criticism of it by know-nothings. Lisa will follow with the last of the supplies.

Pierre Chouteau came to me recently and asked for more cash for trade goods; there simply were not enough wares to meet the British competition's generous disbursements. Nor enough powder. Word has come downriver that the Sioux and Arikara are determined to stop the company.

Reluctantly, I have offered him an additional draft for five hundred dollars payable on the account of the secretary of war, and another for four hundred fifty, with which to purchase additional powder and lead. I have no choice. The allegiance of the Plains tribes will tilt one way or another, depending on the success of this venture.

I have given Pierre explicit instructions regarding the conduct of the venture, but I have left the field commanders room enough to use their own judgment. I toiled long over this set of instructions, wanting it to be a paternal guide from the seat of government yet not so binding as to defeat the purposes and judgments of the officers, including my brother Reuben.

I see them inviting Big White and his entourage to board the second keelboat, so I know the moment has arrived. It is a fine, breezy morning that promises to make the rowing and poling cool and easy for the horde of boatmen and riflemen and trappers crowding the keelboats.

A great crowd has gathered. St. Louis loves mighty events, and nothing mightier than this army has ever pushed off from its levee. What a sight! Thirteen keelboats and barges in all will head upriver, and seven of them leave today. One last boat, carrying Lisa, will leave in a few days after he has completed some last-minute purchases.

I have already said my goodbyes to Reuben; he is on the riverbank, in charge of two keelboats, directing the last flow of materiel. He has, on one of those boats, a formidable medical chest and I do not doubt that the ailments and wounds of so large a force will tax his supply of powders and his skills to the utmost. I am rather glad he is not my physician; he does not approve of the courses I choose for myself.

What a city this is! Ebony carriages have drawn up to the levee, and ivory-skinned Frenchwomen in silks watch events from behind their folding fans, while sooty slaves hoist the last of the casks and crates aboard. Rough men in tan buckskins jostle powdered men in black beaver hats, and riflemen in blue chambray shirts and slouch hats stand aboard the planked hulls of the keelboats. Many of them are Delawares.

Oarsmen have settled on the cross benches, preparing to flex their muscles against the mighty flow of the Father of Waters, while other Creole water men hold poles in readiness. Red men, white men, blacks, French, Spanish, Yanks, gentlemen and ruffians have all congregated on this mucky bank, not only to see the armada off but to pray for its success, because all of St. Louis will profit—or suffer—from what is starting on this day.

I find Will standing beside me. He and one or two other partners are not going; his duties are in St. Louis. Lisa and Menard are below, at water's edge, directing the stream of casks to the keelboats. Sweating Creole boatmen are balancing the loads in the holds, shouting in volleys of explosive French.

Sunlight glints from brass swivel guns mounted on the bows of some of the keelboats. There is muscle here, lead and gunpowder, lance and staff. Snugged into the holds are thousands of pounds of Missouri lead and many barrels of good Missouri gunpowder, the finest that the partners could buy.

In spite of all the hubbub, there is no cacophony, just a quiet hum of activity, and the low murmur of the spectators. Every shop has emptied; every parlor and kitchen in St. Louis is vacant. I see, standing back a way, my namesake, Meriwether Lewis Clark, and his lovely mother, and half a dozen servants attending her and the baby.

It is so bedazzling, so clear, so bright to the eye, that I marvel at the sight that burns into my head.

Then, suddenly, everything is ready, and a pregnant hush settles over the crowd.

"Au revoir, mes amis," Chouteau cries.

Lisa waves from the shore. A river man touches a fuse to a brass swivel gun. The explosion startles us all, violence in a peaceful moment. Then the hoarse cries erupt from every quarter, the shouts of the Creoles whip across the wind, and the first of the keelboats lumbers painfully away from the levee, jabbed forward upon the poles of the river men, while the oars bite the brown water.

Now there is a great cheer, and hats sail. Another boat sucks free of the levee and lumbers outward, the men straining every muscle against the current. And another and another, until at last this formidable force, close to three hundred men, is loosed from the nurture of St. Louis and is toiling northward to the confluence, and then into the mighty wilds a thousand eagle flights from this last outpost of civilization.

I watch the Mandan, standing like a statue on the second boat, all the mysterious forces of national power and prestige gathered about his person like some halo. Yes, truly a halo. A great yellow glow radiates from him.

It is a sight so brilliant that I close my eyes against it.

I shake hands with Auguste, and then with Will.

"Gentlemen, luck," I say.

"Luck is the last thing to count on," Auguste says somberly.

"Powder and lead, then!"

"Ah! Now you talk business," Chouteau says amiably.

"I hope She-He-Ke has the gift of gab," Will says.

"Who?" I ask. The name puzzles me.

"Big White."

"Oh, yes," I say. "Big White." Somehow, I had forgotten the Mandan version of his name.

Will is staring at me. I smile. He is looking at my mouth, so I wipe my lips. What a bright world, everything etched so sharply in the clear air. The crowd lingers, watching the keel-boats grow small and finally vanish into pinpricks on the blue water.

I need to escape from the sun. I am feeling feverish again.

I see Bates; he turns to avoid me.

The Chouteaus excuse themselves; they and Lisa must fill one more boat and set out within a day or two. It bobs there below, a forlorn remnant of the flotilla.

I catch up with Will, who has joined his wife and child.

"Ah! There's my namesake!" I say cheerfully. "And how are you, Maria?" I ask.

She eyes me oddly.

"Maria! Did I call you Maria? Forgive me. Julia, how do you fare this May day? I must have been thinking of my old sweetheart."

She edges apart from me.

In truth, I have been thinking much about Maria Wood, for whom I named Maria's River far up the Missouri. I don't know why. By the time I returned she had married, and there went my hopes and dreams, and that is why I am a musty old bachelor now. I never courted her in the first place, though I thought of it long before the expedition. She didn't know I cared. She had been a dreamy, peach-fleshed young thing who caught my eye before the trip, and I kept her virgin image before me, like an icon. Now she is an excuse I use to explain everything.

Never was woman more pure and virtuous than Maria Wood, and that is what I said in my journal. I am quite sure I said it, anyway. I would have to go back and look at the entry for that day in 1805 when we were advancing toward the mountains. I have an altar in my heart, and it is dedicated to her, the bride I shall never have.

I look at the journals these days and marvel at them; that Meriwether and this Meriwether are different people. Someday, I will figure them out and send my material to Conrad, and they will be published. But now I need a pill.

31 CLARK

York returned this Saturday, May 20, in the nick of time. A day or two more, and I would have posted runaway notices and a reward. But he appeared at my office door one afternoon, and I let him in.

"You're late," I said.

"Got took here by a keelboat," he said. "They stopped lot of places on the way."

"You have a letter for me?"

He dug into his duffel and produced a battered envelope. It contained his travel papers and a letter from my brother Jonathan, saying that he was sending York to me on the Charles Brothers boat, passage for his hire. He enclosed a draft for $36.50, York's hire in Louisville while visiting his wife, minus one dollar for food on his return. He had been hired out to his wife's owners, the Chartres family, for $2.50 a week plus subsistence. My brother said that York had performed his service in the tobacco fields faithfully, but his mind seemed elsewhere and his attention was not on his work.

"I earn you some money, mastuh?"

"A little. Did you have a good visit?"

He smiled for the first time. "Emily, she wasn't so happy to see me. She tired of babies."

"You make one?"

"I sho' try."

"How is my brother?"

"Mastuh Jonathan? He looking good to me."

"And the general?"

"I don't see the general. They don't take me there. They tell me he got the gout."

"Do you bring any news?"

He shrugged. "Not much rain in Louisville. That tobacca not coming up proper."

"Did you see my sister?"

"No, boss. I be taken right to the Chartres place and they put a hoe in my hand before I even get to see Emily." He smiled a little. "They gave me next day off, and her, too. We go out into the woods and have us a picnic."

"All right, York. You go on to my house and report to your mistress. Then I want you to find Manuel Lisa on the levee and help him. He's still loading supplies in the last keelboat."

"Last keelboat, mastuh?"

"A company's gone up the river. They're taking Big White home."

"Big White!" York grinned. "Taking the old chief back. Ah wish you'd hired me out."

"I need you here," I said.

Immediately a curtain fell and he was a stranger again. I knew that he had changed in some unfathomable way. We had been boyhood companions, protective of each other, and now that was gone. The bond could not survive childhood, but until the trip west there had been some old and continuing understandings.

"Yes, suh," he said, as if talking to a stranger.

"York, the letter from my brother says you were not attentive to your work."

"I work hard in them fields, hoeing all them weeds." There was heat in his response.

"But your work was not satisfactory."

He retreated deep into himself again.

"York, you do my bidding. And be quick about it." I didn't like disciplining the man who had been my servant from birth, and so I softened. "I'm glad you're back safely. And in good health."

"Yes, suh, you get nothing outa no sick slave," he retorted.

Before the Corps of Discovery, he never would have said that to me. I let it pass. He probably would settle into routine. But if not, I would not hesitate to auction him at the New Orleans market, and then he would find out what defiance would bring to his unmarked black back.

I knew somehow that soon he would beg again for his liberty, and I knew I would again turn him down. I could not afford to release a fifteen-hundred-dollar slave; not with my finances in precarious condition. And in any case, I had too few hands for my household. Julia and her baby required four, and I needed two, so that I might escape such sundries as getting stove wood.

I knew, right down, to my bones, that York was not fit for freedom; that without the succor I provided him he would careen from one crisis to another and starve himself. He was not competent to handle his affairs or run a business. He was not able to do sums or read and could be gulled by any white man who wanted his labor and didn't feel like paying for it.

I intended to tell him so when his petition came, as I knew it would just as soon as he had gotten back into his daily routine. I again rued the day I had taken him with me; it had put ideas in his head I could never rout out. I hated the idea of auctioning him. I hated the idea of freeing him. I hated his increasing uselessness. He was aggravating me, and my thoughts ran from whipping to manumission. Let the wretch go and just see how he fares in a mean and tricky world.

Had I discovered a cockiness in him? I sprang to the window, hoping to see his sauntering figure in the street, but he was gone. I intended to ask Lisa about him after York had put in a few days loading the boat.

It wasn't too late to send York up the river on Lisa's keelboat. He was an experienced mountaineer and river man, and would be valuable. It certainly would have pleased York, and I could hire him out to the St. Louis Missouri Fur Company for twenty a month. That would be less than it was paying freemen, thus benefitting the company. But the thought roiled my mind. He was half ruined already and another trip would destroy his usefulness. No! He would stay in St. Louis and I would have plenty for him to do.

I stretched, and then, unaccountably, I laughed. It was good to have old York back, safe and sound. I decided to go tell Meriwether. He had counseled patience and he was right.

I stepped into a splendid spring day, bright with promise and the fragrance of lilacs in the air. It wasn't far to the governor's office, and I wished it were longer, so I might stretch my legs.

I was in luck. The usual gaggle of petitioners was nowhere in sight, perhaps because it was noon, and Meriwether was alone.

"Governor, I have momentous and urgent and entirely amazing news," I said.

He looked alarmed.

"York's back."

He grimaced, and finally laughed in syncopation with my own gusts of delight. I sat myself in a chair without his invitation.

"And how is he?" Meriwether asked.

"Exhausted. He spent the whole of his visit manufacturing."

"Manufacturing?"

"Manufacturing labor, my friend. Labor."

Meriwether smiled crookedly. His pearly teeth were as white as ever, and I had long since dismissed Bates's vile accusations as the remark of a venomous man.

"Labor! Labor! Ah, that does exhaust a man," he said.

"He did quite a bit of manufacturing with the Corps of Discovery, but it didn't seem to wear him down any," I said.

No man on the voyage had found his way into so many lodges as York, and I was of the belief that he had singlehandedly darkened the hue of every tribe we encountered.

"Remember how the Mandan ladies bid for him?" he asked. "They put their husbands to it: come visit my wife, they said, and old York was only too happy to comply." Meriwether laughed, and it sounded like old paper rattling in the breezes.

His eyes went dreamy. "Those were the days," he said, and I knew what he was thinking. Fresh breezes, a dancing sea of grass that made a mere mortal seem as small as an ant, the sparkling river, mysteriously carrying water from some place no white man had ever seen, silently carrying it endless leagues, across a continent, to St. Louis.

"He's older now," I added. "I expect I will have to feed him up, extra rations, good pork fat and beans to get him back into condition. The manufacturing business turns fat bulls into scarecrows."

Lewis grimaced again, and I thought maybe I should change the subject. He was more and more melancholic about his bachelor estate, and not even my efforts to cheer him, or introduce him to the Creole belles who drifted up from Ste. Genevieve to stay with their assorted cousins, seemed to lift his spirits.

"I wish I could do it all over," he said. "I wish I could start upriver with the Corps of Discovery again, and try it once more."

"What for?"

"To avoid the mistakes I made," he said.

"Mistakes are what a discovery trip is all about," I said. "I don't know of any anyway. There was not a decision, an act, a choice, that you would want to change."

He looked at me so desolately that I felt chilled.

Then he gazed out his window, and I sensed that old sadness was stealing through him again. I had seen it so often, but I had always seen his own vital force, his enthusiasm, his strong character triumph over the perfidy of his feelings. He could be melancholic for an hour or two, and then spring into action as if no gloom had ever filtered through his mind.

"You know, Meriwether, nothing prevents you from going upriver again," I said.

"Bates does. I cannot leave here with Bates undermining everything I am and every step I take."

"No, not even Bates keeps you here," I said. "If you need to walk that ground again, walk to the shining mountains, see the black herds of buffalo, then go walk it. Resign. I wish I could go with you."

He said nothing, but somehow I knew his mind was far upstream.

The intermittent fever afflicts more and more; I have had moments when I am delirious. To-day, Monday, June 19, has been such a day. I saw Lisa and the last keelboat off on Saturday, but came only briefly to the levee because I am indisposed.

I have debated for weeks about seeing Dr. Saugrain again. I have dosed myself with my mother's simples rather than submit myself to another misdiagnosis. But now I'm at wit's end and scarcely know how to treat the disease. He is, after all, one of the most eminent physicians in America, and I thought I might consult him about doses.

I visited him at his chambers near me on Rue L'Eglise, and found him occupied with a Creole mother whose infant wailed pitiably through the varnished door. He bade me wait in his anteroom, and was in no hurry to see me. But at last he dismissed the woman and welcomed me coolly.

"Your Excellency," he said, without warmth.

"I am here about doses," I said abruptly.

He nodded, his sharp eyes taking in my entire condition in a glance.

"Sit yourself there," he said, rummaging among his diagnostic tools.

"I'm not here for an examination. I'm here because my extract of cinchona does not seem to be controlling the fevers."

He grunted and ignored me.

"Open your mouth wide," he said, and peered in, using a small mirror to see what was to be seen.

"Quinine is not the only powder you are taking," he said. "You are taking heavy doses of mercury."

"That's because I need a purgative."

"Is it?"

He peered at my eyes. "Enlarged pupils," he said. "Which opiate is it that you employ?"

"Dover's powder."

"Ah."

He listened to my chest with his horn, and ran his practiced finger over the lumps in my face, examined my hands and feet, and looked at my nostrils.

Then he straightened, his small body radiating his special dignity.

"Your Excellency, it is time to face what must be faced," he said.

"It's ague. Malarial fever."

"If it was ague, the quinine would be sovereign. Do you suffer chills so violent that no blanket warms you and you shake for hours under a heap of them, and then suffer high fever and profuse sweating?"

I had no reply to that, and stared mutely.

"Then perhaps your self-diagnosis lacks science," he said archly.

He turned his back to me, perhaps to free me from that piercing gaze that seemed to unearth everything within my heart. He stared out the window, and then began softly.

"*Lues venerea*. Just as I have said, monsieur."

"No!"

"How much mercury chloride do you take?"

I started to reply, but he interrupted. "It is ten times too much. So much mercury in your brain; it ruins you even before the venereal does."

I started to protest, but stopped. He was all wrong.

He spoke gently now. "I can perhaps help a little. In the third stage, Governor, mercury does little good. It helps momentarily, yes. It provides less and less relief, and then no help at all. You are there, at that lamentable point, most regrettably. The disease advances on its own schedule, shall we say. I recollect cautioning you to keep the doses small; that would have been better for the sake of your mind. Now I would prescribe no doses at all."

"It's not the venereal," I said.

He simply ignored my protest. "How much of the powder?"

"I don't know. Whenever I need it."

"Two a day; three a day?"

"One at night."

"And how many by day?"

"I don't know," I replied.

"Nothing is gained by not knowing. Something is gained by knowing every fact, every dose, every risk."

"Two, three."

"I advised, Your Excellency, that you not imbibe spirits, because they hasten the disease. I trust you have abstained?"

"No, and don't speak of it again!"

He did not recoil from my biliousness, but let it pass.

"A gill, two gills a day, perhaps?"

"Wine and porter."

"A carafe or two?"

"I have no idea." I was utterly out of sorts and ready to throw on my stock and coat and escape. But in fact a great heaviness was stealing my resolve from me. I felt ashamed of my maltreatment of him.

"Forgive me," he said. I felt his hand on my shoulder. "I am merciless, but with a purpose."

I watched motes of dust play in the midday sun pouring through his window, and felt the ticking of the eternal clock.

"May we proceed, Your Excellency?"

I nodded.

"You ask about doses. Ah... The dose I recommend, I plead with you, is nothing of mercury. Nothing of the Peruvian bark. Nothing of Dover's powder or laudanum. Nothing of spirits or wine or ale. Sunlight, fresh air, putting aside that which worries you, vegetables . . ."

I knew I would not heed his prescription, but said nothing.

"You spoke to me once of your mother's simples, the herbs she gathers. Try them without the mercury, Your Excellency, but let science be your guide. Experiment. Observe results. Discard the failures."

"You have no cure, then."

"The disease sometimes cures itself. Pray that it will."

"You have nothing to offer me."

He stared again out the window. "No. Some physicians are experimenting with toxic metals. Poisons. Small doses of arsenic. I see little in it. I do not recommend it. *Mon Dieu!* The risk! Medicine is in its infancy. Someday there will be cures. I am a rationalist."

I sensed the man's helplessness.

I have an *incurable disease*. All that remained for me in this savant's lair was a schedule for my doom.

"What will happen?" I asked curtly.

"You might survive many years. Then again, you might not."

"Do better than that, Doctor."

He shrugged, that petite Gallic expression of submission I knew so well. "The disease attacks each mortal differently," he said.

"I am talking about me, not the human race."

He nodded. "When your mind is clouded, when your memory fades, when your judgment lapses, when your hand disobeys and your handwriting falters, when your phantasms and demons crowd your mind, you will know that *paresis* is upon you." He anticipated me. "Paresis is the madness often resulting from the final stage of *lues venerea*."

"I'll know? Some mad people don't know it."

"The paretic usually knows."

"And others? Will they see it?" I asked, for that was the crux of the matter.

He nodded.

"It can't be hidden?"

"Not to the discerning eye."

"And it will be visible in my flesh?"

He sighed. "It already is, Your Excellency."

"Will they be studying me, hunting for the lumps in my face, the oddity of my conduct?"

He stared out the window. "It is a cruel disease and the world treats its victims with utmost cruelty. They condemn the victim. They even laugh at him, for his indiscretions are naked before the world. The moralists rant. The gossips buzz. The ladies flee. Daughters receive lectures from their mothers about the secret vices of men and how to spot them. It is the snake in the Garden of Eden, slithering through good society, reminding them all that it could strike them dead. It is a pity, this barbarous intolerance, monsieur. No one pities the victim. No one tenderly assists him."

"What is done with such people?"

"They are hidden away by families. The uncle in the attic."

"The musty old bachelor."

He tried to reassure me. "Do not despair. You will have good times. Maybe years. Live well and slow the progress of the indisposition."

I straightened. "I am a public man. What is your advice?" I asked directly.

"When the time comes to withdraw from public life, you will know, Your Excellency. It will be plain. But even after you withdraw into private life, you will have good days, time to write and think and prepare your papers. The disease will not kill you soon. It often takes eight or ten years from infection, and you have been infected only four."

"You are treating John Shields. How is he doing?"

The little Frenchman paused, trembled, and summoned his courage, plainly seeking words. "He is gravely ill, my captain. I do not expect him to last a month."

"Of *lues venerea?*"

The doctor nodded.

"The same as mine?"

"From his liaison with the Shoshones, yes."

I had no time at all. I thanked the diminutive doctor, dressed, and headed into the bitter sunlight, a doomed man, bearing his badge of shame for all the world to see.

33 LEWIS

I don't remember such a beautiful summer, the breeze so caressing and the mornings so aglow. The presence of death gilds the world. This July of eighteen and nine I have taken to walking the verdant bank of the majestic river, the mightiest artery of the republic, marveling that so much water from such distant country is rolling toward the sea. What small slice of it is from the headwaters of the Missouri? From the Jefferson River, where we left Louisiana to cross the continental divide?

What stories that restless water could tell me; of painted Indians warring on its banks; of shamans praying to their spirits; of fat beaver patiently building their dams of aspen; of countless buffalo drinking from it or paddling across it; of cottonwoods toppling into it; of dust storms turning it to mud; and of the bones of the dead that it rolls and tumbles to some great continental grave in the delta beyond New Orleans.

I walk through tender green timothy and bromegrass and orchard grasses and rustling leaves and thickets of brush and cattailed swamps, stirring up moths and butterflies, so that I might embrace a clean world and leave a befouled one behind me. I am finding sanctuary in nature.

I have always walked. On the great trip I walked while the

others rowed and poled. My legs still sing under me, enjoy the rhythmic steps, sweep me along and never tire. I have spotted species of sedges and swamp flowers and lilies that tax my memory and might be unknown to botany; but now I do not pluck them. I reverence them alive and let their discovery await other eyes and other times. I have a horror just now of plucking anything to its death. I want to leave each bloom unmolested, and to see alertness in the eye of each creature. Life itself is the greatest gift.

Sometimes the past clasps me until I groan with memories. If I were to keep on walking I would arrive at the confluence of the Missouri, and if I never stopped, I might make the Mandan villages by fall and find a lodging with Big White; the captain and the chief united once again. I might taste succulent, tender buffalo hump again, and live in buckskin clothing that armors against the wind, and watch the savages howl and dance around their fires as sparks fly into the night. But the yearning passes, and I return to St. Louis after each hike, weary but uplifted by every natural thing I meet. For a little while, anyway, I will free myself from the webs of fate.

This is the river of death. I see mutilated catfish, their bellies chalky white, drifting toward the bayous. I have watched dead crows and terns and sparrows drift by, feathery on the water, en route to the sea. In time, the waters that flow by me will rifle every vault, melt every bone, and empty all the death of a continent into the Gulf of Mexico. I have watched the water flow through the ribby ruins of a buffalo, and watched the waters sluice the naked skeletons of cottonwoods and willows to the sea. All manner of things pass St. Louis, but death most of all.

I am reminded of these things but do not dwell upon them.

For even as disease devours my flesh and eats my soul, I redouble my efforts to strengthen Louisiana. I have called a territorial council this summer. There are urgent matters to attend. The British furtively war upon us and mean to take us back into their empire. They have never believed their own defeat and will need another lesson.

The embargo has stopped our shipments of furs to Europe, so St. Louis languishes in debt and despair. Its warehouses bulge with rank-smelling peltries and skittering bugs, and some prominent citizens cannot afford the meanest tax.

I have seen Antoine Saugrain frequently, and he has gently and tenderly taught me the signs of my own decay: memory loss, lapses of judgment, difficulty with speech, an uneven hand that shows up in blots and tiny or oversized letters or crossed-out words, fits of unseemly passion, ranting, puzzlement, and above all, incoherence. I face those things. I, Meriwether Lewis, face *incoherence*, when I will blubber out words that do not connect and defy logic. I face the end of my very *self*, and that thought is more than I can endure.

He teaches me to understand my decline, for it is the only thing he has still to give me: the stigmata of my doom on my hands and feet, the cruel ciphers of the devil getting his usury for one voluptuous moment. That is the medicine the doctor portions out for me; that and a profound and sad affection he has formed for me, and a willingness to share in my desolation. The little doctor has become the physician of my soul. He charges but little now, but always manages to comfort me.

I do not always heed his counsel, and he has stopped chiding me. I take my powders when I need them because I am desperate for them, and I drink spirits at the balls and parties I attend to conceal my affliction and drug away the pain and fever when they pounce. The world sees nothing of any of this, for I still cut a fine figure, but no one, especially the women, has ever looked deeply into the eyes of their governor and seen the hell within.

Mr. Bates braced me again the other day. He has a catalogue of injuries which he writes down in the ledgers of his soul, and now that list is heavier than he can carry. He imagines himself a good official watching zealously over the public purse. I see him as an obstructionist, stopping my projects, quibbling about authority, finding fault with my every act, and spreading his toxins through St. Louis. He would have me leave for Washington so he might govern in my absence. I have no plans to go, but he has found the perfect way to force me: I will have to go east to answer his complaints.

"Do you think I don't know about your powders? I have friends all over St. Louis!" he snapped. "You have no secrets from me, sir. Not all your high connections can save you!"

"My ague?" I asked.

"Ha!" he snapped.

"Mr. Bates, do you want my office? Is that what this is about?"

"Never, sir. I am no usurper. I would be your loyal second, if you were but to consult me, but you never do."

"What can I do to reconcile us?"

"Nothing. It is a breach that cannot be bridged. You have earned my enmity, sir, and your very presence offends me."

I kept trying. "I assure you, sir, I am willing to listen and consider, and if I am misguided, I am willing to undo my arrangements."

He paused, nonplussed for once.

"Give me specifics, Mr. Bates. Would you care to discuss

my diplomacy with the Upper Missouri tribes? Are you content with the agents? Do I coddle the hostile tribes too much?"

"I have no desire to press my views upon you; it would only stay your course."

I proceeded doggedly. "My appointments to office. You object to most of them. Pray tell me, what is wrong with, say, Boone?"

Bates drew himself up. "We have talked too much. I will not give you one bone to chew on. Go counsel with the high and mighty."

I saw how it would go. "Set your own course, then," I said sharply.

That is the polite expression of a complete rupture. Except for our official duties, we need have no other congress. He stalked out of my office, as if even that final caution was an insult to his prickly person instead of a way of accommodating each other while harnessed to the same wagon.

I stood at my desk, processing this latest bloodletting, and slowly took heart.

I plan to endure. I will heal myself and proceed. I have let nothing slide and prosecute all manner of agendas to make this western border safe and secure and profitable, and a gem in the diadem of the republic.

I sometimes think the madness is upon me. I often walk to a place three miles up the river where there is a certain stony bluff that affords a view of the great blue Mississippi and the distant shores of the Illinois country rolling away. And there, I gaze upon life and death and think that the world is indescribably beautiful, that all of creation sings to me, every bumblebee and tern and eagle and field mouse and daisy. I go quite mad with joy, feeling the blood pulse in my veins and the moist earth-scented wind inflate my lungs, and the voice of the wilderness clawing my bosom.

And there I know I am a man, and will fight a man's fight, and will depart from a better world than the one into which I was born because I have set my gifts upon its altar. No matter that disease robs me of all but youth; my name will be remembered.

Someone will prepare the journals after I am gone and catalogue the plants after I am gone, and write a history of Louisiana after I am gone, and they will find my hand in it all, and none of it done on my account, but for Mr. Jefferson and the republic.

I never want to leave that sacred place where the world is inexpressibly beautiful, but the rain drives me off, or a passing fisherman breaks the spell and I am among people again. When I leave it is like descending a long path from a tabernacle to the mundane world, and I am no longer with the eagles, and at the end of the path is only Secretary Bates, and Dr. Saugrain.

34 CLARK

John Shields is dying. George Shannon sent word, and asked if I might go see the doughty private in the Corps of Discovery. I sent word that I would.

We in the corps look after each other, or at least those of us in St. Louis. We were bonded into a rare brotherhood by three years of trial and fire; now we have settled into our vocations. Some have married. A few, like Sergeant Gass, have gone east. Most have foolishly traded their warrants for three hundred twenty acres of public land, awarded by a grateful Congress, for a few dollars. Frederick Bates bought some of the warrants for very little. Several men have entered the fur trade and gone upriver. John Colter is such a one, George Drouillard is another, Shannon another, and it cost him a leg which had been amputated after the fight with the Arikaras.

I have watched over them fondly, and with a deep affection and pride. They were good men to begin with, and some of them had been transformed into exceptional men by our common ordeal. I try to watch over the Field brothers, Private Labiche, and all the rest, and I know Meriwether does, too. Never a letter goes east from either of us but that we don't inquire after those loyal and greathearted men.

I had heard Shields was sick, but the news that he is sinking shocked me.

"Are you sure?" I said to the black boy who had brought me the message.

"Mr. Shannon, he asks you to go right quick, sir."

I nodded.

Shields has a smithy at Fort Bellefontaine, a few hours' walk from my office. He had traded his land warrant for a complete smithing outfit and is a respected gunsmith and blacksmith in the area, employing the trades he gave the Corps of Discovery. He had been a lean, muscular man with powerful shoulders and an iron grip. I could scarcely imagine such a Hercules sinking into the Stygian depths.

I saw nothing on my desk that required attention. The mid-July heat had already built, and I would be in a sticky sweat by the time I reached there, even if I should summon a carriage or a wagon. But I would walk. Walking keeps me hale.

I sent word to Julia that I might be detained and headed for the governor's lair, down the street, intending that we both should go and pay our respects to our corps man.

I found Meriwether studying a petition. The windows were open and he looked flushed by heat.

"Ah, Will!"

"You have a little time?" I asked.

He nodded.

"John Shields lies ill; they say he won't last. I have in mind paying him a call. Would you join me?"

"Shields? Shields?" Some strange light filled his eyes. "No. Busy, can't."

"I'll get a carriage and trotters, Meriwether. It won't be but three or four hours there and back."

"No!"

That rejection came so explosively that we stared a moment.

Then he retreated.

"I regret that I can't. Tell him so. Give him my heartfelt apologies and high regards. He's a good man. None better. He was our salvation several times when he made ironwork to trade to the Indians. If he dies, I'll grieve his passage. If I can help find his heirs, count on me. If I can do anything . . ."

He subsided into a blank gaze. I did not know what was amiss, but Meriwether was acting strange again.

"You go; tell him his old captain honors him," Meriwether said. "He gave his life for the corps."

"He gave his life?"

"He wouldn't be so ill now if he hadn't come with us."

"What is it that he suffers?" I asked.

"Fevers."

I ransacked my memory. "You treated him and MacNeal and others with mercury for the venereal at Fort Clatsop."

Meriwether nodded curtly.

"Do you suppose it's the venereal?"

Meriwether shrugged.

"Well, I'll find out and do what I can. Will the army or the territory bury him?"

Oddly, Meriwether didn't reply. He had slipped into his own world, and was slumped deep in his chair.

"My regrets, Will. I'd see him if I could," he said.

I left him lost in reverie, went to my house, kissed Julia and peered at the sleeping infant, collared York, got a hamper of ham and bread and stew and jams from the kitchen, and we set off through a muggy morning for the cottage of John Shields, not knowing what we would find there.

We hiked north on a military road. The army had bridged Coldwater Creek, corduroyed over some marsh, and widened a horse trail into a wagon trace from the city to the fort that governed access to the Missouri River and did a lively Indian trade as well. Shields held a smithing contract there, and lived nearby.

York followed along behind me a few paces toting the hamper. We hadn't talked much since his return from Louisville and I knew he was still looking for a way to be set free. He had been careful to fulfill his duties and to escape my wrath, but something between us had vanished.

The lifeless air seemed oppressive and forbidding.

I was perfectly familiar with Fort Bellefontaine, although it was a regular army post and not a militia site. And I knew Shields's cottage, so I headed there directly rather than paying my respects to Colonel Hunt, First U.S. Infantry, inside the post.

The stained log cottage baked quietly in the sun. Its shutters were open, letting light in and releasing silence to the world.

Someone must have seen us coming, because a door opened quietly, and a small composed woman greeted us.

"Gin'ral," she said, her glance sweeping me in. I heard Ireland in it. She was no doubt some noncom's wife, hired to look after the dying.

"We've come to see Mr. Shields, madam."

She nodded and motioned us in.

"I am General Clark."

"Oh, sir, I know, and I'm Mrs. Tolliver, and me man is Corporal Tolliver."

I glanced toward the bed. "How is he?"

"Oh, sir, you can see." She spoke softly and tenderly.

In spite of the open casement, I smelled death.

Shields lay in a narrow bunk on the far side, his eyes open but staring sightlessly. His mouth had curled into a permanent O, and his face had shrunk around his skull, save for some thick lumps along his neck and cheeks.

The woman started to retreat, but I stayed her.

"Madam, please . . ."

She stood back. York hung back, too, and I motioned him in. He put the wicker hamper on a rude table.

"I brought some ham and some other things," I said.

Shields didn't move; life was visible only through the slight rise and fall of his chest. I took off my hat and stood there before the ruin of a splendid soldier and a fine companion of three years of travel. Here was a man who had gone the whole route, across the prairies, over the mountains, down the Columbia to the salt water, and all the way back, as valuable a man as we had with us.

"Who's attending him?" I asked Mrs. Tolliver.

"The little Frenchman," she said. "Saugrain."

"What does he say?"

"I ask him, and he just shakes his head. He comes up to my neck, sir, and I look down upon him. I say to him 'What is this malady, Doctor, that robs a good smith of life?' And he just pats my hand gallantly and says it is a certain fever of soldiers. Oh, may my man never catch such a thing!"

I stood over Shields again, trying to discover awareness in him.

"John, it's your old captain. Clark here. I'm here to wish you all the blessings God can bestow on a good man. You walked to the Pacific with me, did your job well, gave more than was asked of you. I remember you looked after your fellows loyally and faithfully, followed our command, used your abilities and trade to make the Corps of Discovery a success, and you stand tall now. You're the best of men."

I discerned nothing at all. Those eyes did not track me. I studied that ravaged face, the lips that puffed oddly, the mouth caught in a death rictus, and I knew he was at the gates of eternity.

York edged close, uneasily, his eyes seeking permission from me and from the woman. He studied Shields a moment and then exhaled deeply, a great long gust of sadness.

"Mastuh Shields, I am saying goodbye. You be a good man, you my friend, and I am wishing you get well, but . . ."

He stopped, fearful that I would rebuke him for being too familiar. But I didn't. They were all brothers on that trip across the continent; strangers at first, brothers by the time we had returned. And York was a brother, too, the brother of us all.

I turned to Mrs. Tolliver. "Have his relatives been notified?"

"I think the colonel is seeing to it, Gin'ral."

"All right. I will do anything in my power to help. Please extend my apologies to Colonel Hunt, but I must return."

"Yes, sir."

We paid our respects a few moments more, and then left.

"Mastuh, what's he got taken him?" York asked.

"Perhaps Doctor Saugrain will tell me."

"You say he walked to the ocean, and he done all things right, and he help the corps, and he give all he got, and he don't need orders but just do it all without asking, and he be the best of men."

I nodded.

"I done that, too," York said.

We buried John Shields today, Friday, July 21, 1809. I wore my blue and white captain's uniform in honor of the man who served in my command. I looked dashing in it and my servant, Pernia, took pains to freshen it and black my boots and brush my tricorne.

They wanted me to do a eulogy and I agreed, though I would not have chosen to do so. There are things a man is required to do, and I do them without cavil. I rode to the post in Chouteau's carriage and took Will Clark with me.

All those from the Corps of Discovery round about St. Louis, save for York, were present to pay our respects to Private Shields, blacksmith, gunsmith, and carpenter, whose skills repeatedly saved us from disaster and starvation during that journey into the unknown.

Last night I went to my journals to refresh my memory. The man was our salvation. We had bartered Shields's skills for corn or other provender in the villages. He repaired the broken rifles and muskets of the tribesmen, or fashioned battle-axes and lance points out of sheet metal from a burnt-out stove, and in return we got what we needed to subsist ourselves. He had made nails and hinges for our winter posts, and carpentered tables and chairs and beds as well. He had been a fine soldier, swift to obey any command and eager to go the extra mile. A hunter too, and a gifted woodsman, comfortable in the wilds.

All this came back to me in a flood as I examined my entries. I turned finally to those of August 1805, when Shields, MacNeal, Drouillard, and I, in advance of the main party working up the Jefferson River, had ascended the eastern foothills of the Bitterroot Mountains and discovered the Shoshones, the Indians we wanted most of all to meet so we could barter for horses. They were shy as deer, and it took all our wiles to persuade them that we meant no harm. But at last we did meet Chief Cameahwaite and his hungry band, and boundless was our joy.

Their joy matched ours because Shields and Drouillard shot deer and pronghorn and fed them all. We all rejoiced in the lavender August twilight. They danced for us around a spark-shooting fire and offered us their tawny young squaws, and I well remember that night, though I have wished a thousand times since then that I had remained steadfast in my resolve. Only Drouillard stayed apart, for whatever reasons only that silent French and Shawnee scout and translator could say. And only Drouillard was spared what followed.

If I could take back that evening, blot away that eager, smiling, raven-haired, yellow-fleshed Shoshone girl with whom I could not speak a single word, repeal the eager smiles and caresses, purge every voluptuous second of it from my life, I would not hesitate to do so no matter the cost. From that moment onward, even though I ascended from triumph to triumph, I sank further and further into a hell beyond mortal reckoning.

My entry of August 18, 1805, caught my eye:

"I was anxious to learn whether these people had the venerial, and made the inquiry through the interpreter and his wife; the information was that they sometimes had it but I could not learn their remedy; they most usually die with it's effects . . ."

I remembered why I had inquired so anxiously.

I sighed and put away the journals. I had garnered enough to offer the assembled veterans a glistening catalogue of John Shields's worth as a man. And I would do so boldly, concealing morbidity of my own soul from them all.

We assembled at the grave on a blistering afternoon.

There was the old corps, or some small portion of it. George Shannon, leaning into a crutch; John Ordway, third in command and a gifted sergeant, and now farming outside of St. Louis; Robert Frazier, private, living in St. Louis; Ensign Pryor, still in the army, a career soldier and skilled noncommissioned officer; William Werner, now one of Will Clark's subagents; and Will Clark, erect and commanding as ever. Of those in Louisiana, only York was absent, and I regretted that Will had excluded him.

Doctor Saugrain was there, enduring the heat in his black suit, a tiny white-bearded presence at the head of the coffin, which rested on poles over the yawning grave. He had removed his top hat, his gaze sometimes shifting to me.

I saw, as well, one of the Creoles who had come with us, and had a troubled moment trying to remember his name. François Labiche? Jean Baptiste LePage, Pierre Cruzatte, who had put a ball through my buttocks? I think it was Labiche. I cursed my bad memory.

We are dwindling.

Potts is dead, killed last year by the Blackfeet though his partner, Colter, had miraculously escaped and I hear from traders returning to St. Louis that he is alive in the West, at Lisa's post. Gibson is dead, succumbing this year, like Shields, of the *lues venerea*. I remember dosing him heavily at Fort Clatsop. I heard of his death too late to attend the service, and I knew his relatives had hidden his sordid sickness from the world and hastened him into his grave. MacNeal has vanished, MacNeal, who was with me in the Shoshone village. I suspect he too has perished of the mortal disease that stalks us. We sought horses among the Shoshones, and instead bought death.

Bratton remains in the army, and so do Willard and Windsor. Joseph Field died in 1807 but his brother Reubin lives in Kentucky. I know nothing of Goodrich. Sergeant Patrick Gass is in the East, enriching himself with his journal and blackening me with every letter he writes to the press. Hugh Hall, Thomas Howard, Peter Weiser, Joseph Whitehouse, all gone from view, some dead I am certain.

I was sweating by the time the preacher summoned me to give the eulogy, and my damp hands blurred the notes I had scribbled, so I couldn't remember what I wanted to say about John Shields. Inside my blue tunic, I was drenched with sweat and I ached to tear it off and let some breezes cool my fevered flesh.

I felt my sweat gather at my brow under my tricorne, and traverse my cheeks, and drip relentlessly into my stock. I felt my armpits leak moisture, and knew it was sliding down my sides, dampening my linens. I felt as if I was standing on the brow of hell, feeling the heat, watching that fine old soldier John Shields slide into the eternal pit.

I gave him a good soldier's eulogy; he was brave, resourceful, obedient, courageous, honorable, an asset to our command. There were no parents and no widow and no children to receive my words; only a few old corpsmen with better memories than I have. So I didn't dwell on Shields's achievements for long; the words were more for us than for his family.

I spoke of what we had done, the odds we faced, the way we came together into an indomitable and well-knit force bonded by danger and brotherhood and sheer joy. I told those privates and sergeants and my officer colleague that we had done something grand, something that would shine forever in the eyes of the people of the United States, and John Shields had marched with us from the first step to the last.

Will spoke a few words, too, plainspoken and true, remembering the good soldier in John Shields and the brave companion of a thousand days of danger. Will looked grand in his Missouri militia uniform, a faint scatter of gray at his temples, his demeanor dignified and serious, his gaze welcoming each man present and acknowledging the gift of that man's attendance at the last.

We saluted. A trumpeter borrowed from Fort Bellefontaine played the dirge. Colonel Hunt and a few regulars stood at a distance, sharing the moment with us.

"Dust to dust," the preacher said, tossing some sand upon that plain plank coffin, the yellow shellac of the pine glowing in the hot sun. And then we lowered it into that yawning hole, a pit that looked all too familiar to me as I peered into its gloom. Who would the Stalker stalk next?

Will and I headed back together in the carriage.

"You look done in," he said.

"Hot in this uniform."

"You sure it's not fever?"

I didn't reply. For years I had blamed the ague, and now I could not.

"Why don't you stop for some refreshment?" he said. "I'll put Julia and the servants to it."

"I'll get to see my namesake?"

Will smiled. "Governor, the baby's fat and happy, and we're calling him Meriwether and he's old enough to respond to his name, and fixing to walk, and before we know it, he'll be walking to the Pacific Ocean and back."

Somehow, all that good news only deepened my morbidity.

I halted the dray horse before Will's house, tied up at the hitching post, and we escaped from the furnace of the sun into a close but cooler climate within.

He studied me. "Are you sure you are well?"

"No, I'm not."

He nodded, and soon was rousting out servants and Julia, making the whole house clatter to life just when it was lost in siesta to the heat.

I waited until I was bidden to the nursery, where Julia curtsied. She wore a shapeless white cotton dress that hid her from an old bachelor's admiration. I wondered if she might be expecting another child.

"Your Excellency," she said tonelessly.

The boy dozed restlessly in the moist closeness, a loose-knit coverlet over him. Meriwether Lewis Clark. New life following death, the endless cycle repeated. This child was as close as I would ever come to a son.

"He is a fine healthy boy," I said politely.

"We'll raise him up to be the image of you, Governor."

Julia looked uncomfortable, and her fingers played with the muslin of her dress.

"Please forgive me, but I think I will forgo your lunch," I said.

"Why, Meriwether . . ."

I retreated as swiftly as courtesy permitted, under the concerned and tender gaze of General Clark.

PART III

36 LEWIS

I stared at the letter from Washington, absorbing the bad news that had reached me this Friday, August 4, 1809. It came from a clerk in the State Department, one R. S. Smith, and with it came a voucher for eighteen dollars and fifty cents that I had submitted in February. The department, the letter explained, was returning the voucher because it lacked the authority to pay it.

The sum was to pay a translator, Pierre Provenchere, to render certain laws into French, something entirely necessary in a bilingual dominion. How could the Creoles know the law if it were not comprehensible to them? But here was this voucher and a note that blandly said I had gone beyond my authority.

Heat built in me. Clerks! They have no more vision than an earthworm. I fumed, reread the letter, and then began to worry about what else might befall me. I had signed hundreds of vouchers for necessary services. My signature as governor was all that any merchant or supplier required to ensure payment. And up to this moment everything I had signed, including the scores of vouchers for the Corps of Discovery, had been honored in Washington.

When I had submitted the voucher for Provenchere last

February, I made a point of explaining the purpose of the expenditure. The French translations of the law were published and distributed for a felony trial. What could be more essential to the course of justice? Any reasonable official, any clerk in any bureau, would swiftly understand the need, the legitimacy. But not Smith.

I sighed, knowing that I would have to compensate Provenchere out of my own purse, and I would have to borrow again to do it. I did not even have enough to pay my manservant, John Pernia. The family estate in Virginia had not found a buyer and I was heavily in debt.

And was this the first? Would more come floating back to me? Was this the work of some conspiracy whose design was to ruin me? Was this Bates's spidery hand at work? He had threatened to protest my expenditures, and I knew he had done just that, appending little notes to each item announcing that it had been submitted over his protests. It doesn't take much of that sort of footnoting of a man's vouchers to ruin his credibility.

I slumped at my desk. If this was the first skidding snow in an avalanche, I was in grave trouble. And so were the merchants who had until now trusted me. What could I say to them?

I plucked up the letter and braved the heat, walking slowly toward Will's office. We had shared everything for years; now I would share this.

I waited in his antechamber while he heard out the petition of a Creole who wanted to go upriver to the Iowa country and trade with the Sauk and Fox tribes. I suspected that Will would turn the man down; the British had been stirring up the two tribes against us and that area was dangerous.

Then at last we were alone.

"Governor?" he said.

I handed him the letter. He frowned, studied it closely, and set it down. "Everything boils down to money," he said at last. He stood slowly, lumbered to a black iron strongbox, which was not locked, and extracted some national bank bills and some coin.

"I haven't asked," I said.

He grinned. "You were working up to it."

I withdrew my pocket ledger, borrowed Will's pen, and entered the debt. There were too many such entries in my ledger.

"What are you going to do about this?" he asked.

"I can't keep it a secret. Bates opens my official mail, and he knows about it, and it's probably all over the city by now."

"It's his doing."

"Yes, and I fear there will be many more of these."

Will nodded. He didn't try to comfort me or pretend that this would be an isolated incident. We both knew it wouldn't be. Not with the malevolent secretary appending his florid objections to my vouchers.

The general ran a gnarled hand through his red hair. "When it comes to money, I have learned not to trust the government, any government," he said.

"Did you ever resolve your brother's case?" I asked.

He shook his head. "George doesn't own ten cents to his name. The best we could do was switch the titles of a few properties to me. I am the nominal owner, and that's the only way we've beat off the creditors and lawyers and courts."

It was a grim tale, and I had heard parts of it many times from Will and his family. General George Rogers Clark of the Virginia militia had staved off British occupation of much of the trans-Appalachian west during the revolution. Because of his determined generalship, and skill at keeping a militia army in the field when most of the men just wanted to go home and plant their fields, and Indian diplomacy, the republic now possessed the vast lands east of the Mississippi.

Operating as a general officer of the Virginia militia, he had signed scores of vouchers for munitions, clothing, arms, camp gear, footwear, horses and wagons, livestock, gifts for the always dangerous tribes, wages, and everything else to field an army in a wilderness owned by savages and British agents.

Then came the reckoning. The commonwealth shrugged off its obligations on one thin excuse after another, mostly having to do with lost records. Frustrated by the commonwealth, Will's older brother then appealed to the Continental Congress and was rebuffed: the debt was Virginia's not the national government's. And then the creditors had moved in, claiming everything George Rogers Clark possessed.

The heap of debt set off a widening collapse, as the merchants who could not be paid by Clark in turn went bankrupt, and spread the bankruptcy to several removes from the old general. Will had spent much of his time before the expedition dealing with his brother's creditors and trying to salvage enough so that the whiskey-soaked general at Mulberry Hill could live in a modicum of comfort.

Somehow it had not embittered Will Clark; he was too great a man for that. But now, when I showed him my rejected voucher, I saw a deep and knowing cynicism bloom in his eyes. He had walked that path, and knew the thousand small cuts of officials and creditors and lawyers, and he knew exactly what probably was in store for me.

"We'll wrestle this together, Meriwether," was all he said to me. I had feared he might lecture me about my land purchases and living beyond my means, but he said not a word.

I was grateful for that.

"What are you going to do?" he asked.

"Pay Provenchere for the translation; let people know that a minor refusal is no ground for alarm."

Will smiled wolfishly. He didn't have to tell me what he was thinking: if Frederick Bates were not stirring up trouble, it might work. But Bates's busy tongue was already undoing anything I might say or do.

"I am an honest man! I will pay every cent!" I exclaimed.

Will's eyebrows arched and he scratched at his newly shaven jaw. "You might go talk to the man."

"He would not entertain my presence in his office. This is his design! His objections did this! He wants to ruin me! He'd stop at nothing! He and his Burrites, still smarting over their defeat."

"How do you know he was allied with Aaron Burr? I certainly don't know it."

"Why else would he be so determined to destroy me?"

Will grinned again. "Wants your office. Can't stand to be subordinate to you."

There was more to it, even if Will didn't think so. I saw threads leading back to shadowy men, leading back to Burr, and maybe General Wilkinson himself, men who wanted to turn the western country into their own satrapy to exploit and suck dry and then toss to the British, or the Spanish, when they were done. I saw design in it; men quietly maneuvering to fill their purses and assume the powers of state, men with stilettos and the will to use them.

But Will Clark, as was his wont, had reduced it to the

boneheadedness of clerks and accountants, bureaucratic nay-sayers, and above all, a pompous, busy, mean-spirited, self-important man who thought himself misplaced as the second in command. One of us was wrong, I thought darkly, and it wasn't me.

"I suppose you had better make some plans," he said.

"Such as?"

"A trip east."

"What good would that do?" I asked truculently.

Will shrugged. "I prefer to sit down with a man and get to know him and get him to listen if I have something to say."

"Do you think James Madison would even see me?"

Will laughed easily, and that was answer enough.

"I want to talk to Secretary Eustis. He's the one I worry about. He reprimands me in almost every letter, and I don't like the tone of his correspondence."

"I worry about him, too. He's trying to trim down the army just when we're facing another war. We're fixing to hand the Louisiana purchase to the British if he doesn't send me materiel."

I glared out the window at unseen knaves. "I have tried to govern this territory on the best model, employing all the wisdom I could garner from Tom Jefferson, from my army experience, from my readings, and now this blowhard threatens to undo my every act!"

Will didn't reply; he simply rounded his desk and clapped me on the back, threw an arm around my shoulder, and let me know in that language of friendship that lies above and beyond words that I could count on him. I was suddenly grateful for this stately, dignified Virginian who looked more and more like George Washington as the years etched him.

"I'll wait and see. Maybe it will blow over," I said.

"My powers with the pen aren't much, but I'll come to your defense if you want me to," he said. There was a question in it.

"I'll fight my own fight," I replied.

"You're outnumbered," he said.

37 LEWIS

I downed a gram of Dover's powder to quiet my racing pulse, and waited for the opiate to steal my anguish from me. The letter on my desk this eighteenth day of August had catapulted my pulse and deranged my every thought.

I paced my chamber, some wildness keeping me from sitting myself down and reading the letter from Secretary of War Eustis a second time to measure its deadly impact. I pressed the lids of my eyes shut, wanting to drive out the sight of that awful missive, which had been written in mid-July but only now found its way to my hands.

Such was my agitation that the powder did not take hold entirely; no peace filtered through me, but only a leaden weariness that did not allay my anxiety at all, but perhaps even deepened it. I was tempted to take another gram, but put the thought behind me.

At last I felt my pulse slow, and my jumbled thoughts slow with my pulse, and I supposed that soon I could reduce the chaos of my heart to good order. Without the powder, I might have suffered an apoplexy beyond repair.

I seated myself again in the squeaking chair and let myself stare at the fluted white woodwork of my office, the seat of government of Upper Louisiana, a territory comparable to the *whole* of the original United States of America, though I don't suppose those back East ever fathomed that.

I watched the progress of my hands, sweaty and trembling at first, and spastic in their motions. They dried. I regained control of them. I could hold the letter without smearing the ink or straining my eyes.

It had been opened by Secretary Bates, who no doubt was even now trumpeting the tidings to his cronies, with many a joyous smirk and expression of hypocritical and pious horror. I reached to the cut glass decanter and poured a measure of ruby port and discovered as I lifted the glass that my hands were once again obedient to my will. I sipped, and again.

The letter from Secretary Eustis professed puzzlement about the expedition I had sent forth in May to return She-He-Ke to his Mandan village. Or rather, it expressed puzzlement about what the hundred and twenty trappers would do once they got above the Mandan villages. He said the government had no understanding of any of that, or where the commercial party was heading, or whether it would even remain in United States territory, and I should have inquired before acting.

This was official dissembling, the genteel lying of bureaucrats; he knew exactly what the trappers of the St. Louis Missouri Fur Company would do after they had delivered the Mandan chief to his village because I had thrice written Eustis in great detail about the arrangement, and what was required because the regular army would not do the job. I had enclosed a fair copy of the contract with the St. Louis Missouri Fur Company.

All this the secretary knew, but now professed ignorance, which is the venerable way of effete functionaries to say no, or rebuke underlings, or express disapproval. James Madison's pinchpenny secretary of war was not only no friend, but was now grimly undermining my every effort to secure the territory from the designs of the British, who continued to stir up the tribes against us.

I detected the Machiavellian hand of Frederick Bates in all this: those snide asides, those grandiloquent objections to my every voucher, those raindrops of dissent descending on the governor, all had their effect. His noose was tightening around my vulnerable neck.

The secretary of war wrote, in that dry, passive voice of his, that after his department had approved the seven thousand dollars for the expedition, "it was not expected that any further advances or any further agency would be required on the part of the United States."

He would, therefore, reject the voucher I had issued at the last moment for the additional five hundred dollars to purchase more gifts for diplomatic concourse with the tribes.

The voucher would be my own responsibility. I now owed every penny of it to the merchants who had trusted my signature on a government draft.

But Secretary Eustis wasn't done with me. "The President has been consulted and the observations herein have his approval."

So Mr. Madison was rebuking me, too. There was no sympathetic ear in official Washington. It was a vote of no confidence. It was a blatant if unspoken suggestion that I resign. No governor can govern without the power of the purse, and Eustis knew it.

It was, I felt certain, Frederick Bates's carefully executed coup d'état.

His office was but a few doors away, but I did not storm toward it. I reread Eustis's letter and resolved to fight. The first step would be a reply in this very day's post. I would again provide the exact details of the fur company expedition, the exact plans of the company after it had fulfilled its official function, and the exact costs. I have never been one to surrender under adversity, especially to the withered gray hand of bureaucracy, and so I wrote, the calmness adding to my lucidity, the powders subduing the clawing at my heart.

I explained to Eustis that the feelings his letter excited were truly painful, and I reminded him that I had always accompanied my drafts with detailed explanations of what the funds were purchasing. And I concluded, "If the object be not a proper one, of course I am responsible, but if, on investigation, it does appear to have been necessary for the promotion of the public interest, I shall hope for relief."

And I reminded him that "I have never received a penny of public money but have merely given the draft to a person who has rendered public service, or furnished articles for public use, which have been, invariably, applied to the purposes expressed in my letters of advice."

I fancied that it was one of the best of my letters to the secretary; and when I was done I signed it, sealed it with wax, and posted it myself rather than letting Bates see my correspondence.

But I was not sanguine about the effect of that letter. If I wished to retain office, I would have to go east, *at once,* and sit down with the president and secretary and anyone else who might help me, and make my case.

I dozed.

Will Clark startled me awake. I peered up at him, shaking the cobwebs from my brain.

"What's this about a voucher?" he asked.

So Bates had been telling the world after all. I handed the letter to Clark, who read it, frowning.

"This indicts us all," he said. "The fur company as well as your offices in setting up the expedition."

He had a steely set to his face I had seen only a few times before. An angry Will Clark was a force to be reckoned with.

"So Eustis is feeding you to the hogs," he said.

"Where did you hear about the voucher?"

"Ben Wilkinson. He asked whether the government would honor your warrants. He has several bills outstanding."

"I don't know," I said. "Who told Wilkinson about the letter?"

"He just passed it off as rumor."

"Bates," I said. "He's the one who received and opened it and placed it on my desk."

Clark grunted. "You can't answer backstabbers by writing letters. If you want to bend an official, look him in the eye. We'll both have to go to Washington."

I nodded.

He stared at me. "Are you indisposed?"

"Just tired."

"How soon do you think you can be off?"

"I don't know. A week, maybe. I hate to leave the territory in his hands."

"Bates is too hidebound to do anything. He's an absolutely rule-obsessed man. Put him in charge of anything, and he'd spend days trying to find a rule giving him the legal right to sneeze. You have no need to fear him."

Will could not have been more wrong, but I said nothing.

"You're indisposed," he said. "Maybe that's best. Go to your rooms and close the door and rest."

He left, leaving me to face my creditors. I drew my ledgers out of a drawer and began totting up my debts, which came to four thousand dollars. If more warrants were rejected, I would owe more. I needed cash, and fast.

There was one hope: I had never made use of my land warrant from the government, the sixteen hundred acres given me as my reward for leading the expedition. Land was cheap. There was more than enough. But maybe if it were auctioned in New Orleans, I might get two dollars an acre for it, a better price than I could obtain here. All right. I would take the warrant to New Orleans, and see what came of it. With luck, that might cover half of my debt—if Eustis didn't reject any more of my vouchers. I had the crawling fear that he would, especially egged on by Frederick Bates. If they wanted to ruin me, they could without much effort.

I drew up a list of creditors, and calculated. If I returned two of the farms I had purchased from Auguste Chouteau, I would cover my debt to him. If I placed the remaining farm in the hands of my creditors, and my several city lots, that would cover more debt. But there would be other debts remaining, such as the back salary I owed my servant, John Pernia. And the warrants. I didn't have enough to cover everything. I didn't have enough to afford a trip to Washington, much less the return to St. Louis.

No one had pressed me as yet. But with every commotion in the corridor, I expected one or another St. Louis businessman to burst in and skin my hide. That no one burst through my door was good. If I wanted to demonstrate my intent and my honor, I would go to them first, before they were forced to come to me.

I examined my ledgers, made my choices, and headed into the suffocating afternoon with the documents in a portfolio. I would see an attorney and draw up some papers empowering certain friends to handle my financial affairs. Then, in a day or two, I would face my creditors. Let no man say I am without honor.

38 LEWIS

I walked through dolorous August heat to the offices of Auguste Chouteau, merchant and entrepreneur, and the city's most prominent and powerful citizen. Some would have called it a fool's errand. My brow rivered water, and dark stains dampened my stock. But the discomfort was a small price to pay.

I entered his gloomy building, found him not present, and remembered that this was the hour of the petite nap; most of the Creoles encouched themselves for a little while in the afternoon. Still, the bells had tolled three, and so I waited in his chambers upon a brocaded divan he had placed there for visitors.

I bent my thoughts to other things to escape the discomfort of that stifling air, and remembered the faces. How many thousands of American faces had gazed upon me since my return? I remembered the admiration in their eyes, the smiles, and hearty congratulations. I remembered the curtsies of the women, their way of honoring a man of high rank.

I remembered the toasts raised by burghers in Virginia, learned doctors in Philadelphia, artists and politicians and poets, raising a glass to Meriwether Lewis, navigator of the wilds, conqueror of a continent, botanist, zoologist, stargazer, cartog-

rapher, youthful exemplar of everything good in the new republic, his reputation sterling, his name unsullied by any
scandal.

Thousands of them, all expecting much from me because I
had accomplished much. Expecting too much. I remembered
their toasts, their joy, their poems penned in my honor. I remembered their respect, the staccato applause of the United
States Congress, Tom Jefferson's hearty public acclaim and his
even kinder private words, in which he called me son, and told
me that I had exceeded his every wish.

I remembered all that, and thought of my dilemmas, and
knew that for the rest of my days I would focus on one thing:
keeping my honor unstained. Whatever else happened, I would
preserve my good name because the beloved republic required
it of me. I would not disappoint Tom Jefferson, writing and
gardening there in Monticello. I would not disappoint my
mother. I had already disappointed myself.

The thought that I would surely disappoint them, or probably stain my name, or shame myself, brought pain to me so
intense that I could not even bear the thought. The thought
that I might have to peer into Tom Jefferson's eyes and see
dismay there was beyond my endurance.

Chouteau appeared, disheveled and yawning.

"Ah! C'est vous!"

He waved me into his ornate and dark chambers, which
lacked and needed light.

Wordlessly he motioned me to a creweled armchair, and
poured some ruby wine from a decanter. Then he cocked an
eyebrow.

"It seems my financial decisions have displeased Washington," I said.

"So I have heard, Governor."

"I am liable personally for some expenses mostly connected to the fur company."

"So I have heard."

"News travels fast. I received the letter only this morning." Chouteau smiled.

"I am extended beyond my means."

Chouteau did not look surprised.

"If I return two of your farms, by my calculation, you will be covered completely and have a gain too. My payments to you suffice to keep the third farm."

The phlegmatic merchant sighed, pursed his lips, and nodded. I had a sense that he had, this very morning, examined my debts and payments.

"I wish to return these to you, in exchange for canceling my remaining obligation due next May."

"You are a man of honor, Governor." The words issued from him in all sincerity.

That compliment brought me to the brink of tears.

We completed the transaction in a few strokes. He got his farms back; my debt was canceled, and he gave me a clear title to the remaining farm.

"There are some," he said, "who would use high office for aggrandizement." He smiled. "You, sir, have a loftier design."

I nodded, miserably. I had surrendered not only several thousand dollars of property, but my hopes for the well-being of myself and my family.

"Alors, there are others, mon ami, who use high office to ruin others, who whisper of afflictions, who claw at those above them."

He was talking about Bates, but in his own civil and

oblique way that I had come to admire in this princeling of St. Louis. The assessment of Frederick Bates was not a kind one.

"Auguste, from the beginning, you and your family have helped me govern, resolved problems, generously assisted me in all my designs, and brought the government of the United States into harmony with the French in Louisiana. I am in your debt, and esteem you for your service and your friendship."

He absorbed that a moment. *"Merci, bien, bien,"* he whispered at last. I saw affection in his rumpled face.

I now had one farm in my sole possession, for one moment. I bade my host adieu after the shortest of visits, and headed up Main to the general mercantile of Ben Wilkinson, partner in the new fur company, brother of the army general who was up to his eyeballs in Burr's conspiracy, and no friend.

Wilkinson was more energetic, but somehow less formidable than Auguste Chouteau, and I found him bustling about his poorly stocked emporium, as if his sheer energy could cause goods to appear on his shelves.

"Ah, it's you, Meriwether," he said neutrally. "What can I do for you?"

I motioned to his cage, a raised and balustraded office overlooking the floor of his sandstone store.

"How much do I owe?" I asked, once we seated ourselves.

He donned spectacles and opened a ledger. "Considerable. There's the five hundred dollars of trading items that Secretary Eustis now rejects. Or so I hear. Is it so? I was thinking of asking you about it—"

"You'll be paid. Yesterday I appointed three friends to look after my debts. I'll give them power of attorney and they will sell such property as will pay my creditors."

"Who, may I ask?"

"Will Clark, and two of my Masonic friends, Alexander Steward and William Carr. The papers are being prepared, and I'll sign them Monday. They'll have a farm of mine and some lots as surety, and there will be more coming. I will not rest until every obligation has been satisfied."

"You're leaving us?" Wilkinson asked.

"I'm going to Washington to straighten out some financial matters. Some of them having to do with your fur company."

He nodded, and I knew none of this was news to him. "The rejected vouchers," he said.

"Yes, and there may be more. I cannot count on the Madison government honoring my warrants. I'm at sea, not knowing what will be accepted and what will fall to my own account, Ben. That's why I'm here. To protect you and the rest as best I can."

"Even Frederick Bates?"

"Even the secretary. I owe him a little, along with many others."

"So I am to press my claim with Steward and Carr?"

"Yes, but I hope you'll wait. If I can reverse the decisions in Washington I may not have to liquidate my holdings. I'll send my land warrant to New Orleans to be auctioned, and that will raise more."

"Does this mean you won't be back?"

I dodged. "I expect to settle this with the president and the secretary of war. It is hard to come to terms by mail."

"That's a long trip."

"Will and I are both going, but separately. Since your St. Louis Missouri Fur Company is at the center of the dispute, the general felt he has to explain things in person, just as I do. He will also see to his brother's affairs."

Wilkinson sighed, smiled, and shook his head. "Who would have thought it?" he said. His gaze slipped away from me, and I sensed all this had been much discussed, maybe even plotted. His closeness to Bates was well known to me.

I braced him: "The governor will pay his debts," I said. "Even when some others set out to ruin him."

That was further than I intended to go. It evoked a catlike grin in the amused merchant.

"Meriwether, old friend, rest yourself in peace," he said.

"I will remember that you are doing me a great service," I replied. "You've waited some while for payment, and now you'll need to wait a while more. I am grateful for your patience."

The kind words surprised him a little. He nodded.

A bleak wind was blowing.

I stepped outside into a different and crueler world, knowing there still were things that needed immediate attention. Raising some cash was one. I owed my manservant, John Pernia, two months' salary. I needed also to persuade him to come east with me.

I found him at my quarters, about to tote a load of my linens and smallclothes to the black laundresses.

He straightened up, the wicker basket in hand, a question in his dark face.

"Set it down, my good man, so we can talk," I said.

I waited while the dusky freeman set down his burden and gave me his attention.

"I would like you to come with me to Washington," I said. "It is crucial to me. I will entrust you with an important task, the most important you have ever been given."

He shook his head; I knew he was on the brink of resigning. A man cannot work for nothing for long.

"You, John, are at the heart of my plans. Come with me, and you will be paid everything owing you when we reach Virginia."

He might never know why I needed him; but someday soon he might.

39 CLARK

It is our custom to be at home Sunday afternoons, and entertain St. Louis. We put out bountiful viands and then await whoever comes, and there usually are a few dozen. Julia loves these occasions and swirls about welcoming the assorted militia officers, clerks and secretaries, old comrades from the Corps of Discovery, trappers, boatmen, merchants, and all their pretty spouses, mothers, aunts, children, and daughters.

This Sabbath, August 27, 1809, in the midst of this cheerful occasion, the governor's manservant Pernia arrived with a message.

He drew me aside. "The governor is indisposed, General, and regrets that he can't come. He doesn't know when he will depart for the East, but will let you know of his progress."

"How indisposed, Mr. Pernia?"

The servant squinted at me, reluctant to talk. His face was a mass of brown and liverish freckles, the result of the union of two bloods, and I saw him retreat into discretion. "I couldn't say, sir."

"Perhaps I should go see him."

"He didn't convey that request, sir, but if you want, I will tell him of your wish."

I smiled. The governor's manservant was not only loyal but protective. "Very good, Mr. Pernia. I'll go see him. Is he very sick?"

Pernia debated a response, and finally nodded. "When he doses himself with the medicines, sir, I know he's indisposed."

"I'll be along directly. I haven't seen him in a week, and I was wondering. Let me tell Julia, and I'll just duck out of here."

I left the governor's man waiting, while I cornered Julia.

"Meriwether's got the fever again. I think I'd better go check on him."

"But General—"

"Ah, Julia, they come to gaze upon your fair and willowy beauty, not see me. In any case, I'll be back directly."

She laughed. She was with child and it showed.

I took off with Pernia, hiking through a sultry August afternoon that threatened to explode in thundershowers. Meriwether's chambers were only a few blocks distant.

Pernia grew agitated as we drew close. "I'll just step ahead, General, and let him know that you wish to see him."

I ignored the servant. Meriwether and I had walked across a continent, shared a tent as well as a command, and he had no secrets from me, nor I from him.

The household was not locked, and Pernia let me in, plainly reluctant. "I'll go see the master," he said, racing through the cluttered parlor toward a bedroom at the rear.

This time I waited. I beheld several black leather trunks, their lids open, their interiors silk-lined. One contained his clothing: pantaloons, shirtwaists, hosiery, boots, red slippers, all neatly laid out by his servant. His two matched pistols rested in their case along with his ornate powder flask. I spotted his sword, which had traveled to the Pacific and back.

Another trunk contained the disputed vouchers and the journals, the battered ledger books stacked in orderly piles within. I itched to know what he had completed; whether some of those ledgers contained an edited version he would now take to Philadelphia and the printer, at long last.

Another, smaller chest contained an amazing assortment of blue bottles and pasteboard boxes of powders, packets of herbs, and a store of spiritous drinks in tin flasks. Plainly, Lewis was taking east with him an array of medicines beyond my fathoming, enough to stock a small apothecary shop. I sensed that here was something I had only vaguely grasped about my old friend. How much of all these was he swallowing, and for what?

Pernia emerged from the gloom.

"He's indisposed, General," the servant said.

"I've seen him in that estate before," I said, overcoming the servant's reluctance. I pressed past the man and pushed through the door into Meriwether's bedchamber. A rancid odor smacked me, along with a fetid closeness. The governor lay abed, his face flushed. A nearly empty whiskey bottle stood at his nightstand, and I wondered if the governor's indisposition was nothing more than his occasional indulgence.

"Meriwether," I said.

He peered up at me from a flushed face, the red barely covering an underlying grayness of his flesh. "I'm fevered. Can't leave yet," he whispered.

"Have you seen a doctor?"

He shook his head.

"Should I fetch one?"

He shook his head again. "Nothing to be done. Fetch my mother."

"Your mother? Lucy Marks?"

He nodded.

"Meriwether, you are in St. Louis."

"Oh," he said. "Tell her to come."

Lucy Marks was in Ivy, Virginia, on the family estate. I pressed a hand to Meriwether's forehead. It was hot and moist.

"Close in here," I said. "I'll open a window."

"No! No, don't let them in!"

I paused. "Let who in?"

"I am indisposed," he said. "The fevers. Don't let any more in."

"Fresh air will do you good. Let me air the room."

"No, I beg of you, don't let them in."

I paused at the shuttered window. "Let who in?" I asked.

He stared at me from dull eyes, and said nothing.

The room oppressed me and I sensed that it was oppressing him, too, so I threw open the shutter and opened the casement. A breath of clean air filtered in.

He closed his eyes.

"You can close it in a moment," I said.

"Don't let Maria see me," he said. "Don't let her in."

"Maria? Maria who?"

"Wood," he said. "Pure and fair."

Maria Wood. He seemed to think he was back at Ivy, in his parental home. I wondered whether he was fit to travel at all.

I studied the array of medicines at hand. Dover's powder, calomel, Rush's purgatives, whiskey, wine, belladonna, ipecac, extract of cinchona, brown liquids I couldn't identify.

"Light hurts my eyes," he said.

That would be the Dover's powder, I thought.

"Meriwether, has a doctor prescribed all this?"

He didn't reply, but I knew the answer.

"I'll ask your man to apply cold compresses," I said. "Bring down the fever."

He nodded, and I bade him good-bye. I intended to check up on him daily. I had treated him many times on the expedition; now I would keep an eye on him.

In the parlor I braced Pernia. "He needs cold compresses. And less medicine. It's quite like him to think that if a little is good, more is better. He lays siege to his own body, with all this stuff. Mr. Pernia, please keep me informed. If the governor's not better tomorrow, I'll see to fetching a doctor. Who is it, Saugrain?"

"Yes, General."

"And take those blasted bottles and boxes away from him. Take everything away but the cinchona."

He hesitated, not wanting to offend the governor.

"For the governor's own good, Mr. Pernia."

Plainly I was intruding. My command had disturbed the man, so I clapped him on the back. "No man ever served better," I said. "A good man looks after his master just as you do."

"He desires me to go east, sir, but I'm not sure I should continue . . ."

"Continue?"

He looked trapped. "Without salary, sir?"

I chose my words carefully. "You are a good and loyal man. I am certain that the governor intends that you receive every penny owed you as soon as he reaches Virginia. His mother will see to it."

He nodded. Again I felt I was intruding in the private life of this old comrade of the wilds. But he lay ill and out of his head, and I was his friend, and no family but my own was there to look after him in St. Louis. Reuben was upstream with the fur company. So friends step in, without a thought, and Meriwether was as fine and noble a friend as I ever had.

"Mr. Pernia, your service to him as he heads to Washington would be invaluable. I can only say, sir, that without you he might not succeed. If you should run into any difficulties, contact me and I will do what I can."

I clapped his shoulder. "You've helped me, and helped him. I need to know how the governor's faring, and you can count on me as the governor's friend. It is not something to share with anyone else."

"Oh, never, General!"

"Good. You probably know what Doctor Saugrain prescribes and also prohibits?"

Pernia seemed to shrink into himself again. "Yes, but if I keep spirits from the governor, like the doctor wants, the governor, he gets upset and then I hear about it."

I nodded. A servant could no more keep spirits and powders from Meriwether than I could.

40 LEWIS

They fished me out of the river with their grappling hooks. They glowered at me, so I explained I had fallen in because I am not steady on my feet. The chill of the Mississippi shocked me back to my senses after my tumble overboard. I don't remember what happened before that. I must have been wandering the plank floorboards of this flatboat while the river boiled by.

The Creole boatmen began to examine me sharply as I dripped water, but I ignored them. I did not change into new clothing, but let the water cool my fevered flesh. The river is tepid anyway. I wrung the moisture from my pantaloons and settled within the cabin, on a crude bench that serves me for a bunk.

Pernia doesn't approve, and rummaged through my trunks to find a change of clothing. But I ignored him. I asked him for my pills but he is reluctant, and finally I rose and found the Dover's powder myself. I asked him to uncork a jug of whiskey because I am shaking, but he seems almost truculent today, and glares at me. I am finding him more and more disobedient.

We traveled but little this Monday, September 4. The sun is so oppressive that the boatmen paused during the midday heat, unable to pole and row and steer the flatboat without wilting.

I am fevered as usual, and spend the lazy hours lying abed in the rude cabin. Pernia roams the deck the way a prisoner walks in the prison yard. He did not want to come. I do not want to make this trip.

In New Orleans I will board the next coaster heading east, and will round Spanish Florida and sail up the Atlantic coast, and in a month or six weeks, depending on the winds, I will enter the Chesapeake and be deposited in Washington, all by sea. That is, if the prowling British warships don't stop us. In my condition, that is the only way I can travel. My exertions are limited to walking the forty-foot flatboat for exercise, but the dazzle off the water is too fierce to permit it, so I huddle in the gloom of the cabin. Outside of this small sanctuary, I lose my balance and need support lest I topple again into the murky river that is carrying me on its shoulders to my destiny. I say destiny, rather than destination, knowingly.

I intended to start for Washington a fortnight ago, but fever stayed me, and also the wall of debt that rises higher and darker than the walls of a prison. I could not raise cash to travel. When I was feeling a little better, Will helped me organize my debt. We found that I owe, apart from my land payments, twenty-nine hundred dollars, of which I could readily cover only part by auctioning off my federal land warrant in New Orleans.

This oppresses me. I have subsequently enlarged my debt to purchase passage for myself and Pernia, and to buy the necessary medicines without which I could not hope to arrive in Washington.

The Creole boatmen have tied up here at Ste. Genevieve for the night, and gone ashore, leaving me to fend for myself. Pernia stays on, and has somehow commandeered a cold meal for me, though I am not a bit hungry. I can scarcely swallow the spirits and pills I require to allay my pain.

But there is so much worse afoot in my poor body: I am confused, and while I usually recover my senses, I remember my confusion and my hallucination, and it is as if I have returned from some distant and bumbling journey. I gazed backward this day, watching the bubbling wake of the flatboat as it rocked slowly along the turbid waters, knowing I cannot return to St. Louis. I did not say goodbye.

My last true friend, Doctor Saugrain, visited me several times those final days. He is humble and discreet, and reluctant to tell me how grave my condition now is. But he shakes his head slowly, and I did get out of him that it can no longer be concealed. If I arrive in the city named for our first president in this condition, I shall be found out. When I ask the little physician how long I might last, he shrugs gallantly. "Who knows?" he asks. "One year, ten years, yes?"

I could retreat to Ivy and become that legendary uncle in the attic, and wobble through a few more years hidden from a sharp-eyed world. I wonder what Maria Wood would think of me, could she but see me now.

Doctor Saugrain was firm the last time I saw him. "Have faith. Do not surrender to it. Do not, my friend, imbibe spirits, or swallow more mercury, or numb your soul with the Dover's powder. Stay yourself, my magnificent friend, and endure."

It was a parson's adieu, not a physician's. Live quietly apart, indulge in nothing, endure the pain of body and soul, and veil myself; let no mortal see the fumbling presence, the darkness of my vision, the lumpy thickenings that twist the flesh of my face, the mad eye, the hulk of a man. Conceal what is left of Meriwether Lewis, hide the pathetic ruins from the world, place myself in the care of my suffering mother, and then die and be furtively buried in the family plot, well forgotten.

Doctor Saugrain told me months ago that I would know when I was losing my mind. The disorder is so slow and subtle that its victim can observe the murderous progress of his own unraveling. Now that time is upon me, and yet I retain hope. Maybe my gifted mother, Lucy Marks, can brew the simples that might heal me. Ah, God!

Here I am, the governor of Upper Louisiana, on a trip east to talk to the president and secretary of war. The world knows it; I wrote letters and announced my intent, and they are expecting me. But what if I cannot talk? What if I am mad of eye? What if every word they say to me doesn't register, and every utterance of mine is incoherent to them? I don't want them to see me, nor my mother to see me.

It would be good to fall again off this flatboat. I am *no longer Meriwether Lewis*, and that answers all questions. If we were to travel at night, I could design it. By day, with their alert eyes following me, I cannot. But I might catch them unawares.

It is dusk and the river men are in town after a miserable day under the hammering sun. They deserve their pints in the local taverns. Only Pernia lingers here. The flatboat bobs next to the levee, fastened by hawsers to pilings set in the muddy shore. A thick plank bridges the gunnel and the grassy bank. We are carrying a cargo of stiff buffalo hides that release sharp odors.

"Pernia, go enjoy yourself," I said.

He shook his head.

"I will be all right."

"No, sir, you won't be all right."

"If you lack money for a glass of porter, I have a little."

"No, Governor."

"I will need something to help me sleep."

He looked torn again, wanting to heed my every wish. "Maybe you should not," he said. "I will fetch you some dry clothes. And a sheet will help. And I will hang up the netting."

Mosquitoes *were* whining everywhere; I was ignoring them, but Pernia was not.

He was being, as always, a faithful servant of his governor, and I forgave him his disobedience.

"I'm sorry to cause you such care," I said penitentially.

He gave me a hard look. "Maybe you try praying. God make the fever go, maybe."

"I have no such beliefs. God is a Creator. He has put the universe in motion. That is all there is. I do not accept the idea of miracles."

"You a Christian, maybe?"

"Superstition."

Pernia made the sign of the cross. He was half Creole, and the French had given him what little he possessed of religious understanding.

I lay back on my plank bench, feeling blood throb in my head. I would soon have a splitting headache unless I took some Dover's powder again.

"Why won't you give me my medicines?" I asked.

"They're bad."

"You go to town and enjoy yourself."

He shook his head doggedly. It was going to be another miserable night.

I lay on the hard plank, listening to the whine of mosquitoes, slapping at them, peering into the moist gloom as night things fluttered. I knew a lamp would attract moths.

I closed my eyes, knowing that John Pernia's devotion was good and important to me.

"John, if anything should happen, if I should take sick and perish at sea, what will you do?"

"Master Lewis, I will guard your trunks with my life. I will deliver them to Mr. Jefferson. I will do that, master, no matter what; for that is required of me."

"Only the journals need go to him, Pernia. The rest to my mother and brother in Ivy."

He nodded.

"But the journals go to Monticello, and I know you will guard them with your life. I am my journals. All that I was, all that I will be remembered for, are there on those pages."

He bustled in the gloom and I heard him opening and closing my several trunks until he found what he wanted, some mosquito drapery. He tied this awkwardly to various items, but it did hang over my pallet and did hold the whining mosquitoes at bay. A misty moon gave soft light, enough for me to follow his movements. He found my coat, rolled it up, and offered it as a pillow. I didn't want a pillow; I wanted the powder. I lurched up in my pallet, ripped aside the netting, and grasped the heavy jug, drawing it tightly to my belly.

He paused, sorrowfully, and then slid into that strange passivity he expresses in every motion when I overrule him.

"Get out, John. I will be alone now."

He retreated through the open rear, and into the soft light of the evening. I watched him settle on the transom, next to the sweep of the rudder. I pulled a cork and swallowed the harsh fluid, gasped, and swallowed again, until it burnt a trace down into my belly.

With luck, I might numb all species of pain, including the new one I have discovered, *Afflictus lewisensis*.

41 CLARK

It was time to report to Secretary Bates. Meriwether had left; I would be leaving on September 18, and the territory would be governed by the secretary alone.

I approached his office gingerly, having heard rumors of his current agitation, but little did I expect when I entered to experience the violence of his passions.

He spotted me at once, leapt from behind his waxed desk where no speck of dust resided without permission, and wagged his finger at me.

"You! You!" he cried. "You have come to rebuke me, and I will not stand for it, sir."

I shook my head. "No, I just came—"

"I know exactly what you came for. It's a canard. I have nothing whatsoever to do with the governor's derangement. Nothing at all. He brought it on myself, and it is the basest, vilest of lies and *insults* to say that I drove him to his current estate because I covet his office. That's what they're whispering, sir, and I *despise* every malicious voice that is engaging in character assassination behind my back! I will not tolerate it!"

He was livid. His eyes flashed. He windmilled his arms more dramatically than any actor playing King Lear. Since I could not speak without interrupting, I didn't, but let him run on.

"Here is the *truth*, sir! I pity the man. I don't wish to put him out of office, wretched as his conduct toward me has been. I am not so base as to conduct myself in such a *vile* manner. The canards floating about are contemptible, sir, and I will push them aside. If any man says it to my face, I will express my unalloyed contempt, sir."

I was grinning, and he took it wrong.

"Ah, so you mock me! You and your pitiable friend Lewis! I am an honorable servant of the government, sir, abiding by its laws, unlike the governor, and I will not *tolerate* your contempt."

I saw he was winding down, so I tried a tentative sentence: "I'll be leaving for Washington on Monday and thought I'd report to you, Mr. Bates."

"Report?"

"On the condition of the territory. On what's pending. On what's in progress."

"Report! You'll report in Washington all manner of base canards about me, and I will *not* suffer it. I will defend myself to the utmost, to the last, sir. You and the governor are going to Washington to do me an injustice."

Bates was beyond rational argument, so I just scratched my ear, rubbed my jaw, and smiled.

Oddly, he subsided, like a teakettle running out of steam so the lid no longer chattered.

"Actually," I continued, "I want to explain the fur company to Secretary Eustis and the president. They've never grasped that the regular army wouldn't take Big White up the river, or bear the cost of it, and we had to find other means. And while

I'm there I'm going to try once again to get my brother's finances in order."

Bates was listening for a malign word about himself, or in fact any word, even a kind word, and when the expected reference to his person didn't emerge from my mouth, he lost interest. In fact I'm not sure he registered anything I said.

"They've never given my brother, General Clark, a penny for the debts he incurred. I've spent half my life trying to help him, and I'm not making much progress. So I'm going to try again."

Bates nodded.

"Now, do you want my report?"

Bates strolled back to his chair and sat, slowly, his gaze suspicious.

"In my absence, you'll handle Indian affairs and the militia. You will also be assuming Meriwether's duties. You may wish to learn how things stand."

At last, he was receptive. I briefed him on my attempts to get cannon, shot, and powder from the secretary of war, the status of various tribes including the fractious Sauks and Fox, on our sources of intelligence about the Spanish probing our southwest border, the licenses to trade with various tribes that had been renewed or issued, the condition of our roads, the collection of imposts and taxes, the peltries heaped in warehouses because of the embargo, and other matters.

"I don't know just when I will be back," I concluded. "I'm aiming to return this fall if I can. Weather may intrude."

Bates was all sweetness and rose from the balls of his feet to his tiptoes. "I will look after the territory with *due diligence*, General, and nurture our national interest to the utmost of my abilities and in the bosom of truth," he said. "You may count on me to do that which you would most approve."

I didn't quite know what I had said or done to garner such florid promises from the man. But neither had I ever understood what Bates had against Meriwether Lewis, apart from envy. But I am good at smiling, and even better at shaking hands, and that concluded my duties.

That done, I hastened home to continue my arrangements. I planned to leave Julia behind this time; she had a child to care for, another coming, and a household to run. And I would not be leaving her for long.

I intended to travel by land, and to go only with my manservant. I could go clear to Pennsylvania by water if I chose, but traveling upstream in a keelboat would take much too long. Years ago I would have taken York especially for his good company, but he no longer offers company. He still does his duties punctiliously; I itch to fault him, but can find no fault. Yet matters have changed radically; he is a stranger to me, silent when we are together.

He would like to visit his wife again in Kentucky, but I cannot spare him the time this speedy trip.

Unlike Meriwether, I intended to travel light; a saddle horse and a packhorse would suffice. I have a good bay Tennessee walking horse that will jig me east, and some sound horses well trained to carry packs and York. I could be in the capital in a month, though I will spend time at Mulberry Hill with my family.

I found Julia couched on the daybed in our bedroom, embroidering. She doesn't weather pregnancy well.

"Where's York?"

"He took your horses to the farrier."

"Good. The traveler needs shoes." I sat down next to her. "Are you comfortable now?"

She laughed as if the question was idiotic, and that was answer enough. It was good to be among people who laughed. I realized just then I had never heard Bates laugh. And Meriwether's nasal whinny had vanished from his person months ago. I counted a good belly laugh better than a gill of spirits. Things were altogether too somber in official St. Louis.

"Julia, I hope you'll continue our Sunday open houses."

She nodded.

"Be my eyes and ears."

"General, I'll leave the affairs of state to the men."

"You'll hear more when I'm not around than when I am. Write me at Mulberry Hill."

"Will you have room in your bags for a few things?"

"A few. I'm packing light."

She wallowed to her feet and pulled some muslin from a drawer. It was bold crewelwork, orange, sea green, azure, enough to cover the seat of a chair. "This is for Harriet," she said. "Can you put it in oilcloth?"

Harriet Kennerly is her cousin, and I have a soft place in me for her. I promised I would. "She'll like it, and like word of you," I said.

"Will you get to Fincastle?"

"I intend to."

"Then I'll have a letter for the colonel. You'll take it, won't you?"

"Julia, I wouldn't miss a chance to see your family. I'll tell Colonel Hancock and everyone there that you're fine, our boy's fine, and Louisiana's fine."

"Are you going to Ivy?"

"Yes. I want to see Meriwether. And his family, too, but I want to check on him."

"Because he's indisposed?"

I nodded. Actually, I feared he might not be coming back to St. Louis, though I had never voiced that idea, even to Julia.

"What is the matter with him, Will?"

"He has a fever. It comes and goes."

"I hear it's affecting him. It's something horrible, isn't it? His mind's going, isn't it? Whatever could it be?"

I didn't illumine her. I was sure it was the venereal but I didn't really want her to know the nature of his indisposition. There are things to keep from a delicate woman. It has been clear to me for some while, but something I keep to myself. His vials and powders tell me much. The bills from Doctor Saugrain we recorded among his debts tell me more. But most of all, the ruin of his face, his eyes, his shuffling gait, his bewilderment, tell me the whole of it.

I marvel that I chose prudence all those days and nights with the Corps of Discovery. I cannot call it love or saving myself for Julia; I am an army man. I have ordinary virtues, and few enough of those. Just caution. Because of my caution, which stayed me for nearly three years, my life is full and blessed and complete.

Because of a moment of incaution, Meriwether is probably lost to public life. I need to know, and in particular I need to know whether that miracle-worker, Lucy Marks, has any remedies. I will stop in Ivy not only to see an old and beloved friend, but to discover a verdict.

Julia caught me in my reverie.

She lifted a soft hand and pressed her fingers to my cheek. "I'll miss you, my general."

I am not a man who fancies up words to present to a lady, so I just smiled and winked. She hugged me, and I hugged her mightily.

We floated downstream in a searing sun, the distant shores lost in white haze, the September light so fierce that even the veteran river men squinted from bloodred eyes and wiped away tears.

I huddled in the cabin of this one-way vessel. In New Orleans it would be broken up for scrap, its planks sold along with its cargo of buffalo hides. Its derangement and mine were fore-ordained.

I too floated down the river of life, helpless in my makeshift body, a prisoner being taken where I would not go. Boulieu, whose flatboat this was, kept a sullen eye on me, his frown shouting invectives at me though he said not a word. The damp heat sucked life from my lungs. My man, Pernia, sat beside me in the choked gloom of the cabin, his furtive glances telling me that I was under guard.

I sweat from every pore, soaking my pantaloons and cotton shirt. I drank, defying their forbidding stares, finding my only solace in the raw Missouri whiskey in my jug. I was fevered again, but what did it matter?

Often the Creoles abandoned the tiller, and the flatboat careened ever southward, the torpid water slapping its planks; but other times when the channel veered into sullen swamps, or rounded a headland, they were all busy sounding and steering and studying the colors of the turgid water.

Yesterday at such a time I slipped to the larboard to relieve myself, and again I careened off the gunnel, the gloomy water inviting my company, but Boulieu spoiled the moment. I saw my face in the dark and mysterious waters. The ripples severed my image and mended it again, and I perceived myself as a boneless specter wobbling on the waters. Then I felt his harsh hand clasp my shirt and pull me back. He pushed me into the bilge and wagged a massive finger.

"Governor, I tie you up, *oui?*"

"Sunstroke," I said.

He grunted.

That was all he said, but he entered the cabin, found my jug, and pitched it into the river. I watched it bob, roll, and sink. I have more in my trunks, a flask of good absinthe. He did not know of my powders. He did not know anything about me except that I am the governor of Upper Louisiana and a noted man he was transporting to New Orleans, not perdition. He did not know that his plank boat and my body were one and the same prison.

Pernia helped me back into the shade, his mottled face fierce with shame. "You lie down; the fever don't go away if you're out in the sun."

I suffered Pernia's rebuke.

We came this afternoon of September 11 upon a curious loop of the river, and for a while bore north and west, the shoulders of the stream carrying me, for the briefest time, toward the Rocky Mountains somewhere beyond a hundred horizons. I thought of heaven. By late afternoon the heat had eviscerated me, the odd fetid smell of the river had nauseated me, and my imprisonment at the hands of Creole warders had driven me to distraction.

But then Boulieu himself was steering the stained and sordid scow out of the channel toward a settlement, odd little houses, innocent of whitewash or paint, with verandas on three sides to ward off the sun, mud lanes with silver puddles, rank green shrubbery choking the yards, and a stench of sewage redolent in the sultry air.

"New Madrid," Boulieu said, in answer to my unasked question.

New Madrid. We had come a long way.

My head was clear. There was something I needed to do, and swiftly.

The boatmen poled the flatboat into a grassy bank, tied it to some acacias, and stepped ashore while solemn boys in ragged pants watched suspiciously. One held a writhing garter snake.

"We stay here tonight," Boulieu announced to Pernia and me.

I stood dizzily. I hadn't shaven, wasn't clean, wore sweat-drenched and river-scummed clothes, and my innards felt as foul as my attire. But the heat was subsiding and my mind was as clear as the sky.

"Is there a merchant here?" I asked a boy, once I stepped out of the prison ship and onto a humped ridge of grass along the lapping waters. New Madrid was oddly bucolic and forbidding, a sleepy hamlet with chickens rooting on the main street, but as sullen as a thundercloud.

He must have regarded me as the equivalent of a pirate, but he pointed at a tired, whitewashed affair a block inland. I walked. Pernia followed silently, his disapproval manifest in his conduct.

The hand-printed sign announced a market whose proprietor was one F. S. Trinchard. I reeled in, unsteady on my feet and no less fevered.

A sallow young man rose from a stool behind the counter. "Writing paper?" I asked.

He surveyed me, probably wondering if I were literate, and opened a glass case behind him. From within he extracted a sheet.

"Pen and ink bottle?" I asked.

He shuffled around, and placed the items before me, along with a blotter. "Half a bit," he said.

I was too weary to protest the inflated price, so I dug into my small coin purse and extracted a one-bit piece. I uncorked the black bottle, dipped the split quill into the bottle, shook it gently, and began my inscription:

Will

I bequeath all my estate, real and personal, to my Mother, Lucy Marks, after my private debts are paid, of which a statement will be found in a small minute book deposited with Pernia, my servant.

Then I signed it, blotted it, and handed it to the young man. "Please witness this," I said. He read it swiftly and signed his name.

"Thank you, Mr. Trinchard. I am fevered," I said. "It's a precaution."

"Glad to be of service, my good sir. Help availeth."

I patrolled his emporium looking for certain comforts of the flesh, found nothing helpful except some cinchona extract, and headed outside.

"Keep this safe," I said to Pernia. "It favors my mother. If anything happens, get this to her at all cost. Do not fail me in this."

Pernia took it. He could read a little, which was good. I watched him struggle through the text.

The whole business had wearied me, so that my sole desire was to return to the plank bunk and collapse there upon the splinters.

"You help me to the scow, and then you are free to go for the evening, John," I said.

"No, Governor, I'm right here looking after you."

He annoyed me. "I am quite safe."

He grunted something unpleasant that I took for rebuke.

The boys had vanished, but a pair of dowdy women in bonnets surveyed the flatboat. Then they, too, hastened away, leaving only a bullfrog for company.

Pernia opened the leather trunk that contained my journals, folded the will, and placed it within the leaf of the top journal, readily available. I watched.

"All right. Go have a mug of stout," I said. "Here's a bit."

"Master, this is a strange place and we don't know who'll steal. I'm staying here to keep an eye on things."

That was my Pernia, a man so loyal he shamed me. But he was also dissembling. He was really there to keep an eye on me, not my chattel. The Creole crew had vanished into a public house off a way that spilled light into the mucky street, leaving only Pernia to see to it that I . . . did not disturb the peace.

"Are you hungry? Thirsty, Governor?" he asked.

I wasn't hungry. "You could find some fresh water."

"There's a spring running from a pipe," he said.

He eyed me, left the flatboat, which was bumping softly against the bank, and in short order returned with a pot of fresh water. It felt cool down my parched throat. I sipped the chill water again, feeling fever slide out of me and my ruined body improve.

"Pernia, go buy me a quart," I said. "There's a public house over there." I pressed six bits into his hand, watching his face writhe in protest. But he did what he was paid to do, trudged through a somnolent twilight in an unpeopled village, and then he disappeared within. I tried hard to remember the name of this place, but it eluded me.

He returned wordlessly with a brown ceramic vessel in hand.

"They were fixing to throw me out," he said. "But I tell them it's for the master. He says it's a dollar a quart, so I says to him, fill it six bits' worth, and he does."

"You are a true and faithful man, Pernia."

I reached for the bottle. He seemed reluctant to surrender it.

"Maybe you should go to sleep, Governor."

"This will help me. I need it for pain."

He handed my bottle to me and shook his head. "I'll be here, outside, so if you're looking I'm right here."

That was both a jailor's warning and a servant's promise of service. He was too faithful, and I would need to devise some other path to gain my ends.

I uncorked the brown bottle, mixed the spirits with the cool spring water, and sipped regularly into the hazy night, slapping at mosquitoes when they whined close to my face. Sometime or other, the Creoles returned and settled on the deck outside the cabin, where my whiskey breath and the close air wouldn't afflict them. I wished I could remember the name of this place, but it did no good to think about it. The only reality was the fever which consumed me.

43   CLARK

River men carried us across the river to Cahokia on September 18, and York and I proceeded eastward through the Indiana Territory at once on two saddlers and with two packhorses. I gave York a rifle and powder flask, and we set off through forested wilderness that invited ambush from renegade Shawnee.

Up in Vincennes, Governor William Henry Harrison was negotiating a treaty with the tribes, but there were dissidents itching to fight the incursions of white men to the death, like the prophet Tecumseh. So we progressed cautiously, our gazes examining every sign of nature, from the sudden flight of birds to unnatural silences.

Both York and I were garbed in buckskins, which turned wind and weather well, and lasted better than fabrics. The trace was well traveled and there were shelters along the way, but there were also long stretches of thick hardwood forest that hid the sun and plunged us into gloomy cautiousness. The whir of an arrow would tell us we were too late and too few.

In spite of the danger, I knew York was enjoying himself. All this reminded him of the Corps of Discovery and his care-free days on the long trail. And of the years when the distinction between his estate and ours blurred in his mind, until he was simply part of the company.

I was thinking about it, too, and though neither of us spoke, we were well aware of the other's thoughts. I enjoyed the road, the acrid smell of a horse, the feel of a good mount under me, and the occasional moments when we dismounted, stretched our legs, checked the packs, watered and grazed the horses, or surveyed the ever-changing skies.

In fact that afternoon we scarcely said a word; nothing passed between us but my directions to him, which he acknowledged with a brief nod of his head, his dark face granitic and wary.

I have been irritated with him for months, in fact years, but now, as he rode beside me, my anger washed away in the soft September breezes. It was a fine time of year to travel, and the forests veiled the sun and kept us cool though the midday heat was oppressive.

The companion of my childhood and youth had experienced things unknown to most slaves, and had shown himself to be a worthy and hardworking member of our band of explorers.

Yet he spoke not a word.

Late that day I ventured to converse with him. "It is much like our trip west," I said.

He caught me in his gaze, his yellow eyes awaiting my direction.

"That was a good trip, and you were a part of it," I said lamely, not wanting to compliment him or inflate him. Why was I having such trouble talking to a slave?

He nodded as if it was all of no account, but I knew he was listening.

We paused a moment, when some mallards burst from a

slough, and then proceeded silently until we had passed the place. He had lowered his longrifle, checked the priming, and was just as ready to defend us as any private in the army.

"We'll quit at the settlements," I said. About nine miles ahead were some farms clustered together for protection. They had been hacked out of forest land, but in between the stumps grew a rich harvest of wheat and corn, melons and squash. We would eat well this night.

He nodded.

I wanted to talk to the man but every time I tried, I stumbled into silence. He pretended not to notice my agitation, but I knew exactly what was going through his mind.

An hour later I fell into a familiar mode of dealing with him: "When we get there, you take care of the horses, rub 'em down and check the frogs and look for heat in the pasterns. I want a bait of oats if they have it, and plenty of good timothy. If any horse of mine lames up, you'll be sorry. Get our truck under roof, and find yourself a place to bunk."

His response was a sigh and a whispered "Yassuh." He kept his nag one step behind mine, which irritated me. I had to turn my head back to address him.

"You'll be wanting to see your wife in Louisville, but there won't be time. I need you. So put it out of your head," I said with a curt edge to my voice.

He didn't respond, but I could feel the hope leak out of him even as he slumped in his battered saddle. He had been counting on it; a swift trip to the tobacco fields south of Louisville while I visited my brother and family at Mulberry Hill.

We traversed another three miles in total silence.

"Now, damn it, you know nothing about freedom," I said abruptly. We were crossing a broad meadow, the browning grasses waving gently in the low sun, the liberty of the place exhilarating after the imprisonment of the dark oaks and walnuts and hickory trees lining the trace like a prison wall.

"You know what it means? You'd have to take care of yourself. I make sure you're fed every day. I keep you in clothing. I put a roof over your head. I do that whether you're busy or idle or sick. Whether you're accomplishing my ends, or fallow. I do that in the winter and summer. I do that on days when I have no need for you."

His response was to tap the flanks of his nag with his heels and pull up beside me so he could hear all this better.

"If you were freed, what would you do?" I asked.

He said nothing, afraid to talk about such a dangerous subject.

"Go ahead, say what you are thinking," I said.

"Mastuh, I'd get me a horse and wagon and be taking goods from one place to another for hire."

"How would you do that? You can't read. You can't sign a contract. You can't do numbers. You'd be cheated. They'd say they'd pay you ten dollars and give you three and you couldn't do anything about it. They'd claim you spilled something, and try to take your horse and wagon from you."

He nodded. "Maybe I just do it for black peoples, not white peoples."

"You'd starve."

"Might be worth the starvin'," he mused.

"You'd be worse off than with me."

He didn't answer that, and suddenly I laughed. He carefully refrained from laughing, too, but I saw the corners of his mouth rise a little, and I reached across and clapped his shoulder.

What I saw then shocked me: there was more pain in his eyes than I had ever seen in him. Pain fit only for the dying.

I hated myself for it, but I knew what I would do, and I knew that I had to tell him then and there, walking across that lonely valley in wooded hills, in a land as dangerous as the one we traversed en route to the Pacific.

"I'll need you this trip and can't let you visit your woman. When I get back to St. Louis, I'll write the manumission papers. I'll do them in triplicate and file one, give you one, and put the other in the hands of Pierre Chouteau for safekeeping. I'll also publish it in the *Gazette*."

He stared at me, unbelieving.

"York, I'm freeing you."

He seemed bewildered. "You mean I don't have to work it off, the money?"

"I'm freeing you. When we get back."

"You mean I don't owe you nothing?"

"You'll regret it. You'll wish you never asked."

He sat there shaking his head back and forth, slowly, side to side, his lips parted, his eyes on some distant horizon.

I don't know what was impelling me, but I wasn't through. The farms were just ahead; I saw light spill from a cabin a mile away. I saw cattle in the field, with a belled cow announcing her presence.

"When we get back to St. Louis, I'll write your papers, and I'll give you a wagon and a dray. You can go into business. It won't be easy. You'll be competing with plenty of others and they might charge less. Hay and feed and pasture and oats cost money. Wagons break down; you'll need a wheelwright now and then. All of that costs money. You'll have to find a place to live, and that costs money. It's called 'rent.' You can own a house or rent one. You try to raise a family, and there's food to pay for, clothing to buy, furniture, cribs, blankets, diapers, coats, and all of it you'll pay for. I won't be providing it. And if you can't pay, someone will come and take it all away and leave you in the ditch looking for wild asparagus or maybe a mallard or catfish to live on or stuck in a shanty, chattering and cold when the snow flies."

I finally wound down as we penetrated the hamlet, and two curs set up a clamor.

"Mastuh Clark," he said. "You gone and make me a man."

"No, York," I said, remembering those years with the corps, "you made yourself a man."

44 LEWIS

On September 15 they put me off here at Fort Pickering along with Pernia and my trunks. It didn't matter much. For days they had stood guard over me; Pernia and the Creoles took turns as warders. The air on the river had been so thick and moist that I could scarcely breathe; the sun so blinding I couldn't bear to abandon the cabin. White haze obscured the distant shores, and I felt myself being carried to the sea in the prison of my body, detached from the world.

Sweet oblivion. To be aware was to suffer. I numbed the pain as best I could, blotted out the horror with powders, and the ghastly ruin of my body with spirits. They didn't stop me inside the cabin; they arrested my trajectory only at the gunnels of the bobbing flatboat, where one or another hung onto my shirt while I performed my ablutions. I lay drenched in my filthy cottons during the midday heat; lay chilled at night even though the air was sultry. My heart beat relentlessly, pumping life into the ruin of my flesh.

When we anchored at night they fed me broth and hung up the mosquito curtains around me, but little good those pathetic veils did. My arms and neck and face soon swelled with welts from ferocious insects, and only the powders were sovereign against the ache. I do not remember much of that journey, and don't want to.

Boulieu must have thought that a desolate and fevered governor was more cargo than he bargained for, because he took the tiller and made for the army post located on Chickasaw Heights in the Territory of Tennessee, on the left bank of the river. It was one of several posts commanding the river and its traffic, strategically located below the mouth of the Ohio.

Of all this I was only vaguely aware. We bumped against the levee under the mouths of iron cannon, and some hushed conversation ensued beyond my hearing. Then four privates in blue appeared with a litter, and they lifted me onto it, and several others began hoisting my trunks off the flatboat and into a mule cart. We ascended a steep grade, but for how long I don't remember. I only know I was threatening to slide off the litter.

So I was a prisoner of the army.

They deposited me in a whitewashed room walled with broad plank, barren and clean and so bright it hurt my eyes. A surgeon's mate examined me, took the measure of my fever, washed me, and then vanished. I heard mumbling in the hall outside my room. I discovered faithful Pernia hovering there, eyeing me solemnly. The room tumbled and whirled, and Pernia loomed over me and vanished. I wanted my powders and knew I would have to discover where they had taken my trunks. I was burning up again.

It didn't matter.

When I opened my eyes again I beheld a man of rank, his gold epaulets announcing his estate. I knew him somehow, and yet I didn't.

"Governor, I'm Captain Russell at your service," he said. "Gilbert Russell, commanding Fort Pickerell."

I nodded.

"The river men have put you in our care," he said. "We've a surgeon's mate here, and he has examined you. Are you following me?"

I nodded.

"He's going to apply cold compresses to reduce your fever, which is elevated."

I nodded.

"Your manservant says you're en route to New Orleans, and then to the Chesapeake. My advice, sir, is that you will need some little while to recover from this attack."

"Thirsty," I said.

Russell nodded. The surgeon's mate brought a tin cup of cool water. I drank greedily.

"I would like my chattel brought here," I said.

Russell paused for just a moment. "Most of it, Your Excellency, will be brought directly. My surgeon's mate believes you are suffering from an excess of some things in your medical cabinet. We will ration those for your own sake. A glass of claret each day will suffice."

"But my pain—"

"We're up above the river, Governor, and it's cooler here. Clean linens and cold compresses and fresh air will restore you directly."

"I want my powders, my snuff. I'm a physician; I dosed the entire Corps of Discovery."

Russell sighed. "And so you did, sir, and brought your corps back safely. I am filled with boundless admiration."

"Is this an infirmary?"

"Actually, officer's quarters."

"Am I free to go?"

He hesitated again. "The boatmen and Mr. Pernia suggest,

sir, that you were temporarily so fevered that you were acting against your own best interest. We have a watch stationed for your own safety. If there's anything you need, why, I am your servant in all else."

Even as he addressed me, my mind was quieting and the coolness of the room was comforting my burning flesh. I lay in a clean squared log bunk between muslin sheets. A breeze billowed through the open windows now and then. His talking wearied me. I nodded.

I remember little of the rest of the afternoon, except that the mate steadily applied cold compresses to my face and neck and chest, and so relentlessly that for the first time in a week I felt cool. I fashioned a vast longing for the powders, but knew I had no prospect of getting them, and lay cool and tense through this afternoon, while my faithful Pernia wandered in and out, studying me. I can imagine what he and the river men had told Captain Russell.

My mind clarified wondrously at twilight, and I was able to look about and see something of the post through the open window. Far below, the vast river glimmered, en route to the Gulf of Mexico and my rendezvous with a coastal packet, which would carry the prisoner, Governor Lewis, across the breast of the gulf, around the dangling organ of Florida, to my destiny.

I knew at once I wouldn't go.

Captain Russell visited me again that evening. It was very quiet. I heard nothing, not even crickets at their nightsongs. An assortment of enlisted men changed compresses every few minutes, cooling my body and mind.

"Would you like some claret, Governor?" he asked.

I nodded.

The surgeon's mate handed me a filled glass; a weighed and

measured portion of wine. I struggled up in bed, took it, and sipped.

"Are you comfortable?" he asked.

"I'm changing my plans, Captain. I'm going overland from here."

He hesitated. "You're not fit, sir."

"I will be. I have my journals of the overland expedition with me. I fear that I might lose them if British men-o'-war stopped us. They'd love to get their hands on something like that. They are all ready for publication. All I need do is deliver them to my printer in Philadelphia. Years of work now ready to be set into type."

I wondered why I was telling him that. Had I lost all honor? But perhaps the end justified the means.

Russell nodded. "It's a prudent idea, Governor. The British would love a prize like that. And they'd make good use of the journals, too. The maps, the botany, the observations. But in your condition . . ." He let the rest of the idea slide away. "You know, the chances of being stopped by a British warship are very slender. I don't suppose they are more than one in a hundred."

"The British have intelligence, Captain. They would know of my journey."

"The sea is a restful way to travel," he said. "You need do nothing but recover your health in your cabin, watch the dolphins, and think about the future."

"I am already better," I said. "I'll go overland."

"Not alone, sir, not alone. In your condition, I could not let you do that."

I saw at once that the webs of fate binding me wouldn't be snipped so easily. I sipped the claret and smiled up at him.

"Is there anything you need?" he asked.

"I need to write a letter to Mr. Madison, telling him of my progress and my change of plans."

"I will supply the necessaries at once, Your Excellency. The post leaves early in the afternoon."

The captain visited with me a while more, and then suggested that I might wish to retire. It was yet light out, but sinking toward a Stygian night. He seemed formal, ginger in his dealing with me, conscious of rank. He bowed, saluted, and departed.

I dozed. A little later, an aide appeared carrying a small, burnished field desk of cherrywood, several sheets of vellum, an ink pot, and a dozen quills.

"The captain, sir, says you requested this," the corporal said.

I nodded. "Please light the tapers," I said.

The corporal nodded, vanished for a moment, and returned with a glowing punk. He lit one candle and then the other, and retreated.

I struggled to sit up in bed, and finally managed to pull the field desk to me, but my mind refused to work. Words had fled me. Phrases meandered through my mind, and I feared I would not be able to write one word.

For some infinity I tried to write Mr. Madison, the words forming aimlessly in my head and skittering away. It was necessary to send this letter; to let the world know I would head for Washington with intelligence of value for the president and his secretaries.

But after half an hour, or so it seemed, I had not managed a word. I pulled the field desk off me, and blew out the tapers. Soon thereafter, in the close dark, I felt cold compresses on my forehead again. They might cool the fever of the body, but not the fever of the soul.

45 LEWIS

I awakened this morning feeling cooler. My fever had abated. I was not gladdened. A white blur of light probed through the window, but it did not hurt my eyes. I discovered Pernia sitting in a chair in a corner, as blurred a man as he always had been, for I knew him by his conduct, and not by his heart.

"Your Excellency—"

"Why are you here?" I asked.

"Governor, we're watching over you."

That seemed odd. "Was I that out of sorts?"

His glance slid away. "You were indisposed, sir. You look better now."

I had been abed a long time. "What day is this?"

"Friday, Governor."

"I mean the date."

"The twenty-second."

"And when did we arrive?"

"The fifteenth."

I measured that, slowly grasping that I had been in this bed for a week or so. I remembered phantasms, the tossing images, watchful soldiers, and the captain, yes, Russell. Captain Russell of Fort Pickering. Not Captain Clark. I remembered talking to

341

Russell about my trip down the river, and my need to see the president, and my fear of the British on the sea, and the valuable journals I bore with me.

I looked about me, focusing eyes that refused to serve me. My trunks were collected in a corner, a black heap. A cherry field desk sat on a bedside table. Yes, I had scratched and blotted a letter to Mr. Madison. I remembered it clearly. It had required relentless effort, and neither my mind nor my hand was quite up to it. I had told the president that I would go to Washington overland; that sickness had delayed me. That I had important matters to bring to his attention. I wondered whether I might retrieve that labored epistle and do better.

"Was the letter to Mr. Madison sent?"

"Yes, Governor. I folded it, addressed it, and gave it to Captain Russell. He sent it in the next post."

I nodded. "Where are my medicines, John? I want to take some powders."

Pernia looked uneasy again. "The captain and the surgeon's mate have them, sir. They took away most everything but the Peruvian bark, for fear you might make, ah, your own employment of them."

"It was ague, then."

"They don't know, sir, but they kept up the quinine you'd been taking. They thought you were dosing yourself rather to excess, and it was afflicting your mood."

"I'll want my powders now." It was a command.

Pernia reluctantly shook his head, fearful to be resisting my direction.

I struggled to sit up, and found myself too dizzy and weak and bewildered to do so. I had been here a week and scarcely knew the passage of time. And yet I did remember most of it after a fashion, the darkness and light in succession, the parade of soldiers sitting there, one after another, never leaving me alone, the wild thirsts, the cold wet compresses, one after another, the nausea, the quaking of my limbs.

I lay in a dry cotton nightshirt. My freshly washed clothing hung from a peg in the whitewashed wall. I struggled to get up and dress.

"No, Governor. My instructions are to keep you in bed," my manservant said, reversing our customary relationship. "I think the captain would like to know you're . . . better."

"Back in my head, you mean. Yes, tell him," I said.

Pernia left the room, and I was alone at last. I found a thundermug and relieved myself. I was heading for my trunks when Captain Russell came in, followed by Pernia.

"Governor, I'm glad you're up," he said. "You asked to see me?"

I sank back onto the bed. "I have to go to Washington," I said. "I need to see the president."

Russell frowned. "You need to recover first. Then I'll help you."

"It was ague."

"Your Excellency, my surgeon's mate tells me it was many things, including the wrong medicines, and they had, frankly, affected your mind. Mr. Pernia's conveyed your request for your powders, and I'm going to say no for the time being. My surgeon's allowing you a glass of wine at evening mess."

The craving for some Dover's powder made me tense, but I could see I had no choice. I nodded.

"When are you going to let me go?"

"When you're back in health, and even then I intend to have someone accompany you. You're not up to traveling without assistance. I thought to join you, because I've some protested warrants too, like you, and we could make our cases together. But I can't get permission. They won't relieve me. So I'll need to find someone else."

"I can go alone; I'll have my man with me."

"Mr. Pernia is an admirable and loyal man, Governor, and he's looked after you for days, going without sleep to see to your safety. But you'll be traveling with someone who can keep an eye on you, when I can arrange it."

I sighed and sank back into my pillow. I was going to be taken where I would not go, watched night and day, treated as a prisoner of disease.

"Have you someone in mind?" I asked.

"Major James Neelly, sir, agent to the Chickasaws. He stopped here on the eighteenth and I've apprised him of your condition and the need for a traveling companion. He's willing to wait a few days until you are able to travel. I think you'll find yourself in good company. He's responsible, eager to serve the governor of Louisiana in any capacity, and beyond all that, an amiable friend who admires you boundlessly for your conquest of the continent."

I had never heard of him.

"I'll wish to talk to him in due course, Captain. But I wish it could be you accompanying me. I prefer regular army."

Major was an honorary title given to Indian agents. The man would no doubt be a civilian. Probably one of the innumerable parasites who sucked a living out of the government and the tribes they served. Maybe a rascal. No doubt avaricious, and probably a conniver. Maybe there would be some opportunity in all that.

344

"At any rate, Governor, I'm pleased to see your progress. My God, how greatly you worried us!"

"I hoped not to worry you at all," I said dryly, knowing he would not fathom my meaning.

I settled back into my bed and he left.

"You can leave now," I told Pernia.

"No, sir, the captain wants a man at your service, and I do a turn; another man will take the night turn."

So I would still be a prisoner. I settled into the pillow, wondering whether anything had changed, whether my life had somehow improved, whether I might better gather my strength and proceed to Washington, dissembling about my purposes, and retreat to Ivy and obscurity.

Nothing had changed. I hated my own dissembling. I had spent a lifetime, a happier time, holding my honor above all else. And here I was, concealing the dark design of my heart, even from my supine position in bed misleading those who were responsibly and affectionately looking after my body and soul.

Did they know? They must! The governor of Louisiana, the celebrated conqueror of a continent, the much-toasted contributor to botany and zoology and other branches of science, was losing his faculties, the victim of his own night of folly, his furtive dalliance with a dusky maiden far from prying eyes.

They could not help knowing. They would know what the calomel meant. They would know what those thickenings about my face meant. They would know, they would not keep it secret, and my honor and reputation would be thinner than an eggshell.

And in Washington they would casually suggest that I retire, and I would no longer hear from my learned colleagues at the American Philosophical Society, and the ruined man,

Lewis, would vanish from sight, to the safe imprisonment of a cubicle at Locust Hill, a babbling idiot, kept by his aged mother and dutiful brother far from prying eyes and malicious tongues. Nothing had changed; and neither would my plans, though I would need to dissemble all the more.

"Pernia!"

My man jumped to his feet and approached me.

"I'm not going to Washington by sea. We'll take the Natchez Trace. I'll get horses somehow for the trunks. Now, do you understand your duties to me?"

He looked bewildered, so I enlightened him.

"You are to take my journals to Monticello, no matter what happens to me. If I take ill again, it shall be your bounden and sacred duty to deliver those journals to Thomas Jefferson. You will keep them dry, wrapped in oilskin if need be, and take every precaution for their safety. And my effects to my mother at Ivy. Have I your word?"

"Yes, sir, Governor, my word."

"Have I your oath, sworn before God?"

"Governor, I do swear it before God Almighty."

I fell back on the pillow and closed my eyes.

"Pernia, it all falls on you," I said.

I turned away from him. Not anyone, most especially my manservant, would I permit to see my face.

Captain Russell and Major
Neelly have deemed me well enough to travel, and I have fos-
tered their delusion. The Natchez Trace will be my route to
wherever I am going. I have let them know that I won't entrust
myself to a barque while the British prowl the coasts, and would
go overland to the City of Washington.

That has taken some maneuvering. I've had to borrow a
hundred dollars from Captain Russell to see me to Washington,
which I secreted on my person, and also I have had to purchase
two horses and tack from him, one to carry two of my trunks,
the other to carry me. All of this came to nearly four hundred
dollars. I've instructed Captain Russell to ship the other two
trunks by sea. I will take the journals with me, plus a trunk of
personal items, including my brace of revolvers and powder
flask.

With a Virginian's eye I looked over the two horses, which
seemed sound enough for my purposes, though neither was a
handsome steed. I spotted no lameness or hoof rot or fistulas
or other weaknesses, and believe that Captain Russell means
to serve me well. Pernia will walk behind, being sound of back
and foot, and will be my third beast of burden. The captain

gave me a bill of sale, and I gave him a promissory note for $379.58 payable before next January 1.

Toward repayment, I wrote Major Amos Stoddard, who commands Fort Adams downstream, and asked that he repay a two-hundred-dollar loan if possible, and to forward the sum to me in the City of Washington. I have little doubt it will end up at Ivy.

I've had a chance to acquaint myself with Major Neelly, the Chickasaw Indian agent, these past two days. He is a smooth man, without a wrinkle of face or mind or soul, and his brow is innocent of all creases. I have little doubt that he smoothly extracts annuities from the War Department, and smoothly distributes some small portion of it to the Chickasaws who reside only a few leagues from here. But perhaps I am jaundiced. My brother Reuben, after all, is an agent, appointed by Will.

I think Neelly will make a good traveling companion. He has shown genuine concern for me, and has expressed his admiration for my command of the Corps of Discovery.

And so, this morning, September 29, we set forth: Neelly and his slave Tom, my manservant Pernia, and myself, as well as a few others heading for the Chickasaw reservation. Both the major and his slave are mounted. They have pack animals as well. The heat still oppresses, though much of our travel is along a trace arched over by oak and maple, so that we progress through a perpetual twilight.

We bade Captain Russell goodbye at about ten o'clock, thanked him for his courtesies, and proceeded east by means of a cutoff from Chickasaw Heights to the trace, a considerable distance, I am told, barely settled, and buzzing with insects. We will have to have our horses and party ferried over the Tennessee River, which will cost my beleaguered purse considerable, but I no longer have choices.

In one of my trunks is my stash of medicines, and once free of the worthy captain, I swallowed some powders intended to release me from the pain that afflicts my mortal coil. I was at once set free. I recovered my flask from my trunk, and slipped it into my coat. I was now armed against misery and fever on the trail.

Major Neelly spurred his fine bay horse forward until he could keep pace with me, where the trace was wide enough to permit it.

"How are you faring, Governor?" he asked.

"I am making progress. It is a terrible thing, having to go clear to the City of Washington to settle accounts. Why will they not accept my word? Am I not an honorable man, Major?"

"I'm sure it's all a misunderstanding. I have the devil's own time getting my affairs straight with them."

"Will is following, you know," I said.

"Will?"

"General Clark. He's coming also. We've left the whole of Upper Louisiana in Bates's hands."

"Bates?"

"Secretary Bates. Acting governor, who this very moment is penning letters to Secretary Gallatin, President Madison, and Secretary Eustis about my neglect, and my failure to imbibe his wisdom."

"Sir?"

"Ah, you wouldn't know about that, Major. No, not here, across the river. We are coming, Will and I, to set Washington right."

"You say General Clark is following?"

I nodded. "Right along," I said.

Neelly looked back, half expecting to see the general cantering up behind.

"Major," I said, "within those trunks rest my journals of the expedition, the ledgers kept by Will and me. Sir, I have instructed my servant to make sure those reach Mr. Jefferson at all cost. No matter what happens to me, those journals must go east."

"I'm sure you'll soon be fine, Governor."

"Will you promise it?"

"Governor, your manservant is as faithful as any on earth. He'll see to it."

"No, Major, will *you* see to it?"

The major nodded. "I promise."

"Good. You are a patriot and a benefactor of science. In that trunk, sir, is a nation's claim to the territory it purchased, but also its claim to the Oregon country, the whole northwest. In that trunk, sir, are a few hundred descriptions of plants, birds, animals new to science. In that trunk, sir, is the defeat of the British fur traders. It contains priceless information, gathered by myself, about each tribe we met; information that will seal the hold of our fur traders on those tribes; information that will keep the grasping British out of the northwest. So I want more than a nod, sir; I want your pledge, your most solemn affirmation—"

"Governor, you have it. But what's this about Clark?"

"He's on his way, sir, and we'll deal with scoundrels and knaves and clerks, which are all one and the same."

"You made no mention to Captain Russell that General Clark would be coming."

"Ah! But he is coming, I assure you."

Neelly stared smoothly at me, his smooth smile concealing

his true self and private thoughts. He could only be an excellent Indian agent, professing smooth affection for his Chickasaw charges.

I am sure Will is coming. He said he would come. He must be right behind now. Odd how it is that I don't see him. I need him to straighten things out. I am weary of sitting this horse. It may be sound, but it has a rough gait that doesn't improve my health. Horseflies attack us, big black flies that bite man and horse alike. I hear slaps behind me.

"What takes you east, Major?"

"Nashville. Business there. I will be picking up some items to distribute to the tribe."

"Will is coming soon," I said. "Then we will settle the protested vouchers. A great injustice, sir. I would be solvent now. I would be a landowner now. I would be laying the foundations for my mother and brother. Bates is a most difficult man, you know. Bates, can you imagine a man like Bates?"

He eyed me. "Would you like to stop and rest, Governor? There's a creek a mile ahead."

I closed my eyes against the sun and nausea. "Carry on, Major," I said.

The leaves along the trace had not yet colored and fallen, and so we traversed a green tunnel through a sweltering day. I was grateful for the shade.

I explained my grievances to the major, but I am not sure he grasped any of it. When we did pause to rest the horses or ourselves, he concerned himself anxiously with my care, and advised me that once we get to the Chickasaw reservation, we should pause to allow me to recover.

"I am well enough," I protested.

He did not reply, and I took it for disagreement.

We rode this whole day, and covered much ground, and

scarcely met a soul. I have not made up my mind about this Indian agent. He is, by turns, solicitous of my health and eager to know what matters are much upon my mind. He calls my affliction the ague, and I wonder whether he means it, or if he and the others have agreed not to say what they must know.

Twilight approaches, and I know not whether we will find a stand where we might rest for the night. Such places are only a shade better than camping, mostly because we have a roof to turn the rain. But Neelly knows this road, and I leave the arrangements to him.

"Your Excellency, tonight we must make camp, but the skies are clear and I do not expect a soaking. From now on, though, we will find shelter. The day after tomorrow, we will arrive at my Chickasaw agency, and there you can take your rest until we're ready to travel again."

"Major, there is no need."

"There is a need, Governor. I am charged with looking after you, and I will keep my purposes before me."

"And what are those, Major?"

He looked at me gently, and I expected the smoothest from him. "Governor, I am taking it upon myself to deliver you safely and in the best health that can be managed. I do this because I want to, as well as from duty. You are a man I admire, the sort this republic elevates to positions of honor. Who is this man who is with me but a conqueror of a continent? And that is enough. I am pledged to bring you safely home. And I will be looking after you, along with your excellent servant Pernia. I'll do everything in my power to bring you safely to the capital, because I am honored to be in your company and honored to do you any small service I am capable of rendering."

I nodded. I found sincerity in every word. So Neelly would stick like a burr. I would have to think of something else.

47 LEWIS

We travel without Major Neelly now. Just my manservant Pernia, Neelly's slave Tom. Neelly stayed behind to catch two strayed horses at Dogwood Mudhole, where we camped for the want of a settlement.

The horses had been well picketed on good grass, but were freed in the night by parties unknown. They were nowhere in sight at dawn. Major Neelly was greatly puzzled by the disappearance.

"I could have sworn I hobbled them," Neelly said, upon discovering his hobbles resting beside his gear. "I must have imagined it."

In the night, I had untied those pickets and pulled off the hobbles, so that I could travel alone, save for the servants. We would leave the Indian agent behind.

This morning I proposed a plan: "Major, I'll proceed toward Nashville while you hunt down the animals, and I'll pause at the first stand I come to."

"Are you sure you're up to it?"

"I have Pernia," I said.

He nodded. I had been doing a little better for several days. We had stopped at his agency for two days, while I overcame the delirium that afflicted me. It was not my choice: as long as

I was in his care, he decided these matters. But he did not take from me my necessaries, the snuff and the powders, by which I dulled the fever of soul and body. It was lying there abed in his Chickasaw agency that I decided what to do, and how to do it.

By the sixth instant I was, in Neelly's estimation, sufficiently recovered to proceed, and we continued west toward the trace, and were ferried across the Tennessee River in a flatboat, by an avaricious ferryman this morning. My horses and Pernia and my person cost me dearly.

This morning, then, my fate has changed. I travel alone, sovereign at long last, east toward my sunset. Later we struck the trace, which burrowed like a tunnel through the golden forest, the air pleasant upon the cheeks, chill in the shade, but warm where the low sun struck my ravaged face.

I have been arguing with myself. Sometimes Pernia glances at me, because my debate rages even to his ears, as he trudges behind us. I go east against my will. Far better to go west, toward the future, toward the setting sun, than east, to Washington and exposure. I will not be the old uncle up in the garret of the family home at Ivy. I will not be that Lewis. I will be only the other Lewis.

The censor in me mocks me: you will defame yourself all the worse, he says.

But I rebuke my censor: one can choose a living death, or one can choose a more honorable one that preserves the name of Meriwether Lewis for posterity. One death is tragic; the other is vile. I prefer tragedy.

But this ghastly judge residing within me will not be stilled. "Ah, they will count it a coward's death, a shameful death, your weak character and melancholia forever on public display."

"Hush! You are wrong! What I must do requires all the courage I possess. I will preserve my name. I will not disillusion Mr. Jefferson. I will not disappoint my friends in the American Philosophical Society; I will not tarnish my honor; I will not mortify my family. I will not blacken the reputation of my Corps of Discovery. Let them call me a coward if they must, though what I intend is a sacrifice to honor. But I will spare my family, spare my friend Tom Jefferson, spare Will Clark, spare the corps. A good officer looks after his men; this is how I look after mine."

I heard laughter from that corner of my soul.

"You would not know what honor is," I said. "I will suffer shame, but preserve honor!"

Who was I arguing with? A phantasm, a nightmare, without flesh.

"You would not know what courage is, either," I continued. "You would not even know what pain is, pain of soul, pain of body."

Pernia said, "Are you all right, master?"

I smiled. "I am debating with myself," I said.

My manservant stared.

That grim judge occupying my heart would not be still. "You, sir, are a coward, deathly afraid of pain."

I acknowledged it. "Yes, I am."

"You won't succeed. You cannot inflict pain upon yourself. You will botch it. You cannot point a loaded piece at your bosom and pull the trigger."

He was nettling me. "I will do what I must do," I retorted.

This specter in my bosom laughed, and it sounded like a flight of honking geese late in the fall.

I turned inward. We proceeded through an autumnal mid-

October day, with iron-belly clouds scudding low. I looked back, half expecting that Neelly would ride up with the two strays, but he didn't. Pernia and the slave followed behind my pack-horse. I could not remember the name of the slave; only that Neelly owned him. My memory was flagging. I didn't doubt that someday I would not remember my own name. I suffered lapses constantly. I spent half an afternoon trying to remember the name of the officer at Fort Pickering, the man who would not let me have my medicines.

We were two or three days out of Nashville, but this country had yet to be settled. The dense oak and maple woods discouraged farming. I prefer open country, not this cloistering canopy. I pulled my flask and drank the harsh whiskey to settle my soul again.

Late this afternoon I espied a clearing ahead in a broad swale set in the oak-covered hills. It had been painfully hacked out of the dense forest, and at the far end of it stood a dog-trot cabin, that is to say, two cabins connected by roof in the manner of frontier dwellings across the South. And far beyond that, a log barn. And I discerned a yellowed corn crop rising among the black stumps that toothed the field.

Whatever the place, it would no doubt provide comforts for travelers such as ourselves. The trace ran along the very edge of the settlement, no doubt drawing trade.

I urged my horse forward, leaving my entourage behind.

At my arrival, a work-worn young woman in brown checked gingham emerged from one of the water-stained log cabins, and she was swiftly surrounded by urchins of stairstep ages.

I halted. "Madam, do you provide lodging?"

"Yes. Not fancy, but a roof. In there." She pointed at the

other cabin. "That's where the children sleep, but I'll move them in here tonight. Are you alone?"

"My servants follow, with packhorses."

She nodded and pointed at the log barn. We negotiated a price for myself, the servants, and the horses. A dollar and two bits in all, grain for the horses extra.

"I'm Mr. Lewis. And you?"

"Mrs. Grinder," she said. "My man's up at the other place . . . but he'll be back soon enough. Very well, Mr. Lewis, I'll shake out the tick and get ready. I'll have some supper in a little bit."

Grinder's stand, then. As I dismounted she vanished into the log cabin that would house me. The children shrank into the other cabin, which was redolent of stewing meat. Pernia and the slave walked up, and I steered them toward the barn.

"But put my trunks in there," I added, pointing to my quarters.

They unpacked the horse and carried my heavy luggage into the dark confines, while Mrs. Grinder finished her preparations.

"Where's my gunpowder, Pernia?" I asked.

"In your canister, sir."

"I want to recharge my pistols. I've neglected it. This is not a safe place."

Pernia eyed me uneasily, and then took my horses off to water and rub them down, as he always did. I entered my new dominion, alone at last. I had not been alone for a month. My two trunks rested in a corner. A not very clean tick lay on the puncheon floor, and I supposed it would have its complement of bedbugs. But that would not matter. I had escaped at last.

Twilight comes swiftly this time of year, and I knew I would not have to wait long for darkness to fall. I pulled off my shirt and put on my blue-striped nightshirt over my pantaloons. Mrs. Grinder invited me in and offered me some stew, but I refused. Her ragamuffins peered shyly at me, astonished at my odd attire.

"Give it to the servants, madam," I said.

"But you should have some, Mr. Lewis."

I dissuaded her. I was not a bit hungry and my fevers were mounting again. "I would take a little whiskey if you have it, madam."

Wordlessly she lifted a jug and poured a gill or so into a cup for me. But once I had it in hand, I didn't want it, and sipped but little.

"Madam, have you any gunpowder?" I asked.

"Gunpowder?"

"Yes. I wish to clean the damp powder out of my pieces and recharge them."

"Oh, sir, Mr. Grinder might, but he's not present now, and it might be a while."

I sighed. Would my intentions be defeated by that? I could not find my powder flask. Perhaps Pernia had it. Or perhaps it was in one of the trunks left at Fort Pickering. My two pieces were not loaded.

"Hidden it, have you?"

"Sir?" asked Mrs. Grinder.

"I was talking to someone else, my servant, madam."

She looked about, saw no one, and stared at me.

"You cannot know what it takes to do what I must do," I said.

"Are you indisposed, Mr. Lewis?" asked the poor woman.

"Madam, it's a very pleasant evening. I think I'll just sit outside and have a pipe before I retire, if that is suitable."

"Oh, of course, sir, of course. I just thought maybe something is amiss. If you're indisposed I have a few simples I might steep for you."

"No, madam, you look after your children, and trust the night."

She backed away, carrying her pot and ladle and a trencher intended for my use.

I watched her retreat, confused, toward the barn with the stew, and settled down on a bench outside my cabin door. I pulled out my old briar pipe and tamped some sweet tobacco into it, enjoying the soft sweet quiet of the fading day, the thickening blue of a lifetime.

48 LEWIS

It came down to duty. I could preserve, for the republic, the Meriwether Lewis they knew and celebrated, or not. I knew what I must do, but didn't know whether I could summon that mournful courage to do it. And so I argued with myself that soft Wednesday eve in the oak groves of Tennessee.

I hated this!

Oh, if only I might repeal three years; but how sad and feckless to think it. I paced and argued, but there was nothing to argue. The nation had built a shrine to me, and I had befouled it. Like the whited sepulcher, it contained corruption within.

I could not go east; I could not ride into the City of Washington without betraying the trust invested in me. I could not sully the Corps of Discovery, my loyal and stouthearted men. I could not beslime my mentor and friend Tom Jefferson. I could not open the floodgates of gossip. I could not babble my case to Mr. Madison or Secretary Eustis, for they would be listening to gossip and not to me. I could not bear the thought of entering into the presence of my mother, with her searching gaze and saddened mien.

I watched night settle and listened to the crickets. I heard the last of a day's toil in the cabin next door, and then the soft darkness settled over the farmstead. It was a gentle night, this eleventh day of October, soft and melancholic, the tang of the good earth in the night breezes.

There were black holes in a starlit sky, where occasional clouds obscured the universe. Even in that infinity, there was no place to go, no escape.

By the light of a stub candle, I stormed through my chattel and found the powder flask, which Pernia had artfully buried under my journals. I grasped the embossed canister and plucked it out of the trunk. In my other trunk I found my two brass-mounted Pennsylvania pistols, encased in a polished cherrywood box. I opened the box and beheld them in the drear rays of the candle. They were costly, reliable pieces, and had served me well during the expedition. They had put balls into grizzlies. They had comforted me in emergencies.

I lifted one, and felt the smoothness of the walnut stock and the coldness of the ten-inch octagonal steel barrel. I lifted the other, two old friends whose loyalty I did not question. The locks and frizzens were fine, the flints fresh. The pistols had been cleaned and oiled, and were ready for whatever use my eye and finger might put them to.

I charged each piece, pouring the full measure of good Missouri powder down the cold muzzle, patching a forty-four-caliber ball and driving it home, and then priming the pan. I hefted them. They felt fine, balanced, formed to my hand, and I pointed them here and there, at the candle, the floor, the wall, my trunks. Everywhere but at their target.

"You are a coward after all," said my censor.

I responded by pointing the pistol in my right hand at my forehead.

Could I not do what needed doing?

I paced again, the pistols putting authority to my every gesture.

"Mr. Eustis, if you will just let me explain. There was no way to execute Mr. Jefferson's design to return the Mandan without some expense. The regular army declined, so we created our own. But it will pay off, sir. And the presents we distribute along the river will ensure the safety of our western flank in the event of another war. The British never stop stirring them up! You will see, sir, how well it was spent. And now I am ruined. It's a burden hard to bear. Can you remedy this?"

No response rose out of the night.

"Who can say I lack courage?" I cried. "I faced savages with drawn bows intent on killing me. I braved roaring white rapids in a hollowed-out log of a canoe. I walked into savage villages even as I saw their warriors spread out and arm themselves and prepare to butcher me. I chose what rivers and paths to follow, often against the perceptions of the rest. I ate dog and horse and other meats that repel most men. I sat next to murderous men armed with long knives. I urged us forward when the faint of heart wanted only to flee. I faced angry bears and buffalo. I suffered a grave wound without complaint. Courage I have, for any good cause. And this is the best of causes."

All this I declaimed into the night, not caring who heard.

But there was only the hum of crickets. A whisp of smoke from Mrs. Grinder's fieldstone chimney eddied in.

And still I loved life too much.

"I am trapped! That is the sole reason!"

Then I thought of the unspeakable disease, of the shame, and thinking of the shame heartened me, and I thought I could do this thing if I could summon one swift moment of inner steel. Ah, that was the secret. One swift moment.

And still I could not.

I stepped to the door. Moist air met me. I saw no stars. The skies had been blotted out. I slumped to the stoop and sat dully, my mind purged of every thought. I knew nothing, scarcely knew my name, and could not even think of simple things. Maria Wood, she did not wait for me.

The calm eluded me. I had no more anodynes. I had snuff, and only a swallow of spirits. Violence was my only salvation.

I stepped into the inky black of the cabin, lifted the pistol in my right hand to my temple, and pulled . . .

49 CLARK

I have tarried here at Locust Hill some days with the governor's family, trying to make sense of it all. Mrs. Marks has welcomed me, along with Meriwether's half brother John Marks. I will stay a while longer in Albemarle County, where the family and Thomas Jefferson are quietly putting Meriwether's affairs in order. But soon I will go to the City of Washington for talks with Secretary Eustis and President Madison.

The news reached me in Shelbyville, Kentucky, only three days after I had departed from my own family at Mulberry Hill, Indiana Territory, and started east to untangle the financial affairs afflicting the Clarks and the governor and the St. Louis Missouri Fur Company.

The blurred story in the *Argus of Western America,* published in Frankfort, shattered my repose, and I read it over and over, trying to draw from it the information I wanted. But it was mute on all the essentials.

I handed the shocking paper to George Shannon, who was with me, and we stared at each other, scarce believing that our captain had left us, and by his own hand. My mind crawled with doubts, but at the same time I was not surprised.

I was so grieved and disquieted by the news that I didn't

know what to do. There was in me a red-haired Clark itch to head south to the Natchez Trace and question all those at hand, rattle their teeth, bang heads together, and get to the bottom of it. Maybe they could tell me what had excited the governor's passion and caused this last desperate escape. But on reflection, I abandoned that course. The governor would have been in the company of his faithful manservant Pernia and others, and I would soon enough get the whole and true story.

I did alter my plans in one respect: I had planned to head directly to the City of Washington for talks with Secretary Eustis, with only the briefest pause in Albemarle County en route. Now I decided to sojourn with the governor's family and help any way I might. Meriwether had given me power of attorney to settle his debts and perhaps I might be of use even now.

In Shelbyville I wrote my brother Jonathan of the horrifying news, and said I thought the report was true. "I fear, Oh I fear the weight of his mind has overcome him, what will be the Consequence?" I concluded. Those last letters from Meriwether, posted en route, asking me to look after his affairs, persuaded me of the truth of it. I will destroy them.

Shannon and I started east again, sharing in all tenderness and simplicity our memories of the great captain who walked the banks of the Missouri while we poled and rowed our vessels into the unknown. There was Meriwether striding before us, pausing at a plant he had never seen, stopping to unlimber his instruments and give us our latitude and longitude, sending Drouillard out to make meat, all of his hunters and fishers somehow feeding us off the land every day. There was Meriwether, bravely treating with glowering savages with arrows nocked in their bows, handing out gills of whiskey along with rebukes and encouragement, for he was always the taskmaster, exhorting us to do better even while commending our successes and rewarding the men any way he could.

I was grateful to have one of the Corps of Discovery with me that long, sad journey east. We comforted each other as we proceeded on, Shannon always on horse, which he managed well even lacking part of a limb. We were remembering a man of unquestioned genius and honor, a man of such rare ability that he took us to the western sea and back without disaster, and left behind him a record of it all.

That brought to mind my deepest concern: what of the journals? Were they safe? Had he finished the editing? The matter had become so tender with him that I ceased inquiring, and I was utterly in the dark about them. Were they too lost?

There were moments when Shannon and I doubted everything we had read: maybe Meriwether had been murdered in a most vicious manner.

"The Burr devils got him, plain got him," he repeated, over and over.

Meriwether did not lack conniving enemies in St. Louis, the Burr conspirators as well as disappointed seekers of privileges and offices. Shannon in particular seethed with the idea that a foul deed had felled the governor. Suicide was improbable. Neither he nor I had ever seen the governor in any great state of melancholia; his nature was to fight on, through the worst of events, until he could see daylight again.

At times Shannon and I speculated: was the governor simply murdered by the bandits infesting the Natchez Trace? Was this Neelly the instrument of an avenging cabal? Was this the work of the Burr conspirators, whose faltering scheme to detach Louisiana from the republic the governor had stoutly defused? Was the crafty General Wilkinson at the core of it? Might the governor's trusted manservant Pernia be a part of it? My mind seethed with possibilities, and yet, in the end, I believed the newspaper accounts were largely true. The governor took his own life.

I knew things about him I felt I could not share with my doughty friend: Meriwether had been overwhelmed by sickness, and he had all too generously dosed himself with anodynes, powders, snuff, draughts of spirits, whatever he felt might release him from the suffering of his mortal flesh. I had seen his accounts: of medicines he had purchased a plenitude. Of visits to the doctor, Antoine Saugrain in particular, he had accumulated an alarming number, and it was plain to me that something was radically amiss.

I thought of the unspoken thing, the *lues venerea*, which had afflicted him first on the Columbia and later at Fort Clatsop, and which he and I concealed from the corps and from the journal. I supposed he had the drips, but I was wrong. Had that vile affliction been his nemesis?

I perused more newspapers along the way. The fragmented and incoherent story had created a sensation everywhere. I learned that two balls had penetrated the governor, and that murder was a distinct possibility. All this aggrieved and disturbed me to the bone. I hoped the answers would come clear in Virginia, at least if Meriwether's manservant, or this man unknown to me, Major Neelly, had carried his possessions and information to the governor's family and to Monticello as I knew the governor intended. I could only hope, and hasten east as fast as Shannon and I could manage in nippy and often wet weather.

When we arrived at Locust Hill, on Ivy Creek, on December 3, Mrs. Marks and John greeted us tenderly, and swiftly brought from the servants' quarters the man I most wanted to see: John Pernia.

"Mr. Pernia's helping us with the estate. He's visited Mr. Jefferson and delivered the journals there," John Marks explained. "He's eager to talk to you, and has tarried here for your coming, just so he could deliver himself of an account of the governor's last hours."

That, indeed, was good news. While the servants hurried some hot viands to us, Shannon and I settled ourselves in the cream-enameled parlor, along with our hosts. In a moment, Pernia appeared.

"Oh, General, General," he said, clasping my hand. "What a painful matter this is! I have stayed here just so that you may learn of everything."

The mottled face of this Creole black man crumpled with feeling. Mrs. Marks and her son settled themselves on settees, all of us in that sun-drenched parlor, our sole focus the witness to Meriwether's death.

There unrolled, tentatively then more confidently, the account of the governor's horrendous last days, madness and delusion plaguing him, fever and sickness felling him, spirits and opium pills and snuff addling him. I listened to the story, believing it all. I already knew most of it.

"He says over and over to the major, to me, you are coming along right behind, and you are going to fix everything," he said.

"Was he . . . mad?"

Pernia sighed. "Ah, my general . . . Sometimes he was raging at the secretary of war for protesting his drafts. He says to Captain Russell that the journals were all written up and ready to publish. General, he never did write a word."

"Tell me about Major Neelly, Mr. Pernia."

"The major, he was no friend of the governor, and had certain failings, sir, but he saw his duty, and he respected the flag. He took care of everything afterward, doing it right and proper. Because of him, the journals are safe."

"Why wasn't he present at Grinder's Stand?"

"Now that be a strange thing, General. Two horses get loose of their hobbles the night previous; we hobbled them up for certain. The major did it himself, he being something of a horse fancier, and next morning two horses had strayed, one of the major's and one of the governor's. That's when the governor is pretty cheerful; he said he would go on ahead and stop for the night at the first stand he came to."

"Someone let the horses loose?"

"Someone did, sir. It was no mishap."

"Who, Mr. Pernia?"

The man looked reluctant to talk, glancing fearfully at Meriwether's mother. "The governor, *pauvre homme*, he had tried to throw away his life several times, and he be carefully watched for his own sake. I kept the vigil, the major watched, back at Fort Pickering there was a regular vigil, and that day, when the governor went ahead and the major stayed back to find the missing horses, that was the first time the governor wasn't watched. He got free."

"But you were with him, watching."

He looked discomfited. "I couldn't. The woman, Mrs. Grinder, she put us in the barn, sir, the people of color."

I nodded. "Was the governor murdered?"

Slowly Pernia shook his head. "All this that happened, it was the most plain thing, after his trying so much, so many times."

"Why didn't you come to him when you heard shots?"

"The barn was *très* distant, General. We didn't hear. I think the governor's powder was damp."

"Why didn't Mrs. Grinder go to him when he cried out?"

"General, she thinks him a lunatic, him arguing with himself and shouting half the night. She thinks only of protecting her children. Her man was away. She didn't unbar that door until the morning."

"How could a man shoot himself twice?"

"The first ball, it creased his temple and tore out bone and exposed the brain, not taking effect, and after a while he found the other pistol and put that ball into his chest. And still he lingered."

"Do you believe a man could do that?"

Pernia nodded. "In his condition, General, he would do anything he had to do."

"Where was Major Neelly?"

"He came up in the morning, sir. Maybe an hour or two after dawn."

"That's a strange hour. Was he present when the governor died?"

"Yes, sir. But it be too late. The governor is breathing his last."

"Did he have the missing horses?"

Pernia nodded. "He found one, his own, but not the other, and came up."

"How could he travel at night?"

"I didn't ask him, sir. It wasn't so dark. He maybe rode early, by moon, to catch up and press on."

"Then he was not far off at dawn. Is there the slightest chance that the major shot the governor?"

"No, sir, not as I know. The governor cut his arms to finish the dying. He lay there, bloody arms, sometimes aware of us, but he didn't accuse anyone from his deathbed. He didn't point a finger, he didn't say you or you or you did it. He didn't curse the major from his bed for all of us to hear. He could be doing that. He is aware enough. His eyes open."

"After he died, then what?" I asked.

Pernia looked uncomfortable. "The major set about digging a grave and getting a coffin. He put his slave to the digging, and me to get nails and all. There was no box, not in a hundred mile, and we got a few nails from a smithy and planks from a farm long ways away and a man there made a box from oak plank nailed up by himself. It be not much, but it's all we got. We buried the governor there, at Grinder's Stand the next day, all of us standing there, hats off to the governor, and the major saying the words."

"Then?"

"Then the major got the trunks and made an account of everything in them, the journals, disputed vouchers, clothing, weapons, and all, and we all set off for Nashville carrying the bad news inside us. The governor's purse was missing, and someone took it, maybe it got lost on the trail, the governor being so out of his mind, so there was no money for me.

"In Nashville the major gave me fifteen dollars to get here, for I had none, and sent the two trunks with me on the horse. And then he wrote the president—I mean Mr. Jefferson, and I brought the letter with me. He and I got the journals safe to Monticello, just as the governor wanted."

"And Mr. Jefferson has the letter from Major Neely?"

Pernia nodded. "He read it while I waited, and then he brought me in and asked me things for a long time, and I answered everything for the president, best I knew how. I give the journals to him, just as my master wanted, and then I went to Washington and talked to the president about it, and came here with the horse and the other trunk, and Mrs. Marks kindly takes me in and bids me to stay."

There were strange circumstances. Missing money. Major Neelly a checkered man of dubious repute. The odd reappearance of Major Neelly soon after dawn. No one helping Meriwether all night. Two shots and yet a suicide. But as I probed Pernia's story the rest of the day, and talked with Lucy Marks and her son, my mind kept returning to the overwhelming truth of it all: the disease whose name no one spoke had killed him.

50 CLARK

That December evening, beside the cold hearth at Locust Hill, Lucy Marks, John Marks, and I sat quietly, our hearts in Tennessee.

I would leave for Monticello in the morning.

"Are you satisfied?" I asked them. "I can ask for an investigation."

"Satisfied, General? Oh, no," Meriwether's mother said. "We'll never be satisfied, not with the reports so sketchy, and the accounts so jumbled, and so many self-serving stories."

"One word from Thomas Jefferson and the matter will be opened," I said. "The administration could scarcely refuse him. There's a good prospect that we can find out exactly what happened."

John Marks raised a hand. "We'd like to let it rest," he said. "Just let it be. My mother and I have come to that. It would be best for us, best for Meriwether, best for Mister Jefferson."

I nodded. I had come to that, too. Meriwether had done what he had to do, caught between terrible scourges, trying to salvage what he could for our sakes.

I had only eulogy to offer them, but eulogy was what each of us craved.

"He was a great man, a great American," I said, my soul

reaching out to these desolated friends. "I remember that great heart, that great mind, that great will, leading us through the unknown with all its perils. I remember his bright curiosity, his wonder at the world and everything in it; the way he marveled at a new bird, or a cloud, or a waterfall, or the way an Indian drew his bow. No man on earth was better fitted to lead, no man alive could have taken us to the ends of the earth and brought us back safely, save for Meriwether."

They smiled.

I knew that Mrs. Marks, even in her grief, was aglow with pride. "You do him honor," she said gently.

"The world will always do Meriwether Lewis honor," I said, "because he earned it."

"Yes, both of you," she replied. "You together."

AUTHOR'S NOTES

The mystery of Meriwether Lewis's death probably will never be solved. The evidence is too tangled, too contradictory, and too old. For generations there were two opposed theories: he died of suicide induced by depression, or he was murdered.

The suicide theorists argued that he had twice tried to kill himself en route to New Orleans and had made a will, and was depressed by his debts. They cite Jefferson's observation that melancholia ran in Lewis's family. The murder theorists argued that a suicide doesn't shoot himself twice, and there were plenty of people with plenty of reason to kill him, and Lewis showed no sign of manic-depressive disorder or any sort of depression.

A few years ago a Seattle epidemiologist, Reimert Thorolf Ravenholt, M.D., examined the journals and other material and concluded that Lewis had contracted syphilis during his 1805 contact with the Shoshones, and by 1809 the result was paresis, the mental deterioration induced by virulent third-stage syphilis, which led him to his death. Dr. Ravenholt pursued this thesis in three brilliantly argued papers that can be downloaded at his Web site, Ravenholt.com. I recommend in particular "Trail's End for Meriwether Lewis," presented to the American Academy of Forensic Sciences in 1997.

This is not the place to debate the issue. Suffice it to say that I found Dr. Ravenholt's analysis the most persuasive and the only one that adequately explains events and fits much of the evidence. But the other theories are plausible and have serious advocates, and must not be dismissed, though the murder theory seems weakest to me. There is too little known, and too many contradictions, to come to firm conclusions. Of all the mysteries of American history, this one invites the most caution.

We might learn something if Lewis's remains are exhumed and tested for mercury and evidence of syphilis, a disease that can affect bones. They might also offer clues as to the direction the two shots took, the size of the ball, and so on, and thus throw light on the question of murder.

I chose to construct the novel around Dr. Ravenholt's superb historical and medical analysis, and also upon a penetrating monograph called *The Character of Meriwether Lewis*, by Jeffersonian scholar Clay Straus Jenkinson, who brilliantly examines every facet of the complex, troubled, courageous, and sometimes repellent man who died on the Natchez Trace in 1809.

I believe that Meriwether Lewis took his life at Grinder's Stand, not because he was depressive by nature (I doubt that he was depressive at all), but because he was desperate and hopeless and fearful that his scandalous disease could no longer be concealed from the public. He feared that the national hero would soon be the national disgrace. By killing himself, he might yet preserve honor, not only his own but that of the entire Corps of Discovery.

Had he not killed himself, he might have lived years longer, even though his syphilis, probably complicated by malaria, was steadily destroying him. He knew he would soon become the demented, degenerate husk of the magnificent man he once was, and that was more than a man of his pride and sensibility could endure. Desperate circumstances father desperate acts.

As I examined the question of Lewis's disease, I found myself discarding the murder theory, and also abandoning the much-publicized idea that Lewis was depressed. Lewis was trapped. He was a courageous young man who was caught in a vise that was steadily squeezing him to death. He could not arrest the course of the disease or halt the decline of his reputation. He turned to one remedy after another, but nothing would heal him. He probably overdosed the mercury and further addled himself. In the space of only three years after his return, his health and spirits were ruined.

And so this novel was born. I came to share Lewis's horror and despair as I walked beside him. I admired and pitied him. Here was a good man, a greathearted American hero, desperately struggling against an insidious disease that was destroying not only his body but his very person. Here was a Homeric story worth telling. I resolved to tell it as a stark chronicle of decline. Lewis never surrendered. His suicide was a last act of defiance of the disease that was robbing him of his soul.

There are no full-scale biographies of William Clark, but his life can be pieced together from various sources, including *Lewis and Clark, Partners in Discovery*, by John Bakeless, and *William Clark, Jeffersonian Man on the Frontier*, by Jerome O. Steffen.

Other useful works include *Meriwether Lewis*, by Richard Dillon, *Undaunted Courage*, by Stephen E. Ambrose, and *A History of the Lewis and Clark Journals*, by Paul Russell Cutright.

There is a vast Lewis and Clark literature, too extensive to be listed here, as well as several excellent editions of the Lewis and Clark Journals, including the majestic and exhaustive new one by Gary Moulton.

A novelist dramatizing history must sometimes depict events for which there is no historical record. The funeral of John Shields, in this story, is such a scene, and there are others. I have also arbitrarily chosen among various spellings and decided which of the many conflicting accounts to use in the novel.

I am indebted to my editor, Dale L. Walker, for awakening in me a fascination with the Lewis question, and offering shrewd and thoroughly researched insights into the various possibilities as well as research material. And I am grateful to archivists at the Missouri Historical Society for pointing me toward various sources about William Clark.

Richard S. Wheeler
November 2001